Daughter
of the
Shipwreck

Daughter
of the
Shipwreck

LORA DAVIES

bookouture

Published by Bookouture in 2021

An imprint of Storyfire Ltd.
Carmelite House
50 Victoria Embankment
London EC4Y 0DZ

www.bookouture.com

ISBN: 978-1-80019-590-5
eBook ISBN: 978-1-80019-589-9

For Rosalind

There was nothing to announce the end of the world. It had been a normal day. The children had walked to the market with Mama that morning. They had eyed the ivory ornaments, the rolls of cloth in all the colours of the rainbow, the squat earthenware pots, the mountains of fruit and vegetables. They'd giggled behind their hands at the market traders – men and women from faraway towns and villages, who wore strange clothes and spoke words the children couldn't understand.

They had sniffed hungrily at the meat cooking over the firepits and begged Mama for a treat, as they always did. Mama had ignored them, prodding and sniffing pineapples, yams and plantains, her slim arms jangling with bracelets as she haggled with the traders. At last, she had relented, as she always did, and bought them each some dried fish. The children had devoured it greedily on the way home, licking their fingers long after any trace of the salty fish remained.

In the afternoon, they had played with the other children while their parents went to work in the fields. They were still too young to work, though Matondo knew that soon he would have to join the adults in planting and picking the crops or caring for the animals. For now, he revelled in his status as the oldest boy in their little gang, teasing his sister and their friends, leading their games, winning their races and play-fights, and proudly showing off the little knife that Papa had made for him.

That day Matondo had played the pebble game. Each child took turns to throw a stone into the air while the others gathered as many sticks as possible in the time it took to catch the stone. Matondo had won, running in circles, hooting with pleasure, holding his stash of sticks high above his head. His sister Malundama, soon bored of the game, sat and drew pictures in the dusty ground with a stick, lips pursed in concentration. Later, the children had dashed home before the sun went down, with dusty hands and scratched knees, breathless with laughter and hungry as a pair of lion cubs.

There was nothing to announce the end of the world. It was night when it happened. The family were getting ready for bed. Matondo and Malundama had washed their hands and faces. Mama had cleared up the remnants of their chicken stew and was throwing the vegetable scraps to the goats. Papa was in the yard, the smoke from his pipe drifting gently up into the quiet night air. The whole village was settling down to rest, only the bleating of a goat breaking the silence from time to time. Without warning, a gang of men burst upon this peace and quiet with violent shouts, with flaming torches, with sticks and clubs.

When they heard the men, Mama opened the back door and forced the children outside. She bent and kissed them both – a quick, fierce kiss – and then pushed them towards the forest at the edge of the village.

'Run,' she whispered. 'Run!'

And they obeyed. Hesitating only for a moment before turning and running out into the dark night, blood pounding in their ears.

They stopped when they reached the first line of trees and looked back towards the village. They saw the men breaking down doors, grabbing whoever they found inside by the hair, the arm, the leg, dragging them outside, beating them, throwing them to the ground, tying them up. They could hear men bellowing in anger. High-pitched screams and shrieks that sounded more animal than human. The dull thud of wooden clubs on flesh.

They gripped tight to each other's hands as they watched a woman wielding a stick, trying to fight off two of the men. It was Mama. Matondo fought the urge to run towards her. If only he had his knife. She was strong and she fought hard but there were two of them and she was quickly thrown to the ground. The boy covered his sister's eyes, clamping his hand firmly over her face, but he found that despite himself, he could not look away.

He watched the men kick Mama. Again. And again. And again. With each kick she moved, her body jerking and twisting this way and that, but then she lay still and the men walked away. Matondo waited for her to get up. He willed her to get up.

One of her legs was bent outwards at an odd angle. It reminded him of a goat that had been born in the village that spring. It had been unable to stand, its legs splayed out to the sides, and so his father had killed it, cutting its throat as the mother goat looked on. He remembered how the mother had searched for her kid for days afterwards, giving out a long, low cry and sniffing at the ground where the kid had lain. Matondo felt his insides turn to liquid and he bent double, retching.

His sister pulled at his arm and he looked up to see flames rising from the huts as the men began to set them alight. Touching their huge torches to the thatched roofs, laughing as those trapped inside began to scream. He grabbed Malundama's hand and they ran.

They ran until their lungs burned, until their shoeless feet were ripped and bleeding. Matondo was stronger and faster but he would not leave his sister, holding fast to her hand and pulling her along behind him. Tears ran down her face and she gulped for air, tripping and stumbling over roots and branches until at last her brother slowed and gestured that they should hide, pointing to the deep, dark undergrowth and pulling his sister under the leaves and twigs, forcing her down beside him, holding one finger to his lips.

There they waited, sweat itching and crawling down their backs. Through the canopy of leaves, they could still hear the men. The crashing of branches as they moved through the forest, the shouts and whistles as they signalled to one another. Sometimes it seemed that the men must have given up and the children looked at each other with eyes wide with hope, but then they heard more shouting and they held each other tight, burying their faces into one another's necks.

It had been quiet for a while now, save for the buzz and click of countless insects and the trilling and cawing of unseen birds. Through the branches, they could see the sky slowly beginning to lighten. Signalling at her to stay still, Matondo uncurled himself from his sister's embrace and slowly, slowly he raised himself up, breaking through their sanctuary of leaves and peering around.

The smell of burning still hung in the air and the thought of their home razed to the ground was like a punch to his stomach. The thought of Mama brought tears, which he fought back, rubbing at his eyes with dirty, scratched fists. Crying would do them no good. He had to think.

Dawn was coming now and there was no sign of the men. Matondo took his sister's hand and drew her gently out from their hiding place. They were both stiff and sore and they stretched their aching arms and legs, and picked thorns, leaves and tiny insects from their skin.

It would be too dangerous to go back to the village – if there was anything left of it. They would have to press on, Matondo decided. On into the forest until they found people and could beg help from some kind stranger. Mama had taught them which plants were safe to eat and how to find water. They would survive. He would make sure of it.

They began to walk but Malundama was tired, her feet hurt and she wanted Mama. Now that she no longer needed to be quiet, she started to cry. Huge, loud sobs that shook her whole body. He tried to comfort her, rubbing her back as Mama used to do, but it did no good. He too wanted to fling himself to the floor and cry and cry and cry.

A sound to his left caused Matondo to look round and as he did, something hard crashed into the side of his head and he felt himself slumping to the floor. The blow to his ear made the whole world silent and, as if in slow motion, he saw the round O of his sister's crying mouth widen in surprise as arms reached down and lifted her up. He felt rough hands on him, ropes tightening and burning around his arms and ankles. Then dizzyingly, sickeningly, he too was hoisted up. The trees seemed to spin and he felt as though he were falling, falling, and then the trees faded and everything was black.

Part One

September 1820

Chapter 1

Mercy started with fright when the horn sounded. Three loud blasts that ripped through the quiet of the still-dark dawn. As the stagecoach lurched into motion, she realised that the sound was just the signal that they were on their way. A signal that her new life was about to begin and that it was too late now to turn back.

Not that she could have turned back, even if she'd wanted to. The house was all closed up, the servants disbanded, the animals – even Mrs Whitworth's parrot, Palamon – all given away. It had been awful to see the house like that, so soulless, so brutally and utterly empty. It was the only home that Mercy had ever known and now she would never see it again. It seemed impossible.

Mercy turned her face to the window to hide her tears. She had already attracted enough attention from her fellow passengers, not only for her black skin, which drew curious stares wherever she went, but also for her outfit of black crêpe and bombazine. Her mourning attire had been hastily pulled together with the help of Old Sarah, Mrs Whitworth's maid. She had soaked Mercy's grey dress in a tub of coal-black dye for a whole day and night and, with a flash of her needle, had transformed the lining of an old cape into a sombre covering for Mercy's bonnet. Her black shawl and gloves had been Mrs Whitworth's own – bought when she herself had been in mourning for her husband, twenty years or so ago.

'She has no need of them now,' said Old Sarah sadly as she handed them over to Mercy.

And indeed, Mrs Whitworth had no more need for shawls or gloves or anything else where she was going. Mercy had read once that the Ancient Egyptians used to put food and drink, personal belongings, even animals and people into the tombs of the dead. It had seemed such an odd idea but, at the funeral, as Mercy watched the soft earth cascading onto the coffin, she had thought how lonely it looked, and the thought of Mrs Whitworth lying down there all by herself in the dark was almost too much to bear.

Her benefactor was – had been – a great collector. The house was a riot of trinkets and oddities of all descriptions: ornamental thimbles, vases and porcelain, a model of the Parthenon made entirely from cork. Mrs Whitworth had been a great lover of animals too. She adopted endless cats and dogs, a three-legged goat called Nelson and of course Palamon, her talking parrot. Mercy had arrived into this chaotic assemblage as a young child of four or five – not that she could remember that far back – and like the various wounded or abandoned animals in her care, Mrs Whitworth had shown her nothing but love ever since. Mercy felt the tears come again and turned her face to the window once more.

The sky was beginning to lighten, though the moon was still visible, floating pale and ghostly amidst the grey. Mercy watched as the gently rounded hills and sheep-dotted fields of Worcestershire flew past. They were so familiar, so ordinary, yet now as they rushed out of view, she tried to take in every detail, to sear the images into her memory. Who knew when or if she would return?

Mercy had tried to picture London, her destination. She saw mansions and palaces, art galleries and fancy tearooms, ladies and gentlemen in all the latest fashions. She had even heard that there was a menagerie of wild animals in London; lions and bears and snakes that one could go and look at. Incredible.

She was nervous – scared even – of what her future might hold. She knew very little about her new home – had never even heard of Dr Stephens, in fact, until the letter had arrived shortly after Mrs Whitworth died, inviting her to come and live with him. He was a cousin of Mrs Whitworth and must have taken pity on her, she supposed. All Mercy knew was that she was to help his wife, Mrs Stephens, with her work and in return she would have free bed and board. What that work was she didn't yet know. Mercy had never given much thought to her future, had imagined she would live out her days in the sleepy village of Hamblin, but now she had the opportunity to meet people, to make friends – to do something with her life. Alongside the fear, she felt a prickle of excitement.

The coach had picked up speed by now and Mercy felt her stomach roll like a tombola drum as they galloped along. It would be fourteen hours until they reached their destination. Fourteen long hours. How on earth would she stand it? She'd chosen a seat inside, given the time of year but she wondered now, as she rattled from side to side, pressed close to her neighbour on one side and the hard interior of the coach on the other, if she had made the right choice. It was already growing stuffy from the breath and bodies of the closely packed passengers and she would give anything for a gulp of fresh air.

Just then the coach lurched suddenly to the right and Mercy felt herself lifting right off the bench, so that for the briefest moment she was floating in the air before she crashed back down with a thud. There were gasps and cries from the wide-eyed passengers and one lady made the sign of the cross. She had heard that sometimes coaches overturned and she had a sudden vision of cracking wood and flailing limbs. And what about highwaymen? It was said there were some of them still about. She closed her eyes and took a steadying breath. *Be brave, Mercy*, she told herself. *Be brave.*

That night, cold and stiff from her journey, she arrived at last at the house that was to be her new home. It wasn't as big or as grand as she had imagined. It was part of a terrace, flanked on either side by identical houses, each with steps leading up to the front door. She took the crumpled letter from her pocket one more time. *17 Cowley Street, London*. Yes, this was definitely the right address.

She took a deep breath, the unfamiliar smog thick in her nose, and went up the steps. A metal plate next to the door read *Dr Edwin Stephens* in curly letters. She knocked gently and waited. Nothing. She knocked again, a little louder, feeling a creeping anxiety as the door remained resolutely closed. What if they had changed their minds? The thought was terrifying yet also strangely exhilarating for, if no one answered, where would she go, what would she do? She lifted her hand to knock for a third time but just then the door swung open to reveal a woman; somewhat older than Mercy and a little taller, with dark, glittering eyes and a ready smile.

'You're here! Come in, come in!'

The woman ushered Mercy into a warm, bright hallway and closed the door behind her, shutting out the cold and the dark.

'I hope you're not too tired from your journey? My, what a long way it is! Put your bag there, yes, that's right, just there. We'll take it up to your room later. And your bonnet and shawl and whatnot can go there for now.'

As the woman swept her through the hall, Mercy glimpsed the impression of a brightly patterned rug, of wall lamps burning brightly, of an ornate grandfather clock. Was this the mistress? The housekeeper? Her dress was very fine – silk by the looks of it – but her manner was so informal.

'Goodness me, how late it is! You must be hungry. Come through and get warmed up.'

'Thank you, ma'am,' Mercy said. She heard her own voice cracking as she spoke and realised dimly that she hadn't spoken to anyone since she had said her goodbyes early that morning. Already, that seemed a lifetime ago.

The woman led Mercy into the parlour, where a fire burned in the hearth, and then stopped, looking her up and down. Mercy was all at once acutely aware of her travel-worn dress, dusty at the hem and creased from the journey. She felt her hands vainly patting at her skirts.

'I have some bread and butter,' the woman said suddenly. 'And tea. We must make some tea! I sent the servants to bed as it was getting so late but I'm sure I can manage tea. Now sit. Sit yourself down there.'

Mercy perched obediently on an armchair by the fire. So, this was the mistress then. Mrs Stephens. She was younger than Mercy had expected, probably only thirty or thereabouts. She had glossy brown hair worn parted in the centre, with tight curls at either side of her face, which bounced and jiggled as she moved.

'Now, please, have some of this. You must be starved!' she said as she handed Mercy a plate with some neatly cut triangles of impossibly white bread, spread thickly with butter.

'Thank you, ma'am.'

She hadn't eaten for hours but Mercy forced herself to eat slowly, taking delicate nibbles of the bread. She didn't want to seem uncouth. Mrs Stephens took a seat on the other side of the fireplace.

'How was your journey?' she asked.

'Very good, ma'am, thank you,' she replied, keen to forget the terrific jolting of the coach, the stares and whispers of the other passengers, the aching in her back and buttocks from hours and hours of sitting on that narrow wooden seat. 'It was most kind of you to pay my fare.'

The woman waved her hand in a dismissive gesture.

'No trouble at all, Mercy. It is Mercy, isn't it?'

She nodded and Mrs Stephens went on.

'Religious, I imagine? Like Faith, Hope and Charity? Well, we need all we can get of those at the moment. Where does it come from? Your name?'

'Mrs Whitworth chose it, I believe.'

'Of course, of course. You lived with her since you were quite young, I understand?'

'That's right. She took me in when I was only four or five. After my father died. She was very good to me.'

The thought of Mrs Whitworth, of her familiar face, was like an unexpected blow and Mercy was mortified to feel tears welling in her eyes.

'Oh dear. I am sorry. You've only been here five minutes and already I'm interrogating you! Here, have this. You can keep it.' She handed Mercy a handkerchief. 'We were so sorry not to be there for the funeral,' she went on. 'You must miss her terribly. But I hope you shall be happy here. Edwin and I are very glad to have you. Very glad.

Now, dry your eyes and I shall go and find my husband. He'll want
to meet you, I'm sure.'

Mercy pressed the handkerchief to her eyes, willing back the tears.
She must make a good impression. This was her chance for a whole
new life, and she mustn't sit there crying like a child in front of her new
employer. But Mrs Stephens wasn't at all what she had expected. When
she had heard she was to work for a doctor's wife, she had imagined
a stern, upright sort of person. A smell of camphor oil and sensible
shoes. But Mrs Stephens wasn't at all like that. She was bright. And
pretty. And that silk dress was beautiful.

Even the handkerchief was exquisite, Mercy thought as she folded
it neatly. It was embroidered with a pattern of ivy leaves and edged
with fine lace. And now it was hers. She tucked it carefully into her
sleeve. She took another bite of bread and stretched out her feet
towards the fire, feeling some life coming slowly back into her cold,
tired limbs.

So this was her new home. She could hardly believe it. While the
outside of the house hadn't been very impressive, the interior certainly
made up for it. The room was furnished in tones of dusky pink and
peach with thick, tasselled curtains that hung all the way to the floor. It
was all so – tasteful. There were vases and vases of flowers – hyacinths
and hellebores and others Mercy had never seen before. A bookcase
lined one wall but the room was dominated by a large cabinet in one
corner that looked like something you might find in a museum.

With no sign of Mrs Stephens's return, Mercy went to have a
look, her reflection glancing darkly back at her from its glass doors as
she approached. The objects were evenly spaced on the shelves, with
rectangular labels, written in a neat hand, laid next to them. It was a
good deal more organised than Mrs Whitworth's sprawling collections.

A plate, decorated with sprays of painted flowers in blue and ochre, was labelled *Porcelain, China, 1700s*, and what Mercy took to be a metal teapot was, in fact, a *Beer-jug, Tibet, date unknown*.

Fascinated, her gaze travelled along the shelf to a wooden cylinder with a narrow slit along its length. At each end a carved wooden head extended, one male, one female, each one with perfectly rendered facial features and curled hair. Tiny jewels were inlaid where their eyes would be. *Slit-drum, Congo Basin, 1800–05*, the label read. It was beautiful and she thought vaguely that she had seen something like it before. Mercy touched her fingertips lightly to the glass.

'Wonderful, isn't it?'

Mercy spun round to see a tall, slender man standing in the doorway. He was dressed in black, and his auburn hair was cut close to his head and receding at the temples. He was old – forty, at least – but he had a kind face.

'I'm sorry if I startled you,' he said. 'My wife suggested that I come and introduce myself. I'm Dr Stephens.'

'Pleasure to meet you, sir,' said Mercy, bobbing a small curtsey.

The doctor looked at her for a moment. She was used to that, of course, but there was something about his expression that she couldn't place. Almost as if he was searching for something in her face. Then he smiled and offered her his hand. He had long, slim fingers, perfectly manicured.

'Welcome to London, Mercy,' he said.

He pressed her fingers gently and then released them. For a fleeting moment she had the oddest feeling that she'd met him before, but just as quickly it was gone.

'I see you have discovered my pride and joy,' he said, gesturing to the cabinet.

'Yes, sir, I'm sorry, I—' Had she been too bold? What was it Mrs Whitworth used to say? Curiosity killed the cat.

'Not at all. They are there to be looked at, after all. I have rather a passion for collecting. That one is from Africa.' He tapped the glass in front of the wooden drum.

'Have you been there, sir?' She looked up at him.

'Africa? Yes. Yes, I have. Many years ago. I worked as a doctor in Sierra Leone.'

Sierra Leone. What a beautiful-sounding name. Mercy remembered seeing it on a map; perched on the coast of the vast Atlantic Ocean. She'd never met anyone that had been to Africa before.

'I should love to hear about it, sir,' she said, but before the doctor could speak again, Mrs Stephens appeared at the door bearing a tray of tea and cups.

'I hope I've got everything!'

She placed the tray down with a clatter and began to pour the tea.

'Well, you must both excuse me, I'm afraid. I have work to do,' said the doctor. 'It is a pleasure to meet you, Mercy. I'm sure my wife will see you settled in. Tell you everything you need to know. Good night.' He nodded stiffly and made for the door.

'Take Mercy's luggage up, won't you, dear? Make yourself useful!' Mrs Stephens called after him.

'Husbands must have their uses,' she said with a smile as he closed the door behind him. 'Do you have thoughts of marriage, Mercy?'

'Oh, I… No – I…' Mercy felt the heat rising to her face.

'You're perhaps a little young. How old are you, my dear?'

'I'm nineteen,' Mercy said. 'At least, I think I am. Mrs Whitworth didn't know my exact age when she took me in.'

'Of course,' said Mrs Stephens. 'There I go again, interrogating you! You must forgive me. But a pretty thing like you must have her admirers?'

'Oh, no, ma'am, no…'

'Such wonderful hair! May I?'

She reached out a plump white hand. Mercy stood unmoving as Mrs Stephens patted and stroked at her hair. She had endured this many times before but it was no less infuriating for that.

'Wonderful! Wonderful! So soft. Like a little lamb. Now sit. Please. Sit.'

Mercy returned to her seat and blew into the cup of hot, strong tea, letting the steam rise up and obscure her face. Mrs Stephens was only trying to be kind.

'So, tell me about yourself,' said Mrs Stephens, regarding her with a beady look that put Mercy in mind of a magpie.

'Well, I…' Mercy stuttered. What did she mean? What was there to tell?

'My husband tells me you're a princess!'

'Oh, well, I suppose so,' said Mercy, trying to draw her shoulders back a little. It was hard to feel regal under the penetrating gaze of Mrs Stephens. 'Sort of. My father was an African prince, you see.'

'How fascinating. Whereabouts was he from?'

'I don't know,' said Mercy. 'I know nothing about him, I'm afraid. He died quite suddenly and I don't remember him at all.'

Mercy had heard the story of her father so many times that she knew it off by heart, and she recounted it now for Mrs Stephens by rote. Her father had been travelling in Europe for trade when he fell ill in an English coaching inn. Mrs Whitworth, who was staying at the same inn, had found a child on the stairs saying 'Papa' over and over again, and had been at her father's bedside as he died. His last words were, 'Take care of her. Please,' as he handed over a leather pouch, full of gold and jewels. The soft-hearted Mrs Whitworth had brought her to live in Worcestershire, and decided to name her Mercy.

Sometimes Mercy thought she remembered flashes of her early childhood, but at other times she wondered if she was only remembering what Mrs Whitworth had told her. She'd been very young when her father died, and couldn't really remember anything of her life before Hamblin and Mrs Whitworth. She had tried to remember her father, strained to conjure up some image of him, but there was nothing. She thought too about her mother; was she still alive somewhere in Africa? Did she wonder what had become of her husband and her daughter so many miles away? But Mercy didn't linger on these thoughts. They gave her a sort of sick, twisting feeling in her gut and what was the use of brooding on the past? No use crying over spilt milk, as Old Sarah would say.

'How very sad.' Mrs Stephens reached out a hand and placed it on Mercy's own. 'I hope you shall soon feel part of our little family.'

'Thank you,' Mercy said. 'Do you have children, Mrs Stephens?'

Mrs Stephens drew her hand away. 'No,' she said, with a tight smile that made Mercy wish she could take the question back. 'No, we don't. Now, tell me, my dear, can you read? And write?'

'Oh, yes. Yes. I can read and write,' said Mercy, bewildered by the change of subject. 'Mrs Whitworth made sure that I received a good education.'

'Excellent! Well, there will be plenty for you to do here. Helping me with my work, mainly – I shall explain all of that tomorrow – but you will also have leisure time. I encourage reading. Don't be shocked!

I encourage reading and I encourage thought. If either of those things interests you, then we shall get along famously!'

'I'm keen to learn, Mrs Stephens. And I will certainly work hard, I promise you that.'

'I'm sure you will, my dear. I'm sure you will.'

Mercy sipped again at her tea. Mrs Stephens watched her for a moment and then glanced at the watch she wore on a chain at her waist.

'I expect you're exhausted. I know I am. My husband often stays up late working. He's a terrible sleeper. But I must have my sleep or else I am a complete buffoon in the morning! Have you finished your supper? Very well, this way.'

She led Mercy up the stairs to the top floor of the house, where two doors stood either side of the landing.

'This one is yours,' Mrs Stephens said, opening the door to the right. 'Bridget's in the other one. Our housemaid. You can meet her tomorrow. She's a good girl, if a little lazy. Irish, you know, but we're doing our best with her. You should have everything you need. I'm out and about in the morning. Meetings and the like. But I'll be back in the afternoon. We can talk more then.'

With that, Mrs Stephens went back downstairs, her candle casting large, looming shadows onto the wall as she descended.

The room was small and plainly furnished – a wardrobe and dresser, a washstand in the corner and a table next to the bed – but it was clean and it was quiet and it was hers. Her luggage was on the floor by the bed and Mercy began to carefully unpack her things, hanging her one good dress in the wardrobe and laying her nightgown across the bed, smoothing out the creases.

Here was her prayer book, given to her by Mrs Whitworth when she was small. She held it to her nose. Did it smell of Hamblin? Of home?

She liked to think it did. And here was her most treasured possession: her sketchbook and pencils. She hadn't had room to bring all of her materials, had cried bitter tears at saying goodbye to her paintings and drawings, even her early attempts that were rather clumsy and unskilled. They were like old friends and leaving them had been hard.

She flicked through the book, which still had plenty of blank pages waiting to be filled. There were studies of hands, which she always struggled to get right, a portrait of Old Sarah and another of dear Mrs Whitworth. She turned the next page. Here was a sketch she had made of the house. How strange to think she would never see it again. She closed the book. This was her home now.

She went to the window and peered out between the curtains. A heavy fog obscured the view but she knew it was out there. London. Where the streets were paved with gold and anything was possible – or so they said. A movement below caught her attention. She had the impression of a dark figure, glimpsed in the greenish light of the gas lamp. But then it was gone. Perhaps it was just a trick of the light? Mercy drew the curtains.

Soon she lay cocooned in the crisp, white sheets that were scented with lavender. Her tired mind darted here and there while her body seemed to rock from side to side as though she were still in the stage-coach. *I'm wide awake*, she thought, and then she thought no more as she fell instantly into a deep and dreamless sleep.

Chapter 2

Mercy was woken the next day by a strange noise. For a moment panic gripped her as she struggled to understand where she was, disorientated to see the door and window not in their usual places. Then she heard the sound again; someone calling. She remembered where she was now and saw that fingers of light were creeping in around the edges of the curtains. It was morning.

'Agaboa!'

There was that calling again. It sounded closer now. Mercy got out of bed, the chill air causing the hairs to rise from her skin, and went to the window to look out. The sky was silvery grey, shot through with rose and apricot. Roofs and chimney pots stretched out impossibly far in every direction. What a wonderful painting it would make.

'Agaboa!'

She looked down and saw a grimy-looking man making his way past the house, a sack slung over one shoulder and a stick with a hook on the end in his other hand.

'Rag-a'-bone! Rag-a'-bone!' he called, more clearly now, each time with the same sing-song quality.

Mercy watched him as he picked through the ashes and dirt discarded in the gutter until, finding nothing, he moved on down the street. Her eye was caught by a movement outside one of the houses across the street, where a maid was vigorously shaking out the front doormat, beating it with one hand so that clouds of dust flew up into the air. Further down, an old man was leading a donkey, laden with vegetables. All around, a growing orchestra of sound: the clip-clop of horses' hooves, the swish-swish-swish of a street-sweeper's brush. A city coming to life.

At home – her old home, she corrected herself – her room had looked out over the garden, with not a building or a person in sight, save for the odd glimpse of the gardener. The only sound had been birdsong or the mooing of the cows from a nearby field. She felt a sudden rush of excitement at all this noise – all this life – and she washed and dressed in a hurry, eager to start the day.

And yet she found the house silent, all the doors closed. Of course, she remembered now, Mrs Stephens had said she would be out all morning. There was no sign of Dr Stephens, either. Which one was his door? Mercy paused on the landing, unsure where she should go. She found herself drawn towards the kitchen, from where the sweet and spicy smell of stewing fruit grew stronger as she went down the stairs.

The kitchen door was open but she knocked softly nonetheless. There was a young woman adding coal to the fire who now turned to face her, hand on hip. 'Oh,' the girl said and went back to her work, shovelling the coal from a bucket next to the fire and prodding it vigorously with a poker, causing the flames to catch and grow, sending sparks flying.

'Good morning,' Mercy said, summoning up her confidence. 'You must be Bridget?'

'Must be, mustn't I,' said the girl. She wiped her hands on her apron and tucked some unruly strands of russet hair under her white cap.

'I'm Mercy.' The girl did not respond. 'I expect Mrs Stephens has told you about me?' Mercy went on, all confidence now ebbing away. 'May I?' She gestured to the table that stood in the centre of the room, flanked by two benches.

'Suit yourself.'

'I wasn't sure what I should do.'

Bridget said nothing but took up a wooden board, on which sat a plump loaf of bread, and put it down on the table in front of Mercy.

'Help yourself. I've work to do.' She threw down knife, butter and plate, muttering, 'Haven't the time to be waiting on everybody hand and foot. Cook's day off, and don't I have enough to do?' She hesitated for a moment and then retrieved a jar from one of the shelves. 'Jam,' she said.

Mercy held out her hand with a 'thank you' on her lips but Bridget sniffed and placed the jar on the table, avoiding Mercy's outstretched hand. She pretended not to notice; it wasn't the first time it had happened, after all. As the only black face in Hamblin – in all of Worcestershire for all she knew – she'd had her fair share of queer looks and unfriendly treatment. She watched as Bridget went back to the fruit that was bubbling and steaming on the stove. Her sleeves were rolled up to her elbows, and Mercy could see the power in her muscled forearms as she lifted up the pan of fruit to pour it into a ceramic bowl to cool.

Mercy ate in silence, watching the girl as she moved about the kitchen. She was a little younger than Mercy, maybe sixteen or seventeen. She was like Titian's Venus, with her red hair and pale skin. No number of milk baths or vinegar scrubs would make her own skin that colour and Lord knows, she'd tried. She recalled with embarrassment how Mrs Whitworth's cook had once caught her dusting her face with flour in an attempt to make it paler. But then again, Bridget's hands were red and chapped, whereas her own were soft and smooth, she thought, as she looked down at her fingers, each with its neatly curved nail.

Bridget now took a huge lump of dough from beneath a cloth and began to knead it on the other end of the kitchen table. Mercy's plate shivered and jumped as the dough was beaten into life. In truth, she jumped a little too; there was a fierceness in this girl and the air around her seemed to crackle. Feeling like an unwanted intruder, Mercy finished her breakfast in haste, her words of thanks as she left met only with an impassive stare.

She hovered again on the stairs before deciding to fetch her pencils and sketchbook. She had loved to draw ever since she was young, and it was a comfort now, in this strange new house, to have the familiar feel of the pencil in her hand, the blank page before her. She liked to draw portraits, and so she began now to create a likeness of Mrs Stephens, calling to mind her sparkling eyes and bright smile, her ringlets that were the colour of conkers and just as shiny.

She was a difficult subject, though, as her face was so mobile and seemed always to be changing. No, that wouldn't do. Her chin was too broad and her brow too low. Mercy began again with a study of Bridget, smiling to herself when she managed to capture the maid's surly expression.

What about Dr Stephens? She'd only seen him briefly but she found that she could recall his face perfectly; the long, slender nose and thin lips, the faint eyebrows and the kind eyes beneath them. As she moved her pencil back and forth across the page, his face came to life, perhaps looking a little younger than he actually was, but yes, that was definitely him.

'My, do I really look so stern?'

Mercy jumped in surprise and turned to see Dr Stephens himself peering over her shoulder. She had been so absorbed in her drawing that she hadn't heard him come in. Mercy closed the sketchbook and sprang to her feet, dropping her pencil in the process. It rolled across the rug and Dr Stephens bent to pick it up.

'I'm sorry, sir—' she stuttered. How she wished that the ground would open up and swallow her whole.

'Here you are,' the doctor said as he passed her pencil back to her. 'And no need to apologise. It's really very good. May I?' He gestured to the book.

Mercy hesitated – she rarely showed her drawings to anyone – but felt she had no choice but to hand it to him. He took it and sat on the sofa, turning the pages slowly.

'My, these really are very accomplished,' he said. Did he really mean it? 'What's this one?'

Mercy moved closer and the doctor gestured for her to sit beside him. He was holding the book open on one of her few drawings that wasn't taken from life. It was a building, circular in shape with a conical roof.

'I don't really know,' Mercy said truthfully. 'I just found myself drawing it.' She had drawn the building more than once, in fact, had wondered herself where it came from – a dream? A fairy tale?

Just then they heard the front door open and Dr Stephens stood abruptly as his wife came into the room.

'Catherine, it seems we have an artist in our midst,' he said.

'How marvellous,' Mrs Stephens said, taking up the book.

Mercy held her breath, praying that Mrs Stephens wouldn't see the rather unflattering drawing of herself. Thankfully, she only glanced briefly through the book.

'Delightful,' she said, closing the book with a snap. 'Now, let's see what other talents you have, Mercy. I think it's about time we set you to work!'

She began selecting books from the bookshelf and piling them up on the table. Mercy spotted the title of one of them, *A Vindication of the Rights of Woman*, and immediately felt nerves bubbling up in her stomach. What if she couldn't manage whatever Mrs Stephens had in store for her? What if she decided to send her away?

'I shall leave you ladies to it,' said the doctor as he rose from the sofa.

On his way out he smiled at Mercy and, as if sensing her anxiety, he mouthed 'good luck' and nodded his encouragement. This small kindness buoyed her up and she held her head a little higher as Mrs Stephens turned to her.

'Now, where shall we begin?'

Mrs Stephens explained that she was a member of several societies and charities, and that Mercy's role would include organising and cataloguing her extensive collection of books and pamphlets, recording appointments in her diary, as well as writing out Mrs Stephens's correspondence, and so on.

'You shall be my very own amanuensis!' Mrs Stephens said. 'Should you like that?'

Mercy nodded and smiled, though she wasn't entirely sure what an amanuensis was. It sounded like some sort of secretary and she resolved to look it up later in Mrs Stephens's tome of a dictionary, just to be sure. An unusual role for a young woman such as herself. But, as Mercy was beginning to learn, there was much about Mrs Stephens that was unusual. She told Mercy that she had been her parents' only child and that her father had brought her up almost as though she were a boy, giving her the best education and talking to her about politics from an early age. She was passionate about equality and even thought that women should be able to vote.

'All are equal before the Lord, Mercy,' she said on that first day. 'Man and woman. Black and white. As Wollstonecraft said, "There must be more equality established in society, or morality will never gain ground".'

Mercy nodded again. What a lot she had to learn.

'Now,' said Mrs Stephens. 'I don't know about you but I could do with some refreshment. Be a dear and go down to the kitchen. Tell Bridget we require coffee – and no dilly-dallying!'

One day, a week after Mercy arrived in London, Mrs Stephens announced that they were going out. Their mission was to persuade sweetshop owners and bakers to boycott sugar from the West Indies. This was all part of what Mrs Stephens referred to as 'the great campaign'; namely the campaign to end slavery for good. Mercy hadn't had much time for drawing since arriving in London and so she was happy to put her artistic skills to good use by making signs for them to hand out to willing shopkeepers: neat rectangles, bordered with black, declaring *We use EAST INDIA SUGAR. Not Grown by SLAVES*.

Mercy had quickly discovered that Mrs Stephens's biggest passion was the abolition movement. Her father had been keenly involved in the campaign to ban the slave trade some fifteen years before and Mrs Stephens was now a leading member of the Female Society for the Abolition of Slavery. Her husband was involved in the movement too, though his work prevented him from being quite so active as Mrs Stephens. In fact, Dr Stephens seemed to support her in everything she did. Mercy hadn't had much experience of husbands – Mr Whitworth had died before she went to live in Hamblin – but she was quite sure they weren't all as amenable as Dr Stephens.

The campaign against slavery was all new to Mercy. She'd heard of abolition but she had never really given it much thought. She knew slaves existed, but there hadn't been any in England for many years; they were far away in some foreign land.

'Slavery is a stain on the soul of humanity, my dear,' Mrs Stephens had said, touching Mercy's face with a gentle hand.

Whenever she said the word 'slavery' in Mercy's presence, there was always that knowing look, the slight tilt of the head. She almost mouthed the word rather than saying it aloud as if just because Mercy shared the same skin colour as those poor unfortunates, she was somehow connected to them. But Mercy could no more feel an affinity with those wretched souls in the West Indies than she could with the man in the moon. She had looked at Mrs Stephens's pamphlets, with pictures of slaves in various poses of servitude and despair, had run her fingers over those black figures, with their strange clothes and bare feet, and felt pity, of course, but she was not like them. Not at all. She was from a noble family. Her father had been a prince.

In any case, she had been lucky that, thanks to her father's money, she had been given a good education and a comfortable life in England. She was pleased that now she could do something for those who were less fortunate than herself and she was learning a great deal from Mrs Stephens. She had never realised that women could do so much. Mrs Whitworth had been active – she'd organised poetry readings and been involved with local church events and so on – but that all felt so small, so insignificant now. Mrs Stephens wanted to change the world and it was exhilarating to be a part of that.

And so they set off, through the busy city streets, armed with their signs and a list of sweetshops and bakeries. Mercy was only just beginning to comprehend the sheer size of this city. The Stephenses lived in an area called Westminster – with the old abbey and the Palace of Westminster to one side and the River Thames to the other – but apparently that was just one small part of London. Dr Stephens had told her that it was the largest city in the whole world and that over a million people lived there. She wasn't sure if he was joking – how could there be a million of anything? – but looking around at the crowds of shoppers and carriages, street-sweepers and beggars, she thought that perhaps it could be true.

With all the noise and dirt and twisting streets, it was a wonder that anyone could ever find their way. But Mrs Stephens seemed to know where she was going and after a few minutes they stopped outside another shop. Above the door was a swinging sign with 'Hannigan's' emblazoned across it in gold paint.

'Here we are. I shan't be long,' said Mrs Stephens.

Mercy waited outside while Mrs Stephens went to talk to the shopkeepers. She was still in her mourning clothes and Mrs Stephens thought that might not set quite the right tone.

'You look rather too severe,' she had said, and Mercy supposed she was right as she caught a glimpse of herself reflected in the shop window.

She turned her gaze instead to the dishes on display on the other side of the glass. There were hard-boiled sweets in bold citrus colours, marzipan shaped miraculously into tiny animals and fruits, gleaming toffees, sugary twists of candied peel. Without noticing, she licked imagined sugar from her lips.

As Mrs Stephens left the shop, the bell above the door gave a cheerful tinkle.

'Success!' she declared, smiling. 'Now, come on. No dawdling!' She took Mercy's arm, leading her down the street at a brisk pace, heedless of the blisters that were beginning to pinch at Mercy's heels.

While Mrs Stephens could be demanding she was also generous, and when they got home after their tour of the sweetshops of London, she announced that she had a treat in store. She asked Mercy to wait in the parlour while she went up to her room, returning a few minutes later and calling to Mercy to close her eyes.

'Ready?' she called.

When Mercy opened her eyes she saw that Mrs Stephens was holding a dress. The most beautiful dress Mercy had ever seen. It was lemon-yellow and made of taffeta and silk with delicate bands of lace adorning the hem and the sleeves.

'Go on, take it,' Mrs Stephens said. 'I know you cared deeply for Mrs Whitworth but I think it's about time you discarded those dingy clothes.'

Mercy hesitated.

'You weren't actually related, after all,' Mrs Stephens went on. 'And this colour will suit you so much better than me.'

Mercy reached out to touch the dress with a careful finger. Mrs Whitworth's death did seem a very long time ago now, though really it was only a matter of weeks. And Mrs Stephens was right, she wasn't related to Mrs Whitworth. Though it hurt a little to be reminded of that, it did mean that she wasn't actually obliged to wear mourning dress. And that colour was quite something.

'Try it on,' said Mrs Stephens with a smile. 'And later I'll speak to Edwin about a proper shopping trip for you. I hear the fashion now is for shorter, fuller sleeves. We can pick out one or two dresses for you. Some shoes. Whatever you like.'

Mercy had to admit that some new clothes would be welcome. In Hamblin, she'd had no one to compare herself to other than Mrs Whitworth's aged friends and the village wives with their plain skirts and knitted shawls. Mercy had always considered herself well dressed, but since arriving in London she couldn't help but compare her own dour dresses with the vibrant outfits of Mrs Stephens and her friends. She was a princess, after all, and it was only right that she should look the part. She must ask Dr Stephens about her inheritance, too. She had no idea how much money was left from her father's bequest. Mrs Whitworth had always been rather vague about the exact amount but now that she was nineteen, she really ought to know.

She accepted the dress and when she had slipped it on, the silk cool and smooth as water against her skin, she twirled before Mrs Stephens, laughing and giddy with excitement, like a dancing doll in a music box.

Those first few weeks with Mrs Stephens passed by in a blur of meetings and talks, of reading books and pamphlets, of lunches and afternoon teas. Each night Mercy practically fell into her bed, exhausted but content. She and Mrs Stephens got along well; Mercy grew to know her foibles, learned how to make her laugh and when she should hold her tongue. Dr Stephens would often find them together by the fire, heads bent over a book.

'Here they are,' he'd say, 'my two Muses!'

Mrs Stephens seemed to know everyone in London. She counted men of business and Members of Parliament amongst her many acquaintances, as well as a number of writers and artists. The former were invariably old and grey and dry as firewood. Mercy attended a number of meetings with them, where she sat quietly in the corner making notes for Mrs Stephens. It was all she could do to stay awake on some occasions, though Mrs Stephens always managed to act as if the gentleman in question was the most fascinating man alive as she cajoled him into signing a petition or giving a donation to the cause.

Mercy was far more interested in the writers and artists, though she was yet to meet any of them. According to Mrs Stephens, while they could be useful for spreading the message and were good at parties, artists were often poor or mad or both. One day, however, Mrs Stephens announced that they would be having a guest for lunch; a Mr James Northbury, a painter and a fervent abolitionist.

'The Alderneys introduced me to him,' Mrs Stephens said. 'A charming gentleman and very interesting. He's a portrait artist. Perhaps we might persuade him to paint me – what do you think, Edwin?'

Dr Stephens was reading the paper and didn't respond. Mercy saw Mrs Stephens's mouth begin to purse with irritation.

'I'm sure he will want to, ma'am,' she said. 'You have such a fine complexion.'

'Oh, Mercy, don't be silly,' Mrs Stephens said, but she smiled as she said it. 'Pop down to the kitchen and tell Mrs Dowers about our guest, would you, Mercy? We'll need something a bit special for lunch. Ask her to come up and see me.'

Mrs Dowers was the cook, a woman of few words who seemed to have taken an instant dislike to Mercy for some reason. Mercy tried to avoid her as far as possible – tried to avoid all the servants, in fact.

As well as the cook and Bridget, there was Martin, Dr Stephens's valet. He was a smooth-faced man in his twenties with a sly smile and a gaze that couldn't quite meet Mercy's eye but which seemed to have no trouble resting somewhere on her chest.

Mercy reached the kitchen door and was about to go in when she heard her name.

'Thinking herself so high and mighty. A regular Jack Brag, that one.' It was Mrs Dowers.

'She won't give me the time of day.' That was Martin now. 'Thinks herself too good for the likes of us. And her with a face as black as soot.'

'You're just sour 'cause she's not interested in your ugly mug!' Bridget chimed in.

The three of them laughed. Mercy pressed her ear a little closer to the door. How dare they?

'Trust you to defend her!' Martin said.

'What's that supposed to mean?'

'Well, we all know why a girl like you would be fond of the blacks.'

There was a shriek from Bridget and then Mrs Dowers spoke, more sternly now. 'That's enough, you two. I won't have filthy talk like that in my kitchen.'

Mercy burned with indignation. She wasn't entirely sure what Martin meant but she knew they were laughing at her expense. She pushed open the kitchen door and, in her most imperious voice, informed Mrs Dowers that her presence was required by the mistress. Then she turned on her heel and left, head held high.

They could laugh all they liked. They were just jealous. She was the one who would be taking lunch with the Stephenses and a renowned artist while they were cramped in the kitchen. And if that made her a 'Jack Brag' – whatever that was – well, then she couldn't care less.

Mercy was disappointed to find that Mr Northbury, rather than the dashing young man she was hoping for, turned out to be well into his forties, with a wife and several children – not to mention a terrible habit of slurping his soup like a hog at a trough. She was sure Dr Stephens had noticed it too, for he had caught Mercy's eye with a look that caused her to press her napkin to her mouth with a feigned cough to hide her laughter.

Yet he was an entertaining guest and genuinely passionate about the campaign to end slavery. As they sipped coffee after lunch, Dr Stephens mentioned that Mercy had a talent for drawing and the artist turned to her with a raised eyebrow.

'Is that so, young lady?' he said. 'And pray, what is your subject?'

'People, mostly,' Mercy answered, feeling suddenly shy.

'Very good. And what is your medium?'

'Oh, well, pencil, I suppose. I like to paint but I wasn't able to bring all my things to London. There wasn't room. And now I'm so busy, there really isn't time.'

Mr Northbury looked as though he were about to speak again but before he could, Mrs Stephens was offering him more coffee.

'And you must try one of these little biscuits, they're delightful. Yes, Mercy is so busy with the campaign, aren't you, my dear? But it's wonderful to have a hobby. I myself used to spend hours pressing flowers as a young girl, and then arranging them, you know?'

Mr Northbury nodded and smiled. 'Yes, how lovely.'

Their conversation moved on and Mercy sipped at her coffee, glad that the focus was away from her but also wishing that she had said more. She was sure that Mr Northbury must think her a complete dunce. But then, as he left, she went to shake his hand and he held on to it for just a moment and leaned towards her.

'No matter how busy you are, you must make time for art. It is what sustains us.'

He smiled and Mercy nodded.

'What did Mr Northbury say to you as he left?' Mrs Stephens asked later. 'He seemed to take rather a shine to you.'

'Oh, nothing,' Mercy replied. 'He just said goodbye, that's all.'

She spent most of her time with Mrs Stephens – shared all her thoughts with her – and yet she found that this was one thing she wanted to keep all to herself.

That night Mercy begged an extra candle from Bridget and, though her eyes were dry with tiredness and she longed to crawl under the covers, she sat up for an hour with her pencil and sketchbook. *Art is what sustains us*, she wrote carefully inside the cover.

Chapter 3

A week later, Mercy watched as Mrs Stephens's fingers tapped nervous as moths on glass against the paper containing the notes for her next speech.

'Are you sure you can bear to hear it again?' she asked.

Mercy nodded. She loved watching Mrs Stephens as she paced about the room, eyes like flint, her voice as soothing as a breeze one minute and as sharp as a whip the next. She was like an actress – no, for actresses were only pretending, whereas Mrs Stephens meant every word.

On Friday she was giving a speech to the Grocers' Company and she needed to practise. Mercy had learned by now that there were companies in London for everything from bakers and brewers to ironmongers and farriers, and that the Grocers' was one of the oldest and most influential. Mrs Stephens wanted their support with the sugar boycott and so this speech was terribly important.

Mercy had helped Mrs Stephens to write it and now watched her rehearsing, signalling with her hand when she thought she should slow down or pause. Mrs Stephens had said several times how much she depended on Mercy, that she couldn't imagine being without her, that she didn't know how she had coped before Mercy arrived. For her part, Mercy had come to rely on Mrs Stephens, taking her recommendations for what books she should read, what clothes she should wear, how she should comport herself.

Mrs Stephens had made her a gift of a set of Jane Austen novels when she realised how much Mercy loved to read, and sometimes Mercy liked to daydream that they were sisters like the Dashwoods or the Bennets. In reality, at thirty-five, Mrs Stephens was almost old enough to be her mother, but she had such a youthful air that Mercy often forgot that. She hadn't dared broach the subject of why she and Dr Stephens had no children of their own. She sensed it was a source of pain for Mrs Stephens; wondered if it was perhaps the reason she threw herself so thoroughly into her campaigning.

Lately, Mrs Stephens had taken to asking Mercy to help arrange her hair. This had previously been Bridget's job, and Mercy couldn't help but feel a prick of triumph when she saw the maid's mouth twist as Mrs Stephens dismissed her.

'Her fingers are just so much more gentle, Bridget. You plait my hair like I'm a prize pony! Now, off you go. I'm sure you've other work to be getting on with.'

Bridget stared at Mercy for a moment before her gaze slid away and she left the room.

'I think I've upset her!' Mrs Stephens caught Mercy's eye in the mirror and they both laughed; conspirators, confidantes.

Bridget was taciturn and sullen in Mercy's presence. She reminded Mercy of Mrs Whitworth's cat, Tansy, who had glared balefully at visitors before slinking off imperiously, tail held high. Bridget even shared the cat's green eyes and thick tawny hair, she thought with a smirk. Though, truth be told, Mercy rather admired those green eyes, that long, straight red hair which could be coiled and plaited in ways that her own could not.

In any case, she had no need of Bridget's friendship. Not when she had Mrs Stephens. And it wouldn't do for her to become too familiar with the servants. As Mrs Stephens's assistant, Mercy was in a different class altogether. It was no wonder that Bridget and the others would be envious.

Mrs Stephens had reached the climax of her speech, her fist in the air.

'Well, what do you think?'

But before Mercy could respond, the doctor came in from the hall where he must have been listening.

'Bravo!' he said, clapping his hands together. 'Bravo! There isn't a grocer alive who could resist you!'

'Do you really think so?'

'Of course,' said Mercy. 'You'll be wonderful.'

'And you'll both be there?' said Mrs Stephens expectantly. 'I need you both at my side. Especially you, Mercy. I can't do it without you.'

Mercy reassured her that of course she would be there, enjoying the warm glow that came of feeling so needed, so valued.

The Grocers' Hall was grand, its walls hung with portraits of kings, nobles and other men of note. Mercy was sure their painted eyes were watching her as Dr Stephens guided her through the crowd. She wondered how many black faces they had seen passing through this hall. Not many, that was for sure.

The place hummed with noise. Mercy felt nerves gnawing at her as they made their way deeper into the crowd. The chatter fell silent as Mercy passed amongst them and she could feel a thousand eyes on her, hear the occasional tut and mutter. She kept her gaze down, glimpsing only an impression of black leather-shod feet, dark woollen trousers, and here and there a silver- or ivory-tipped walking cane. The air was thick with the scent of cigar smoke, of expensive cologne, of money. Only the reassuring pressure of Dr Stephens's hand on her arm kept her from turning and running out of the door.

They arrived at the platform that had been set up at one end of the hall and found themselves a place to stand where they could get a good view of Mrs Stephens, who was now taking to the stage. She cut an impressive figure in the dress Mercy had picked out for her; oxblood silk that gleamed in the light of the chandeliers. She wore a large silver medal at her throat that read *Am I Not a Woman and a Sister?* above the image of a kneeling woman, her uplifted arms in chains. On the stage, Mrs Stephens seemed somehow taller – more solid – and as she stepped forward the crowd began to hush. Mercy heard one or two scoffing at the idea that they should be lectured by a woman but, undeterred, Mrs Stephens began.

'Gentlemen. Friends. I thank you most heartily for being here today. Never has a matter been of more import than that of the pernicious, inhuman and hateful matter of slavery.'

Mercy could hear mutterings of agreement amongst the crowd as Mrs Stephens went on, though many remained silent.

'Perhaps some of you are not well acquainted with the subject, so please permit me to explain to you what it is and what it means for those who must suffer it. First, let us imagine a child who is born a slave. From the day of his birth he is considered a brute – a beast. From that very day he becomes property, the property of a master, who may sell him and do with him what he pleases.'

How Mercy wished that she could have the same courage as Mrs Stephens. The idea of being up there with all those men staring was unbearable. She felt herself grow hot at the thought of it, felt the itch of sweat at her armpits.

'He works, but he is not paid for his labour. He works not freely and willingly, as our labourers do here in England, but he is followed by a driver, whose whip leaves the marks of its severity upon his back. And if he resists? If he is found to be obstinate? Chains, iron collars, shackles – and other vile modes of punishment.'

Mrs Stephens dabbed at her eye with her handkerchief. She always did that at this bit of the speech. 'You would be amazed, Mercy,' she had said, 'how a few womanly tears can work upon a man's conscience.' The crowd shifted and murmured to one another. It seemed to be working.

'And there are other evils belonging to slavery,' Mrs Stephens said, dropping her voice lower so that the crowd leaned in to listen. 'Perhaps a slave has a wife and family. He may be sold at any moment to go to a plantation a hundred miles away, never to see them again. The wife may be severed from her husband, the children may be severed from their parents. I ask you, gentlemen, to consider your own wives, your own children, and to imagine being separated from them in this most cruel and pernicious manner.'

That was Mercy's favourite bit; she had suggested the line about their own wives and children. She sneaked a look at the men standing nearby, their faces upturned towards the stage. One, a barrel-chested man with bushy sideburns, shook his head from side to side, clapping his hand upon the shoulder of the young man next to him – his son perhaps. Were those tears in his eyes?

Mercy looked at Dr Stephens who was watching his wife intently. Feeling Mercy's gaze, he turned to her and nodded. It was going well. Mrs Stephens was speaking now about the Slave Trade Act that had passed some thirteen years ago. The Act had banned the buying and selling of African slaves, and Mrs Stephens had told Mercy that back then they had all thought it would bring an end to slavery itself.

'But, no,' Mrs Stephens was saying now. 'Like an unstoppable plague, it grows and grows, polluting our very souls with its continued existence. Right now, in Guyana, British plantation owners, unable to purchase slaves from across the sea, are buying up land – and slaves – from the Dutch and the French, so they can convert this land to grow sugar. The trade in people continues, the raising up of profit over people continues, and the subjugation and murder of thousands and thousands of innocent people continues!'

She paused, her gaze travelling across the crowd before her, as though daring them to look away.

'And that, gentlemen, is why I am here. I do not doubt your willingness to pity the oppressed at home – I know of the charitable work that you undertake for the poor and destitute here in London. And I commend it. Can you, then, overlook this monstrous oppression, these atrocious outrages upon human nature, simply because they take place in a foreign land? Christianity, true Christianity, does not confine its sympathy to country or colour, but feels for all who are persecuted wherever they may live.'

To her left, Mercy could see a cadaverous old man with wisps of hair brushed across his scalp, who was bashing his cane on the floor. He shook his head, his lip curled in a sneer, and Mercy realised with a shudder that he wasn't agreeing with Mrs Stephens – quite the opposite. She looked away, instinctively stepping a little closer to Dr Stephens, who glanced at her with a smile.

Mrs Stephens was reaching the end of her speech now. She finished with her fist held aloft, just as Mercy had seen her do before. Tendrils of hair had escaped from under her hat, and her cheeks and neck were flushed pink with emotion. Most of the crowd cheered and applauded and Mercy waited for Mrs Stephens to bring out her handkerchief again, as she always did at the end of the speech, and dab at the tears which brimmed in her eyes. But for once she didn't. Instead, she held up her hand, requesting quiet, and then strode to the edge of the platform where Mercy and the doctor were standing.

Looking up at Mrs Stephens, her dress blending in with the dark red walls, Mercy had only the impression of her face, a white oval, and her two gleaming eyes. She reached down and Mercy, hypnotised, took her hand and felt herself being pulled up onto the platform. The crowd was quiet now. Mercy looked out over a sea of white faces. Her heart thumped in her chest and she held fast to Mrs Stephens's hand, her palm slick with sweat.

'Gentlemen, look at this young woman.' Mrs Stephens's grip was like steel. 'She is one of the lucky ones. She has a life of comfort and contentment. An education and the knowledge of Our Lord Jesus Christ. But just think how different her life could be. Enslaved, beaten, whipped, defiled.'

Mercy lifted her gaze from the faces that seemed to float before her. The same white face repeated over and over. She could feel humiliation like a burning poker thrust into her gut. She tried to release her hand but Mrs Stephens held her fast.

'If my words have not moved you, then let this young woman work upon your conscience! For she is an example of what we can achieve when we free the enslaved, when we educate, enlighten, enrich them. With a decent Christian education, the dear blacks can be just the same as you or I. This young woman is the living proof that the African is not our inferior but our brother, our sister – our equal!'

There was more applause; a cacophony of voices. Mrs Stephens let go of her hand and the crowd surged forward towards the stage. For a moment, Mercy was rooted to the spot. She looked at Mrs Stephens who winked and smiled, then turned away to unroll the pledge so that the men could sign it. Her part played, Mercy was forgotten.

She stumbled down from the stage where Dr Stephens was waiting for her.

'Mercy, are you quite well?'

'No, not really.' She desperately needed to get out of here. 'I think I need a little air.'

'Of course, let me help you.'

Despite Mercy's protests that she could manage on her own, he took her by the arm and led her through the crowd. Again she kept her gaze to the floor, unwilling to meet the curious glances no doubt being cast in her direction. Outside, Mercy took several gulps of air and slowly the hot, shaky feeling subsided.

'Mercy?' The doctor looked at her with concern.

'I'm quite all right, thank you. I'll just take a moment,' she said, wanting only to be alone.

He nodded and went back inside. Mercy tipped her face up to the grey sky, watched a solitary gull circling slowly overhead as she tried to calm her thoughts. How could she have done it? How could Mrs Stephens embarrass her like that? Perhaps she had just got carried away. She would feel terrible and apologise and all would be forgiven. But Mercy remembered how keen Mrs Stephens had been for her to come today. *I can't do it without you*, she had said. Had she planned it all along?

In the carriage on the way back, Mrs Stephens said nothing of what had happened. Instead, she talked incessantly about how well it had gone, how many signatures they had got, how much money had been pledged.

'Whatever's the matter, Mercy?' she finally asked. 'You've been very quiet.'

'I'm sorry,' Mercy said, unable even to look her in the eye. 'I have the most terrible headache.'

'Oh dear,' Mrs Stephens said. 'I'm sure Edwin can give you something for that when we get home.'

And on she went about the campaign and her speech and what a great success the day had been. Mercy closed her eyes and pressed her face up against the side of the carriage. How could she not realise how awful it had been for Mercy to be hauled up onto the stage like that? To be used as a prop for the colour of her skin? Mercy had dared to believe that she and Mrs Stephens were friends, equals even. Now she saw that she was just a useful pawn in the great campaign. She felt – betrayed. Yes, utterly betrayed.

When they got home, Mercy excused herself and went straight to her room. Where else was she to go? She couldn't bear to hear Mrs Stephens's voice for a moment longer, and she knew she wouldn't be welcome in the kitchen where Bridget and Mrs Dowers treated her like an unwelcome guest. She had dreamed that her new life in London would be one of happiness and opportunity, but now it felt as though all that promise had turned to ash. Mercy got into bed, fully dressed, and pulled the covers up over her head, as if by doing so she could hide from the loneliness that stretched out around her, wide and deep as the ocean.

Chapter 4

The next morning, Mercy's anger had cooled a little but she could still feel the injustice of the day before, like a pebble lodged in her chest. She sat up in bed for a while, reluctant to see Mrs Stephens just yet, and took up her sketchbook. But she found her fingers wouldn't obey and everything she drew came out clumsy and wrong.

There was a knock at her door. It was Bridget.

'Mistress wants you. Better get up.'

It occurred to Mercy then that Bridget would have already been up for hours, cleaning out the grates and setting the fires, sweeping and scrubbing and preparing the breakfast. She felt a twinge of guilt – shame even – as she put aside her sketches and pencils and got out of bed.

Mrs Stephens was waiting for her in the parlour.

'Good morning!' She beamed as Mercy came in. 'How's your head? Feeling better?' She took Mercy's hands in her own. 'Gosh, how chilly you are! Come over here by the fire.'

She led Mercy to the chair by the fire, rubbed Mercy's hands between her own.

'I'm feeling much better, thank you, ma'am.'

'I'm so glad. It occurred to me that perhaps I owe you an apology. Well, it was something Edwin said. That perhaps I was a little thoughtless. I should never have got you involved like that. Not without asking you first. I was carried away by the moment! You understand?'

'Well, I—'

'I could feel that I had them in my grasp – the audience. And it is so, so important that we get them on our side, do you see? We must do whatever it takes! I'm sure you agree?'

'Yes, yes, of course, ma'am.'

What else could she possibly say? And maybe Mrs Stephens was right – they should do anything to achieve their aim, even if it meant a little personal anguish. And yet. And yet she couldn't shake the feeling that Mrs Stephens had engineered the whole thing, had thought it easier to ask for forgiveness after the fact than to seek permission before it.

'I knew you would understand!' Mrs Stephens was smiling now. 'You're such a good girl. Now, I have a treat for you.'

She went to the door and called for Bridget, who arrived with a tray bearing two cups and a plate of muffins.

'Thank you, Bridget,' Mrs Stephens said, gesturing for her to leave.

'Yes, thank you, Bridget,' Mercy added, shreds of guilt still clinging to her, but Bridget didn't notice, didn't even glance at her.

'Now, tuck in. We must build up your strength!' Mrs Stephens passed her a cup. 'Hot chocolate – made with the finest *East* Indian sugar, of course!'

'Thank you.'

The chocolate was delicious, she had to admit, smooth and sweet and creamy. And the muffins were soft and spread thick with butter. Mrs Stephens wasn't so bad, Mercy told herself. She had just got carried away. And it was all for the greater good of the campaign.

'Now, this morning you may rest,' Mrs Stephens said. 'I have a lunch appointment but I shan't need you for that. We can set to work this afternoon. I'll need you to copy out all those names from yesterday's pledge. Now, drink up! Don't let it go cold.'

Her relations with Mrs Stephens soon slipped back into their familiar and comfortable rhythms, and Mercy tried to put the memory of that day in the Grocers' Hall behind her. In fact, Mrs Stephens seemed to go out of her way to be kind to her and even bought tickets for the two of them, and Dr Stephens, to visit an art exhibition. This would be Mercy's first, and she couldn't wait. She still took up her own pencil when she found the time, but to see the works of professional artists – to actually see them in front of her rather than in the pages of a book – would be quite something.

'It's some French artist,' Mrs Stephens said. 'The whole of London is talking about it. And anyone who is anyone has been to see it.'

Dr Stephens had been reluctant, muttering something about being too busy, but his wife had a habit of getting her own way, Mercy realised, for after a hushed conversation between the two of them, the doctor had announced that he would be 'delighted to accompany them'. And so it was that the following Saturday the three of them travelled by carriage to Piccadilly.

'Here we are,' said Dr Stephens, as the carriage pulled up outside the most extraordinary building.

The doorway was flanked by two fluted pillars and above these two giant statues, one male and one female, gazed out across the street. Above these were two sphinxes, back-to-back, with some kind of bird in between them. And right at the very top of the building, the word 'MUSEUM' was carved in large letters across the façade. The building was positioned amongst a row of quite ordinary shops which only served to make it all the more startling.

'It's quite something, isn't it?' said Dr Stephens.

'Yes!' Mercy agreed. 'Those figures, are they Egyptian?' She had seen pictures of similar statues, of pyramids and sphinxes, but never thought she would see them with her own eyes.

'That's right,' the doctor said. 'In fact, it's known as the Egyptian Hall. It was built as a museum to display objects from all over the world.'

'Come along, you two. I want to get inside.' Mrs Stephens began to herd them towards the entrance. 'I think I just saw Lydia Hazelwood going in.'

Inside, they found themselves in the main hall, which, like the exterior, was ornately decorated with carved columns. The walls were painted with symbols and strange figures that were half-human, half-animal. There was a buzz of conversation from the people that milled about inside, many, like Mercy, with eyes wide as they looked around them.

Mrs Stephens was in pursuit of Lydia Hazelwood, the wife of a prominent MP whom she was trying to recruit for the campaign, and Dr Stephens and Mercy tried desperately to keep up with her as she led them through the crowds.

'Catherine, darling,' Dr Stephens said, and she stopped and turned to him with an impatient, 'Well?'

'Why don't you go and speak to Lydia, and I'll show Mercy round some of the exhibits?'

Mercy was relieved when Mrs Stephens agreed. She would much rather look at the paintings than meet yet another well-meaning, middle-aged white woman who would pat her hair and speak to her as though she were a child. They agreed to meet back at the same spot in an hour, giving Mrs Stephens plenty of time to speak to Mrs Hazelwood and find any other influential people who might be here.

Mercy and the doctor chatted as they wandered through the various rooms that led off from the main hall, and for once Mercy really didn't care about the sideways glances she was attracting. Here she was in a London art gallery, wearing a beautiful dress and accompanied by a distinguished physician. She held her head a little higher, let people stare.

Dr Stephens was explaining how the place had once been a museum of natural history with animals from all over the world stuffed and displayed as if in their natural habitat.

'There were other things too; weapons and musical instruments, crafts, that sort of thing, from all over. Once, they even displayed Napoleon's carriage here. Taken all the way from Waterloo!'

'Really? I should have loved to see it all.' Mercy looked around at the now empty rooms, trying to imagine how it would have been.

'They auctioned it all off last year so you just missed out,' said the doctor. 'Look! I believe this is the Haydon room, come on.'

He had explained that the museum was now used for temporary exhibits, mainly paintings, and though the chief attraction at the moment was by a Frenchman named Géricault, there were also some works by a British artist, Haydon, that Dr Stephens wanted to see. The room wasn't very busy – everyone else seemed more keen to see the Géricault – and so they were able to get a good view of the paintings. One work dominated the room: a huge canvas showing Christ riding into Jerusalem on a donkey, crowds of people surrounding him.

It was incredible. Mercy drew closer, fascinated by the colours, the detail, the expressions of joy and awe and wonder in the faces of the crowd, the amazing sense of perspective that made the painting seem to stretch back and back. She could never imagine creating anything of this scale. How would you even begin?

'Impressive, isn't it?' said Dr Stephens, who stood before the painting, hands folded before him.

'Yes, it's wonderful,' said Mercy. 'The red in that child's cheek, there. And the detailing on this fabric – see how it hangs and drapes just like real fabric would?'

He smiled at her enthusiasm. 'I like this figure here,' he said, pointing at a woman who was holding up her daughter's hand towards Christ, her face full of anticipation.

'What is she doing?' Mercy asked, peering closer.

'Waiting for forgiveness,' the doctor said solemnly. 'The painter has captured the moment just before Christ responds. He is poised to forgive. But does he? It is up to us to decide.'

'I see,' Mercy said.

'What do you think?' asked the doctor. 'Does he forgive her sins?'

In the painting, Christ's face was calm, a halo of light spread out around his head. But his face was turned away from the woman. Did he know she was waiting for his forgiveness? Did she deserve it?

'I suppose he does,' she said eventually, though she felt unsure.

'I'm certain of it,' the doctor said, his eyes fixed on the painting.

They moved on to look at the other works but none of them were quite as impressive. They left the Haydon room and found themselves moving along with the crowd towards the main event: the Géricault.

'Perhaps we should wait for Catherine,' said Dr Stephens, looking around for his wife, who was nowhere to be seen.

'We could always have a little peek now and then come back for a second look with Mrs Stephens?' said Mercy, buoyed up with excitement. 'Please, sir?'

He hesitated and looked at her gravely. Had she been too forward? But then, with a smile, he said, 'Very well, just a little peek,' and they continued towards the doorway.

She couldn't see it at first, there were so many people. She could hear gasps as they caught their first glance of the painting, saw one or two women hurrying away, fanning their faces as they rushed to get out. What was this painting? They picked their way through the room and gradually it took shape before them.

If she had thought the Haydon was big, this painting dwarfed it by comparison. It took up one entire wall of the room and must have been at least twenty feet wide. And whereas the painting of Christ had emanated a feeling of calm exultation, this was like a nightmare. Naked and semi-naked figures writhed in agony or lay dead across one another upon a raft that was tossed about in a stormy sea.

'Mercy.' It was Dr Stephens, his hand upon her arm. 'Perhaps you shouldn't. It's not – seemly.'

He had turned his face from the painting but she felt unable to drag her gaze away. She found her feet stepping closer towards it, her stomach a knot, the back of her neck prickling and cold.

'I want to see,' she said.

Oblivious to the glances from the other visitors, she pushed her way through to the front of the crowd. Technically, the work was a masterpiece; the figures were painted with such vigour, such muscularity, they made Haydon's figures seem flat and dull by comparison. And the expressions on their faces – such anguish and pain, such hopelessness. How had he done this with just a brush and some paint?

She let out a gasp as she noticed that the figure at the top right of the picture, a figure waving at the tiniest speck of a boat on the horizon, was black. The muscles in his back seemed to move as he waved, one foot planted on a barrel, the other on tiptoes in his effort to be seen. He was the only one who hadn't given up hope.

The sounds of the people around her in the gallery faded away. All Mercy could hear now were the cries and moans of the desperate men, the creaking of the makeshift raft as it strained under the barrage of wind and wave. She felt as though she had stepped through the frame and into the painting itself, the boards wet beneath her feet as she suffered the slap of seawater and breathed in the stench of death and decay.

She felt an elbow in her side and with a start she came to, became aware once more of her surroundings. There were people on all sides, jostling to see the painting, and she felt suddenly trapped. Unable to move, unable to breathe. Her mouth was dry and there was not enough air in the room. How could there possibly be enough air for all these people? There were so many of them.

Her heart was beating so fast that she could swear it was going to jump right out of her chest or simply stop. She couldn't breathe. She couldn't breathe. She couldn't breathe.

'Mercy. Mercy? Are you all right?'

It was Dr Stephens, fighting his way through the crowd towards her. He held her arms with a firm grip and led her away from the painting. Her chest was tight. She couldn't breathe.

'Look at me. Look at me.'

She raised her gaze to his. Eye to eye. Dark brown to icy blue.

'Mercy, I'm here,' he said.

And she breathed.

Chapter 5

That evening, Mercy went to bed early, pushing her face into her pillow to muffle her tears. She'd had fits like that before, though they'd never been as severe as today's. She didn't know what caused them exactly and had hoped they were behind her.

A few years ago, Mrs Whitworth's doctor had sternly told her it was a form of hysteria. It was common in young women, he said. He had prescribed bitter-tasting nerve tonics, hot baths, mustard compresses, a sweet syrup that made her sleepy for days. None of them seemed to make any difference. Fear could still grasp at her unexpectedly; a dark monster, always waiting just out of sight. And today had been worse than ever before. That terrifying sensation of being unable to breathe, unable to move. She prayed she would never feel like that again.

Dr Stephens had been so kind to her. He had taken her outside and told her to take several deep breaths of the cold air. The panic had slowly subsided but her legs were weak and her hands wouldn't stop shaking. Then he had led her back inside and found her somewhere to sit while he went to look for Mrs Stephens, who was deep in conversation. When she realised that Mercy had been taken ill she was sympathetic, of course, but Mercy was sure she had seen a flash of irritation – of anger even – in her face.

There was a knock at the door and Mercy wiped away her tears before calling, 'Come in,' aware that her eyes would be puffy from crying. Bridget appeared, bearing an extra blanket and a bowl of broth. She said nothing, simply placed the bowl at the side of the bed and laid the blanket carefully over her.

'Thank you,' Mercy said quietly, unable to meet her eye.

Bridget turned to go but then stopped at the doorway.

'If you need anything. In the night, I mean. Well. You know where I am.'

Before Mercy could reply, she was gone, closing the door behind her with an unaccustomed gentleness.

After she had eaten the broth, which was silky and comforting, Mercy drifted in and out of a fitful sleep until she suddenly found herself open-eyed and awake. Had she heard a noise? She couldn't be sure. She lay very still, listening, but the house was quiet.

She went to the window and looked out. The moon hung full and heavy in the sky, casting a faint light upon the street below. Something about the silence, the still, dark silence, told her it was the early hours of the morning. The houses opposite were shrouded in shadow like widows in mourning. Was that a figure, hiding in the darkness? Two figures? No. It was her imagination. She thought again of the figures in the painting, their twisted limbs, and she felt bile rising in her throat.

Mercy lit a candle with shaking hands, the bobbing orange light bringing some small comfort. She thought of knocking on Bridget's door but knew she could never bring herself to do it. She could just imagine Bridget's smirk of derision. *Frightened of the dark? How ridiculous.* She would go down to the kitchen, she decided. Yes, a mug of milk might help her to sleep.

She was surprised to see a thin line of light shining from underneath the kitchen door – surely Bridget couldn't be up and about already? Mercy pushed the door open slowly. At first she thought it was Martin, whose room was just down the passage, but no, it was Dr Stephens who sat at the kitchen table, his back to the door.

He held a glass in one hand, the other hand cradling his forehead. Two candles were burning on the table and Mercy could see that wax from one of them had started to spill onto the wooden surface, unnoticed by the doctor. She began to back away – what was he doing here? – but then he turned towards her.

'Mercy.'

The candlelight cast angular shadows across his face. His eyes were hollows, his mouth a gash.

'Couldn't sleep either, eh?'

'No, sir.'

'How are you feeling?'

'Much better now, thank you, sir.'

'Come and join me,' he said, indicating the bench opposite. 'I'd appreciate the company.'

Mercy hesitated, her hand still on the doorknob.

Then, 'Yes, sir,' she said, and sat down, acutely aware of her thin cotton nightgown and bare feet, her hair wrapped up in a muslin cloth. She pulled her woollen shawl further around her shoulders. Dr Stephens looked at her, though his gaze seemed to slide right through her.

'We should never have gone to that dreadful exhibition,' he said. 'But what Catherine wants, Catherine gets. That blasted painting. Horrible.' There was a bitterness to his tone that Mercy had never heard before. Then, 'I have the most terrible dreams,' he said abruptly, before draining his glass.

Mercy didn't know what to say so she said nothing. He poured himself another drink.

'Some nights I can't bear to go to sleep. Because I know they'll come. The dreams.' His voice was thick, his words slightly slurred. 'Do you dream, Mercy?'

'Sometimes, I suppose,' she said.

'And what do you dream of?'

She hesitated. She dreamed of a woman. She could never see her face. Could only see her slim arms encircled by beaded bracelets. And a sense of reaching, reaching, but never managing to touch her. Then Mercy would wake to find her face wet with tears and a feeling of sorrow, sweet and dark as a ripe plum.

Instead she answered, 'Well, I sometimes dream that I am back in Hamblin, I suppose. That sort of thing.'

'Do you miss it? Your life in Hamblin?'

'No. I'm very happy here, sir.' And she was happy, wasn't she? Hamblin, with its woods and green fields and the little stone church perched on top of a hill, felt a lifetime away.

'You had a good life there,' the doctor said.

It was a statement but a question seemed to hide behind it.

'I did. Oh dear…'

The candle had sputtered, causing more wax to pour down upon the table.

'Mrs Dowers will be after you if she sees this mess.'

They shared a smile and the doctor sipped his drink as Mercy took another candle and lit it, before blowing out the old one and replacing it. She scraped the soft, warm wax from the table, careful not to scratch the wood. All the while, she could feel the doctor watching her.

'I should go back to bed, sir.'

'Stay a little. Talk to me,' he said. 'Please.'

She returned to her seat, hands folded in her lap. She couldn't refuse, after all.

'When Mrs Whitworth wrote to tell us that she was dying, we were only too happy to offer you a home here, you know.'

'Thank you, sir. I am very grateful.'

'We were close when I was a boy. She was my cousin, but of course she was a fair bit older than me. We hadn't seen each other for many years when she died. But we always wrote to one another. She was a good woman.'

'She was.'

'Did she tell you anything of how she came to take you in?'

The doctor's slender fingers traced the whorls and knots of the wooden tabletop.

'A little. She told me that my father was an African prince. He came here for trade, I think. He was travelling but then he fell ill. When he died he left money for me to be raised and educated. And Mrs Whitworth had taken in other girls before. Orphans, like me. And so she took me too.'

'Do you remember him? Your father?'

'No. I was very small when he died.'

'And your mother, what happened to her?'

'I don't know.'

'My parents died when I was young, you know. I know how it feels to be alone.'

A soft silence fell between them.

'It can be very hard, can't it, Mercy? Being alone?'

Instinctively, she reached out and touched his hand. He looked up at her then placed his other hand on hers. Softly stroked her fingers with his thumb. They sat like this, silent, content, for several moments but then the candle sputtered and went out, and just like that the spell that had fallen over them was broken.

He pulled his hand away and rose abruptly to his feet.

'Well. Good night, Mercy. I'm glad you're feeling better.'

And with that, he was gone.

Mercy sat for a moment, her heart racing. Then she picked up the glass he had left on the table and gently touched her lips to the place where, just a moment before, his lips had been. She tipped back the glass, draining those few sweet drops.

Later, as she lay sleepless in her bed, she could still feel the touch of his fingers on hers with a dark thrill that coursed through her. What did this mean? Men had noticed her before, of course. The lingering glances of the Hamblin farmhands as she passed them by; the hands of her art tutor that sometimes strayed a little too close to her waist or the curve of her hip. But this was different. When she and Dr Stephens had looked at each other, there was a real affinity. A sense of – belonging.

Chapter 6

It was foggy the next day. A dense, yellowish fog that seemed to cling to Mercy's clothes and skin as she made her way through the early-morning streets. In Hamblin the fogs had been white and soft; they hung above the fields in the early morning and would burn away by midday. But this fog was heavy, malevolent. A fog that rendered the world unknown. The buildings, trees and passers-by became vague and insubstantial shadows, and Mercy felt as though she too were insubstantial and might be swallowed up and never seen again.

She had slipped out of the house before anyone else was awake, craving the bracing, cold air. Something to 'blow the cobwebs away', as Old Sarah used to say. She had barely slept, the events of the day before replaying in her mind again and again in an endless loop. The face of Christ with its halo of light. The tortured figures on the raft. Dr Stephens's hand on her arm. The soft touch of his fingers on hers. She increased her pace, as if somehow she could outrun her own thoughts.

The once-familiar streets were unrecognizable in this fog. She had planned to go as far as St James's Park and then to turn back, but now she had lost her way. A drayman's horse and cart became a looming monster, clattering out of the mist; a street-sweeper's brush rasped like some huge unseen serpent; even the tapping of her own footsteps rang out hollow and eerie in this altered world. She felt the panic rising.

The constriction in her chest. She took a deep breath, remembering Dr Stephens's instructions from the day before. And another.

She couldn't be too far from home. She hadn't been out long. Had she? If she could just stay calm and retrace her steps then surely – and yes, there was the big house with two lions either side of the gate. There was the house with the bright red door. And, yes, there was the entrance to Cowley Street. Home.

As she reached the steps to the front door, she collided with someone. She felt the breath knocked out of her as a man's elbow connected sharply with her side and the stale smell of unwashed linen assaulted her nose. She stumbled at the blow and, looking up, saw a man who stared at her with a wild expression. His face, pale as a mushroom, was covered in a sheen of perspiration. His black hair stood out in tufts around his head.

She waited for him to apologise for barging into her but he just stared at her. He looked – afraid.

'You've come for him,' the man said.

'I beg your pardon?'

'Dr Stephens. You've come for him.'

'I work for him,' Mercy said, doing her best to imitate the sneering tone Mrs Stephens adopted when talking to people she considered beneath her. 'I am Mrs Stephens's assistant. Now, if you don't mind, I would like to get past.'

As she moved past him he grabbed her arm with his grubby fingers. Now it was her turn to feel afraid. Fear that was sudden and shocking, like a splash of ice water. She tried to pull her arm away but he held her fast.

'I must see him. I must. "If anyone sins and does what is forbidden in any of the Lord's commands, even though they do not know it, they are guilty and will be held responsible." Do you see? It was a sin!'

Mercy could only nod, bewildered. She had no idea what he meant but she was loath to antagonise him. The man eyed her suspiciously then let go of her arm. He thrust his hand into his inside pocket and drew out a scrap of paper, clumsily folded.

'Give him this,' he said, waving the paper in Mercy's face. 'Straight away. S'important. Tell him he must come or there'll be more of this.'

Perhaps he was a patient. He certainly looked ill.

'Very well, I will give it to him.'

She took the paper from his outstretched hand, noticing that the cuffs of his once-white shirt were yellowing and greasy.

'I have your word?'

'Yes, sir, you have my word.' She smiled at him, as though he were a simple child, and saw the fear creep back into his eyes.

'Don't mock me. For God's sake, don't mock me!' And then he was gone, disappearing like a phantom back into the fog. Mercy exhaled with relief, rubbing at her arm where she could still feel the imprint of his fingers in her flesh.

She was shaken by the encounter. There was something about the man's bloodshot eyes and fearful expression that unnerved her. And the way he had grabbed at her – how dare he? But she should be more charitable. More Christian. He was probably very unwell. She had heard there were asylums for people like him, awful places where the lunatics were tied up like dogs. She should feel sorry for him.

It was still early and the Stephenses wouldn't be up yet so she went back upstairs, the note stuffed into her pocket. Once in the safety of her room, she took out the crumpled piece of paper. Perhaps she ought to read it before she gave it to the doctor. Perhaps she ought to just throw it into the fire. She turned it over. It had no seal. The man hadn't said that it was private and she was sure that Dr Stephens wouldn't mind. And yet it was with a tingle of something like danger that she unfolded it and began to read.

It was a yellowish, brownish colour and crisp to the touch. As she unfolded it, she saw that one edge was ragged as if torn from a book. The page was covered with faded brown lettering in a neat, small hand and was dated 23 September 1806. That was nearly fifteen years ago. Why on earth was the man delivering this now?

Some of the writing was indecipherable, the letters long since worn away or smudged, but Mercy could make out a small fragment.

it was too hot to admit the wearing of any clothing but a shirt, not-withstanding which I was so overcome by the heat, stench, and foul air that I nearly fainted

Was that it? Mercy was disappointed; she had hoped the paper might contain something more interesting. A lurid confession of crime or illicit love. She squinted as she tried to read more but it was no use. Turning the paper over, she saw that there was more writing on the other side, this in a fresher ink, a more untidy hand. It simply said, *11 a.m. Garraway's. JB.*

She supposed she had better give it to Dr Stephens. He would probably be in his room by now, as he usually did a little work before breakfast. She checked herself in the mirror, smoothed her hair and pinched her cheeks, as she had seen Mrs Stephens do, though her cheeks refused to glow with the same rosy colour that Mrs Stephens's did. Then she went, heart racing, to his room and knocked with a nervous hand on the door.

'Come!'

The irritation in his voice made her pause but she opened the door nonetheless.

'What is it?' he said sharply, then seeing it was Mercy, his expression softened. 'Oh, Mercy, it's you.'

'I hope I'm not disturbing you, sir?'

He looked tired as he passed a hand across his face. She could make out a light stubble of golden hairs on his chin.

'No, no, come in,' he said, closing the door behind her. 'I'm just catching up with one or two things. And feeling the effects of my sleepless night.'

He caught her eye and smiled, and her heart leapt a little in her chest.

'Did you manage to get much sleep?' he asked.

'Not much, sir, no.' She thought of them both lying awake in their beds, each thinking of the other.

'Well, Mercy.' His cheeks had grown a little pinker, she was sure of it. 'What can I do for you?'

She felt suddenly awkward in front of him, clumsy – she didn't know how to stand or what to do with her hands. She haltingly told him about the man who had approached her that morning and about the piece of paper he had given her. How he had grabbed her by the arm so she couldn't get away.

'Did he hurt you?' he asked, with genuine concern in his voice. It made her happy to see that he cared so much about her.

'Oh, no. I'm all right.'

'You're sure?'

She nodded. 'He said to tell you that he must see you. Or else there will be more. I think he may be quite deranged.'

'Very well. Let me see,' Dr Stephens said, and she passed him the paper.

He looked at it and instantly, as if it had scalded his fingers, he dropped it to the floor. Mercy wasn't really sure what happened next. Instinctively, she bent to pick up the paper but at the same time he moved to put one booted foot over it. Somehow, she collided with his leg and lost her balance. There was a thud and an explosion of pain as her head struck the edge of his desk.

'Mercy!'

She sat, stunned, on the floor. Then, wincing, she touched her head with shaking fingers, felt a warm slick of blood slide down her face.

'Are you all right?'

He bent down towards her and she flinched instinctively. Had he kicked her? No, of course not. It had been an accident.

'Come on, come on. Let's get you up and have a look.'

Dazed, she let him raise her up and guide her to the chair.

'Let me see.' He held her face gently with one hand and dabbed at the blood with his handkerchief. 'Always a lot of blood with head wounds,' he said matter-of-factly. 'But I don't think it's too bad. Here.'

He gave her the handkerchief and took off his jacket, rolling up his sleeves to the elbow. She watched as he unlocked a cabinet to reveal rows and rows of small glass bottles.

'Arnica oil,' he said, selecting one of them. 'Very good for cuts and bruises.'

He dabbed gently at her head, his face very close to hers, first wiping away the blood with his handkerchief, then applying a little of the bright yellow oil with a clean cloth.

She had the strangest sensation that she had experienced this before. All of this. The knock to her head, the blood, the doctor bending over her, the earthy, sage-like smell of the oil. She gripped tight to the arms of the chair, feeling the room begin to tip and spin, feeling her stomach flip and churn so that she feared she might be sick.

'Mercy?' Dr Stephens said sharply.

Just then they heard the loud tap-tap of footsteps on the landing. A brief knock and the door was flung open.

'Edwin, I've— Oh!' Mrs Stephens's eyes widened a little as she took in the scene; Mercy in the doctor's chair, he with shirtsleeves rolled up, bent closely over her. 'What on earth?' she spluttered. 'What has happened?'

'Nothing to worry about,' the doctor said. 'Mercy tripped and knocked her head on her washstand. It looks worse than it is.'

'Mercy! However did you manage that?'

Mercy swallowed, looked briefly at the doctor who had turned away and was retrieving a bandage from his medicine chest.

'I tripped,' she said. 'I'm not sure how.'

'You clumsy thing! Well, it's a good job my husband is here to help, isn't it?'

Her brittle smile didn't quite reach her eyes.

'A very good job, indeed!' Dr Stephens said. 'Now, I'm just going to bandage up the patient and then I shall join my beautiful wife for breakfast. How does that sound?'

Mrs Stephens hesitated but the doctor stepped forward to usher her out of the room.

'Yes, yes, darling, that sounds lovely,' she said as she made her way out onto the landing. 'Mercy, would you mind taking breakfast in the kitchen today? I need to discuss a few matters with my husband.'

Mercy nodded dumbly. She always breakfasted with Mrs Stephens. Why was she being punished?

'And then you can begin making up some new signs. It looks as though we had better keep you out of trouble.'

She smiled again, lips pressed tight together, and went out, leaving the door open behind her. Mercy looked at Dr Stephens but he avoided her gaze, applied a dressing and bandage to her head in silence. Why had he lied?

'There, all done.'

'Thank you, sir.' She turned towards the doorway but Dr Stephens stopped her.

'One moment, Mercy. I just wanted to say...'

'Yes?' She looked up at him. They were standing very close. She held her breath, waiting.

'I just wanted to say, I would appreciate it if you would say nothing of your encounter with that man to my wife. Or to anyone else. It wouldn't do to scare them, you understand. There's absolutely nothing to worry about, of course. But all the same.'

'Oh.' Was that it? Was that all he was going to say? 'Yes, sir.'

'You promise?'

'Yes, sir. I promise.'

'Very good, Mercy. I knew I could trust you. It can be our secret, can't it?'

He smiled and ushered her out, closing the door firmly behind her.

A little later, after she'd eaten her solitary breakfast in the kitchen and was half-heartedly inking more signs for the sugar boycott, she heard the front door slam. She looked out to see Dr Stephens, coat-tails flapping, as he dashed down the street. The clock in the hall chimed the half-hour. Half past ten. She recalled the note that had read *11 a.m. Garraway's.*

She gingerly touched her head. The cut throbbed dully beneath the bandage, from where the faint smell of sage still emanated, tugging at her with threads of nausea. She sat back down and closed her eyes for a moment. She thought again of how she had fallen, how she had felt the doctor's leg hard against her side. Had he kicked her? No, it was unthinkable. He was such a kind man. It had all happened so quickly and she was probably still shaken from meeting that stranger in the street.

There was something in the note that had rattled Dr Stephens. Perhaps he would tell her if they had another of their midnight meetings in the kitchen. The thought was exciting, and it gave her a buzz of pleasure to think she was the only one who knew that he had gone to meet that man. *Say nothing to my wife.* She smiled to herself. *It can be our secret, can't it?*

'Ah, Mercy, there you are!' Mrs Stephens came bustling into the room. 'How funny you look with that bandage. How are you getting on with the signs?'

She looked them over, her lips sewn tight. 'No, no, these won't do.' She pointed here and there at the lettering, as neat and perfect as always. 'The letters are a little small. And this one is slanted, do you see? No. You'll have to do these again.'

Mercy bit back any retort and nodded her head.

'But before that, be an angel and pop down to Mrs Dowers, would you? Tell her we are one less for lunch. Edwin remembered an important appointment at the Foundling Hospital. He won't be back until later this afternoon.'

'Yes, of course, ma'am.' Mercy smiled inwardly. Only she knew where he really was.

'It's not like him to forget such a thing. But he's been working so hard lately!' Mrs Stephens went on. 'Not to mention dealing with all your little incidents.' She smiled but the look in her eye was hot and sharp as a poker.

Mercy smiled sweetly back at her. 'Yes, ma'am.'

'Oh, and tell her to keep something back for him. He's bound to be starved when he does come home!'

Little incidents? How dare she? Only the thought of Dr Stephens stopped her from crying out at that. The trust he had placed in her. The bond between them. The faint covering of fair hair on his forearms. She shook her thoughts away.

'Yes, ma'am,' she repeated, and left to do as she was told.

Chapter 7

Something in her relationship with Mrs Stephens shifted that day. Her employer was still outwardly pleasant, still took her to meetings and talks, still asked for her help with her hair and her dress, but more and more Mercy felt that she was play-acting. The smile was a little too wide, the eyes too bright.

She watched Mercy with the vigilance of a cat watching a mouse. Never let her and Dr Stephens be alone together. She must be able to sense that there was something between them, Mercy thought, as she stood in her room, looking out over the roofs as she often did. Mercy did feel a little bad for Mrs Stephens: after all, they were married and it must be very hard to watch your husband falling in love with someone else. Someone younger and prettier, Mercy thought with a smile. For she was sure that's what was happening – why else did the doctor's gaze linger on her as it did? Why else had he held her hand and told her he felt lonely? Why else did he now seem to avoid Mercy, as though afraid of his own feelings?

There had been no repeat of their encounter in the kitchen. Not yet. But she was sure there would be. Like two magnets she and the doctor were drawn, one to the other. How had it taken her so long to see it? How painful it was now to spend a minute out of his presence.

The day he had gone to meet his odd patient, he had come back later in a sombre mood, locked himself away in his room for the rest of the day and barely said a word at dinner. Then he had gone out again – much to Mrs Stephens's surprise. It was as though he couldn't bear to be in the same room as his wife, Mercy thought.

Mercy had been in bed when she heard the doctor return that night. The clunk of the front door closing was followed by his footsteps up the stairs, a little slower and heavier than usual. It must have been well past midnight. She had blown out her candle and settled down under the covers. She hadn't realised she had been waiting for Dr Stephens to come home but of course she had.

Through the floorboards she had heard the low rumble of conversation. Then the raised voice of Mrs Stephens.

'Where on earth have you been?'

The doctor's response had been muffled. Mercy strained to hear.

'It's long past midnight!' Mrs Stephens again.

Then something else she couldn't quite catch. She had hesitated for a moment and then climbed out of bed and put her ear to the floor.

'Have you been drinking?'

Still she couldn't hear Dr Stephens's reply and so she had tiptoed to the door and slowly opened it. She had stepped out onto the landing, treading carefully over the one creaky floorboard.

'Please don't take me for a fool, Edwin.' Mrs Stephens was close to tears. Mercy had held her breath and leaned out a little over the bannister. Were they talking about her?

'Oh, for God's sake, woman!'

The door of their bedroom had opened then and Mercy darted back into her own room, heart hammering in her chest. Had they heard her? She had stood motionless, waiting. There was the loud slam of a door followed by Dr Stephens's uneven tread along the landing below. Another slam, then silence.

For the rest of that week Mercy had tried to find a way to engineer a moment alone with him, but there was never the opportunity. She found herself thinking back over all the times they had been together; that first night when his eyes had lingered on hers, the trip to the exhibition and the way he had cared for her when she was taken ill. That night in the kitchen, their fingers locked together. She thought too of their encounter in his study, his face so close to hers as he tended to her head. How she wished she could have kissed him. She tried to distract herself with her artwork, and yet the only thing she found she could draw was his face over and over again. It was as though she had known him always.

That evening she joined the Stephenses for dinner. The doctor was in a more jovial mood than he had been for days, and he poured them all a glass of wine before asking them both to close their eyes.

'I have a surprise,' he said, darting from the room and returning a moment later.

Through her fingers, Mercy could see that he was holding two boxes, each one tied up with a ribbon.

'What is it? What is it?' Mrs Stephens squealed.

He put a box in front of each of them and stood back. 'Go on,' he said, 'you may open them now.'

Mercy carefully untied the blue velvet ribbon and rolled it up – she could wear that in her hair. She lifted up the lid and saw that it contained a set of a dozen pencils, and not one but two sketchbooks. There was a new rubber, too. And some charcoal sticks.

'Thank you, oh, thank you,' she said. It was the most perfect gift. He knew her so well.

'Goodness,' said Mrs Stephens, throwing a look at her husband. 'How very generous. What a lucky girl you are, Mercy.'

'Open yours, darling,' said Dr Stephens, and she lifted the lid to reveal rows of sweets, glossy and gleaming. Mercy supposed he had to buy something for his wife or it would have looked suspicious. Her own gift was definitely the better of the two.

Mrs Stephens frowned as she looked into the box. 'I hope this sugar is not—'

'Don't worry!' Dr Stephens interjected. 'I looked out for the sign in the window. You can enjoy these with a clear conscience.'

Mrs Stephens clapped her hands together like a child. 'How wonderful! Shall we?' She picked one out and then passed them to her husband who held the box out to Mercy.

'Go on, Mercy, you have one too.'

Mercy picked out a bottle-green sweet, round and bright as a glass bead. An image flashed into her mind of a slender brown wrist encircled with beads, but just as suddenly it was gone.

The sweets had quite an effect on Mrs Stephens, who smiled and laughed all through dinner. Mercy couldn't wait to unpack her present, to try the pencils and the charcoal. She might try to recreate the Haydon painting Dr Stephens had liked so much. She couldn't remember every detail but the main figures were clear in her memory. How impressed he would be, if she could do it. She could present it to him, as a gift. He could hang it in his study.

'What do you think?'

Mrs Stephens's question interrupted her thoughts and she realised she hadn't been listening to anything she had said. She floundered for a moment, then Dr Stephens came to her rescue.

'I'm sure Mercy agrees that a dinner party would be a great idea.'

'Oh yes, very good.' A dinner party? She had never been to one before. Not a proper one.

'Yes,' Mrs Stephens went on, 'we can ask the Alderneys, of course, and the Hazelwoods – I'm making real headway with Sir Jonathan. His support could make such a difference to the campaign.'

'Are you sure?' Dr Stephens replied. 'About the Hazelwoods? He's an awful bore.'

'An awful bore? What on earth are you talking about? He's a Member of Parliament with a great deal of money in the bank, and if he lends his support then we have every chance of getting a Bill through Parliament to end slavery once and for all. I can put up with a bit of boredom for that – and I'm sure you can too!'

The doctor looked as if he wanted to say more but didn't. He took a long draught from his wine glass.

'We can ask that nice Mr Northbury too – you remember, the portrait painter who came to lunch? It's always good to have an artistic guest to liven things up. We'll need to get the best table linen out and aired. Mercy, please could you run down to Bridget? Ask her to come up to see me after she's cleared the dinner things?'

'Yes, ma'am, of course.'

But she found the kitchen empty. And the scullery. Where was Bridget?

There were signs of activity; dishes stacked up on the table ready to be put away and Bridget's apron lying untidily across a bench. But there was no sign of Bridget herself. Mercy felt a sudden rush of cold air and realised that the back door was open. She thought of the strange man who had grabbed her in the street and, with a flood of panic, ran out into the garden.

It was dark, the garden a greyish-black expanse spread out before her, but through the gloom she could see Bridget, grappling with a man. He had pushed her up against the apple tree. She made to run towards them – should she grab some sort of weapon? Call Mrs Stephens?

But, no – they weren't fighting, she realised now. Bridget's head was thrown back a little and her red hair flowed out from under her cap and over her shoulders. Her arms were wrapped tightly around the man, her hands moving up and down, her fingers digging into his back.

Mercy stood transfixed. The man had pressed himself over Bridget, one hand flat against the bark of the tree, the other roaming across her body, clutching at her hair. He was making grunting sounds as he kissed her. Should she call out? Do something? Then she heard Bridget moan, a soft sound that was so unlike the sullen girl Mercy knew. A soft sound of happiness, of pleasure.

She wasn't sure how long she stood there, gazing at the pair in the moonlight. But suddenly, Bridget opened her eyes and, seeing Mercy, pushed the man away.

'Go!' she hissed, and Mercy saw the man's dark silhouette make his escape up the garden where a gate opened out on to the alleyway behind.

Bridget came towards her; angry, fearful, her breath coming in gasps. They stood for a moment staring at one another, neither speaking, neither knowing what to say.

'I'm sorry—' Mercy began.

'You mustn't say anything. I'll lose my job.' Bridget fumbled to pin her hair back up with unsteady fingers. 'Please.'

'Of course. Of course. I'm sorry, I— I shouldn't have seen, I shouldn't…'

She quickly delivered Mrs Stephens's message before turning and fleeing back into the house.

For the rest of that evening, her thoughts returned again and again to the scene she had witnessed in the garden. Bridget's hair hanging loose. Her clenched fingers. The man's hands all over her body. What would it feel like, Mercy wondered, what would it feel like to be touched like that? And she thought again of Dr Stephens's bare arms, his hands with their long, delicate fingers, and she shivered, whether with trepidation or with desire she couldn't be sure.

Chapter 8

Over the next few days there was a frenzy of activity in preparation
for the dinner party, and Mercy couldn't help but get caught up in the
excitement that seemed to infect the whole household. She thought of
the dinners she had read about in her Jane Austen novels; saw herself
all dressed up, glittering with jewels, delicately sipping the finest wine
from the best crystal glasses.

'Mercy, get your pen and ink. We need to make a list!'

Her daydreams interrupted, Mercy did as she was told.

Mrs Stephens issued orders as if she were the Duke of Wellington,
with Mercy – her second-in-command – making notes of all the
things they needed to do and buy. Martin was in charge of candles
and lamps, of ordering the wine and the brandy – under Dr Stephens's
direction, of course. Bridget was kept busy polishing the silverware,
laundering the tablecloths, and generally scrubbing and shining every
inch of the house.

Mrs Stephens decided that this dinner would be beyond Mrs
Dowers's culinary skills and so hired in a French chef for the evening,
much to Mrs Dowers's disappointment. Monsieur Babineaux had
worked in some of the city's best hotels, apparently, and came highly
recommended. He would bring his own assistant and said he would
need exclusive use of the kitchen for the whole day. He would bring

his own knives and pans, and would require a quart of brandy in addition to his fee.

A few days before the dinner, he came to the house to discuss the menu. He was a large man with oiled hair in a perfectly straight parting. Mercy showed him through to the parlour where Mrs Stephens was waiting to receive him. They spent hours going over recipes and, under the chef's careful instruction, Mercy drew diagrams of how everything would be laid out on the table, with each dish arranged precisely, so that it would complement its neighbour.

Then there was a trip to the draper's for Mrs Stephens to be fitted for her new dress. It was made from toffee-coloured silk, trimmed with gold, with a gauzy fabric at the sleeves and throat and a gold ribbon at the waist. Mercy enviously ran the silk between her fingers, marvelling at its sheen and softness. She would have to content herself with some new buttons for her dress.

On the day of the dinner, Monsieur Babineaux and his assistant, a lad of fourteen or fifteen who seemed to speak no English, arrived first thing and everyone was banned from the kitchen while they began to set up. Mrs Dowers was given the day off. She had huffed and puffed like a disgruntled hen the day before, furious that 'some man' was to be let loose in 'her kitchen'.

Martin was away too – his mother had fallen ill and Dr Stephens had given him permission to visit her. This was not received well by Mrs Stephens, who was of the view that he could have waited one more day. Mercy and Bridget were kept busy answering the door to the various delivery boys, each bringing armfuls of supplies that were ferried into the kitchen, which was now a hive of culinary activity.

Then there was the dining room to prepare, candles to trim, the silver to be finished, fires to be laid, flowers to be placed artfully in huge jugs, and the best tablecloth – freshly steamed and ironed – to be spread and smoothed onto the table, like royal icing onto a Christmas cake.

Bridget and Mercy worked mainly in silence. They had barely spoken since that night in the garden but Mercy had kept her promise and said nothing to Mrs Stephens. She sometimes found herself sneaking a look at Bridget, envious of her secret love affair. Mercy was nineteen – a full two years older than Bridget – and yet in this area of life she was ignorant. If only she and the doctor could find time to be alone together, then they could tell each other how they really felt. Perhaps she would get to sit beside him at the dinner party. She imagined their fingers reaching for each other below the tablecloth.

Mercy took special care with her appearance that evening, sewing her new buttons carefully onto her dress. She tied the ribbon from Dr Stephens's present into a bow around her waist, the royal-blue velvet complementing the yellow of the dress. She spent an age trying to roll and curl her hair just like Mrs Stephens's but her unruly mop simply wouldn't obey. She had spent her whole life wrestling with her hair – 'as tangled as a bird's nest', Old Sarah would say as she had tried to brush it while Mercy squealed in pain. She had tried flattening it with a hot iron, smoothing it with butter, but nothing seemed to work. Tonight, almost tearful with frustration, Mercy finally managed to secure it in a bun with a vast quantity of hairpins.

The cut on her head had healed by now, just a tiny scar remaining to remind her of what had happened in Dr Stephens's study. That and the faint sense of unease she had whenever she thought back to that day, to the doctor's booted foot and the explosion of pain as her head hit the desk. She touched the raised line of skin gently with her fingertip. Then, in a moment of daring, she took a violet from the jar at her bedside and tucked it into her hair, so that the scar was obscured. Yes, that was perfect.

She went downstairs, finding Mrs Stephens in the parlour giving Bridget some last-minute orders on which wine to bring in with each course.

'And don't slouch when you serve! Shoulders back, that's it. Ah, Mercy – there you are!'

Mrs Stephens was resplendent in her gold dress, shimmering in the lamplight. She appraised Mercy with a quizzical look.

'Very good. Though I'm not sure why you bothered with that bow. It'll be covered up by the apron, in any case.'

'Apron?' What did she mean?

'Yes, apron. Without Martin there's far too much for one person to do tonight. You'll be serving with Bridget. You didn't…? Oh, my dear, you didn't think…?'

Mercy felt as though the floor was sliding away beneath her. She wasn't to be a guest after all. Humiliation flooded over her like an April downpour. How could she have been so stupid? How could she have thought that Mrs Stephens would want her at her dinner party?

'No. No, of course. I never imagined—'

There was a knock at the door.

'Oh, goodness. How I hate an early guest! Mercy, you go. Bridget, fetch her an apron and cap and tell Dr Stephens to hurry down here.'

Mercy walked to the front door as though in a trance. There was a lump in her throat and she could feel tears threatening to fall. She blinked them away. She barely knew what she was doing as she answered the door, but there was her hand upon the handle, there was her mouth stretched into a smile, and her arm that gestured at the guests to come in, come in.

The first to arrive were Dr Snell and his wife. He was an acquaintance of Dr Stephens and was apparently very wealthy. There was something rather reptilian about him, with his pale green eyes that never seemed to blink. Mercy welcomed them with a smile but she felt numb inside.

Bridget arrived with a white cap and apron. She handed them over without a word but there was no smirk from her and Mercy was grateful. She tore the violet out of her hair and crushed it in her hand, tied the apron over her best dress and placed the white cap over her carefully arranged hair. She caught a glimpse of her reflection as she went into the parlour: just another black maid, one of many in London, she supposed. Who was she to think she was any different? She wasn't Mrs Stephens's friend, wasn't her equal, no matter how much Mercy might like to think otherwise. She was her staff. She was her servant.

The next guests soon arrived; Sir Jonathan and Lydia Hazelwood and their son. Mercy took their coats and directed them to the parlour, a smile stitched to her face. Then came Mary Alderney and her husband, good friends of the Stephenses. They were both short and a little fat – they matched each other so completely that they put Mercy in mind of a salt and pepper set.

Last to arrive was Mr Northbury, the artist who had been to lunch all those weeks ago. He was the first to greet Mercy with real warmth and he asked her how her drawing was coming along. She, embarrassed in her apron and cap, mumbled some brief reply. How she wished she could sit at the table with him, talk to him about Haydon and Géricault, about his work and her poor attempts to draw. But no, she showed him into the parlour and then retreated. Down to the kitchen. To the servants' quarters.

Once the guests were all seated in the dining room, it was time to serve the soup, its creamy surface decorated with slivers of almond.

Mercy hadn't eaten all day – had thought she would be sharing this meal – and her stomach growled as she followed Bridget, who was carrying the soup tureen, into the dining room. Bridget placed it down next to Dr Stephens, who began to ladle out the soup for the guests while Mercy poured their glasses of wine.

For the most part, the guests ignored her and Mrs Stephens gave only a small wave of her hand by way of thanks. The only person who really looked at her was the Hazelwoods' son. He was probably around the same age as her with a wave of fashionably unruly curls and a ruby-red cravat. As she poured his wine, Mercy could feel him looking at her, and when she raised her eyes to his he smiled. She smiled back politely but there was a directness to his gaze that she didn't much like, and as she moved down the table she could feel him watching her still.

Back down in the kitchen, the chef and his boy were plating up the dishes onto Mrs Stephens's best tableware. There were larded oysters, small pies filled with pigeon, griddled leeks in a mustard dressing, boiled turkey, and Monsieur Babineaux's famous curried mutton cutlets. Mercy and Bridget loaded up their trays and made their way upstairs. The chef tapped his finger at the table diagram as they went.

'Exactly like this! Don't forget. It must be exactly like this!'

As they made their way to the dining room, they could overhear snippets of conversation and laughter.

'She's been with us a few months now, hasn't she, dear?' Mrs Stephens was saying. 'Fantastically helpful. And so good for the campaign.'

They were talking about her. She couldn't bear it. Couldn't go back in there. But Bridget nudged her with an elbow, and like actors stepping onto a stage they went into the room.

The conversation turned briefly to the food as soon as Bridget and Mercy made their entrance, with Mrs Stephens proudly telling the guests about her French chef, *Mon-surr Babi-noe*, 'the best chef in London, so they say'. *She has on too much make-up*, Mercy thought, as she placed a platter of chicken livers down beside Mrs Stephens. Powder had settled into the wrinkles around her eyes, making them appear more pronounced, and her cheeks, red with rouge, had grown redder still after a glass or two of wine.

Then it was back to the kitchen to load up again, and back up the stairs, trays groaning with food.

Mr Northbury was talking about the Géricault exhibition – he was a great admirer of the Frenchman's work. 'It's as though you are there on the raft with them,' he said.

'Oh, I didn't like it at all,' said Mrs Alderney. 'So much nudity. Quite unnecessary.'

Mercy laid down a dish of glazed carrots next to Mr Northbury and he nodded his thanks.

'I never actually got to see the painting,' said Mrs Stephens. 'But Edwin's been several times.'

Mercy glanced at him; she didn't know he had been to the exhibition again. She thought he hated the painting. Dr Stephens was busy carving the pork loin and didn't respond.

'The painting's based on real events, of course. Terrible business,' said Dr Snell. 'I read about it in the papers at the time. Off the coast of Africa, it was. Appalling. But that's the French for you.'

Perhaps keen to steer the conversation away from such a gruesome topic, Mr Alderney loudly cleared his throat. 'Yes. You were in Africa once, Stephens, weren't you?' he said.

Dr Stephens looked up from the carving, knife held aloft. 'Oh, yes, I was. Many years ago.'

'Whereabouts?' asked Mrs Snell.

'I spent some time in Freetown, Sierra Leone. As I say, it was a long time ago.'

Mercy never had found the opportunity to ask Dr Stephens about his time in Africa and she hung back, keen to hear the rest of the conversation.

'Don't be modest, dear,' said Mrs Stephens. 'He went there to tend to those in need. This was before the Slave Trade Act came in and Freetown was a safe haven for escaped slaves. Edwin worked as a doctor there, didn't you? Only for a few months, mind. You couldn't stand the climate, could you, dear? I imagine he must have been as pink as this lobster!' The guests laughed as Mrs Stephens went on. 'And I for one am glad he came back or else we would never have married!'

She began to tell the story of how they had met when she was only nineteen and how he had proposed just eight days later. She accepted but didn't tell her family, and when her fiancé sailed off to work in Africa she half expected never to see him again.

'I gave him a lock of my hair to remember me by,' Mrs Stephens continued. Mercy saw that Dr Stephens continued to carve the meat into thin slices, saying nothing. 'And it must have worked! Nearly fifteen years together now, and as happy as ever!'

If only she knew, thought Mercy, if only she knew how her husband had sat hand in hand with her that night.

As the conversation went on, Mercy made her way round the table, refilling their wine glasses.

She found herself next to Master Hazelwood and he nodded at her to fill his glass. As she began to pour, she felt his hand creep onto the back of her leg. Frozen, she looked at him but he simply smiled and slid his hand further up until it rested just beneath her buttock, his fingertips on her inner thigh. Her hand shook and the wine spilled onto the pristine tablecloth.

'Mercy!' Disappointment rather than anger in Mrs Stephens's voice.

'I'm sorry, sir.' Mercy couldn't look at him. Couldn't look at anyone.

'No harm done,' the young man said. 'No use crying over spilt wine, as they say!'

They all laughed again. No one had seen his hand on her. No one would believe her if she told them. Bridget hurried over with a cloth and Mercy moved away to let her mop up the wine, her face burning. As they left the room, she heard Sir Jonathan remarking to Mary Alderney how hard it was to get decent domestic staff these days and she agreed.

'So true, so true. And when you do find decent ones, it's "may I have a day off?" every five minutes! Oh, Sir Jonathan, you must try this mutton, it's divine.'

Mercy hurried down the stairs and stepped out into the garden. The kitchen was hot and stuffy and the smell of all the rich food was overwhelming. She held her face up to the dark sky and took several lungfuls of air. She wanted to scream. How dare he touch her? How dare he? After a few minutes, Bridget came out.

'I'm going to go back up,' she said. 'See if they need anything. You can stay here if you want.'

Mercy looked at her and Bridget smiled. She knew what had happened. Had probably suffered it a hundred times herself.

'No. Thank you. I'll go.' She had to face them. Had to get through this awful evening somehow.

'Suit yourself,' said Bridget with a shrug.

Mercy went up and paused outside the dining room door, gathering her courage.

'You know *I* agree with you,' Mr Alderney was saying, 'I'm just telling you what *they* said; slavery's been going on for hundreds of years, so who is to say they haven't adapted to it by now?'

'I think that's a most unchristian attitude.' That was his wife.

'Indeed,' Mrs Stephens joined in. 'I think this idea that they are somehow lesser than us is absurd. Just look at Mercy – she can read and write, she can conduct herself in society—'

'Apart from when pouring wine!'

Guffaws of laughter at that. Mercy clenched her fists, hardly noticing as she dug the nails into her palms.

'She can conduct herself in society,' Mrs Stephens went on. 'She really is an example of how with the right upbringing and education they can be just the same as you or I.'

'I'm not sure I'd go that far.' That was Sir Jonathan, his speech slightly louder and more slurred than before. 'But I do take your point. I'm just not sure it needs to be done so quickly, that's all. I think a gradual phasing out would be far better – and far more likely to attract the support of my colleagues in the House.'

'Oh, no,' said Mrs Alderney, 'I really cannot agree with you there. It must be stopped and it must be stopped immediately.'

'Quite right!' said Mrs Stephens.

'Well, it seems we have married a pair of radicals, eh, Stephens?' Mr Alderney said with a laugh.

Mercy peered around the door and Mrs Stephens beckoned to her.

'We're ready for dessert, Mercy,' she said as the others continued their conversation. 'And thank you, you're doing a marvellous job.' She squeezed Mercy's hand.

On and on it went, this interminable evening. The dessert, a huge blancmange decorated with candied fruit and nuts, was carried in to 'oohs' and 'aahs' from the guests. Then the men took their port in the dining room, while the ladies went into the parlour for cups of tea. Mercy had lost count of the times she had been up and down the stairs; her arms and legs ached from all the fetching and carrying, and she was sweating beneath the clinging fabric of her best dress.

Now the men had called for some cheese – how could they possibly eat any more? – and so while Bridget made tea for Mrs Stephens and the other ladies, Mercy went to fetch it. The kitchen was calmer now; Monsieur Babineaux sat at the table sipping a glass of brandy while his boy cleaned and dried their knives, laying them carefully into a wooden box inlaid with velvet.

On arriving back in the dining room, Mercy carried the cheese plate over to the table, purposefully staying out of reach of Daniel Hazelwood. The room was a haze of cigar smoke and, in the absence of the ladies, the men had stretched back in their chairs and loosened their cravats. They were talking about crime and how the streets of London weren't as safe as they used to be.

'Pickpockets and swindlers everywhere!' Dr Snell declared, topping up his port from the decanter on the table.

'And worse!' said Mr Alderney. 'Did you hear about the murder in Pimlico yesterday? It's all over the papers.'

The others shook their heads and Mercy lingered on her way to the door. *Murder?* The word sent a shiver through her and yet, despite that, she wanted to hear more.

'Poor chap found beaten to death in his own home. Naval man, he was. Dudley, his name was. Awful business.'

'Dudley?' Dr Stephens asked.

'Think so. Why? D'you know the fellow?'

'No, no, I don't believe so. What happened? Do they know who did it?' Dr Stephens tapped at his glass with his fingertips, eyebrows pinched together in concern.

'That's all I know, I'm afraid. Terrible times! What's the world coming to when a man's not safe in his own home?'

The men murmured their agreement and Dr Snell began extolling the virtues of a professional police force, saying it was high time they had one in London.

Mercy left them to it and had just arrived back in the kitchen when she realised she had forgotten to take up the chutney. It was Dr Stephens's favourite, made with apples and tomatoes; he would be so pleased she had remembered. As she made her way back up the stairs, she heard lowered voices in the hall ahead of her. Something about the whispered, fervent tone made her stop, out of sight on the stairs.

'We will not discuss this!' That sounded like Sir Jonathan. Arguing with his son, perhaps?

Mercy continued up the stairs, clearing her throat loudly so that they would hear she was coming. But it wasn't Daniel Hazelwood that Sir Jonathan was deep in conversation with, it was Dr Stephens. They both turned to look at her; Sir Jonathan's face was flushed with alcohol – or anger – and yet the doctor looked pale, drained.

'Excuse me,' Mercy said. 'I thought you might like... your chutney, sir.'

'No. No!' Dr Stephens said. 'Just leave us, will you?'

Mercy stammered an apology, backed away and almost tripped down the stairs in her haste. He had never spoken to her like that before, never.

'Everything all right up there?' asked Bridget as she came back into the kitchen.

'Oh, yes, yes. Everything's fine.' There had been such a hardness to his voice. And the way he had looked at her, it had been so cold.

'The men'll be heading in to join the ladies soon,' Bridget went on. 'Then you can make a start on clearing the dining room and I'll finish up down here.'

'Yes, yes.' Normally she would have bristled at being ordered about by Bridget, but she no longer cared.

In the deserted dining room, the guests now gathered in the parlour for their final farewells, Mercy began to stack the plates, absent-mindedly eating leftover bits of cheese and candied fruit. She heard the door open.

'I'm nearly finished, Bridget. I'll bring these down.'

But when she turned it wasn't Bridget. It was Daniel Hazelwood. He closed the door behind him and smiled at her.

'Oh, I've found the little monkey, have I?' He began to approach her, his steps unsteady after an evening of drinking.

'Excuse me, sir, I must get on.'

Mercy backed away so that the table was between them. She circled round towards the door but he lunged at her, and before she knew what was happening, he had his arms around her. She struggled to get free but he held her tight.

'Now, now, don't make a fuss. Let's see what the little monkey has under her skirt.'

She could smell the alcohol on his breath, the smoke from his cigar. She tried to cry out but found she couldn't – no sound would come. Her limbs felt weak, drained of all energy, like a bad dream. She kicked feebly at his leg as he pressed his wet mouth against her neck. With one hand he started to tug at her apron.

'Get off!' she managed, struggling again now, like a swimmer struggling against the tide. 'Get off!'

But she couldn't get away and now he had his hands at her buttons, fumbling to undo them. With a sudden burst of energy she got one arm free, flailed desperately to her side and, finding the edge of the sideboard, grasped the first object that came to hand. Before she knew what she was doing, she had swung it at him. He gasped as she made contact with the side of his head. Stunned, he released her and she staggered backwards.

Just then, the door swung open. Oh God, for them to see her like this! She couldn't bear it. But it was Bridget. She was holding a tray and she brandished it now, putting herself between Mercy and her attacker, like an avenging angel with her fiery hair and silver shield.

'Leave her alone!' she hissed.

For a moment he looked as if he would strike her, but Bridget stood her ground. Then he shrugged and pushed his way past her. He stopped next to Mercy, glared at her.

'Black bitch,' he said, spitting the words at her, and then strode out of the room.

'You'd better put that down,' said Bridget.

Mercy looked down at her hand, still clutching what she now saw was a candlestick, heavy as a cudgel. She put it back with an unsteady hand.

'Sweet Jesus,' Bridget said, 'you could have killed him.'

Mercy looked at her. What had she done? But then Bridget smiled, a warm genuine smile.

'I'm impressed, girl. I'm impressed.'

And she took Mercy by the hand.

'Come on, let's get you out of here.'

They waited until the Stephenses had gone to bed, which wasn't long after the guests had left. Monsieur Babineaux and his boy had packed up and gone home – the chef kissing each of them on both cheeks – and they had cleared away the remnants of the party.

'They'll be out like lights,' Bridget said. 'They'll never know we've gone.'

'But what about the night watchmen?'

'Don't you worry about them. I know how to avoid the Charlies. What do you say?'

Mercy hesitated but there was a fire inside her now and she needed only a little encouragement before she agreed.

'But where will we go?'

'You'll see,' Bridget said. 'Come on!'

And they were off. Out of the back door, through the garden, and out into the alleyway beyond. Unseen. Free.

Chapter 9

Soon Mercy was gulping for breath, half laughing, half screaming, as she and Bridget raced through the city streets, hand in hand. It was November and the cobbles were icy. She slid giddily along, feeling fear and elation in equal measure.

'Slow down! Slow down!' she cried. 'My hat!'

The hat, which she had been desperately clutching with one hand as they ran, had flown out of her grasp and landed in the gutter. They stopped and she dashed back to get it, brushing it off before retying the ribbon firmly beneath her chin.

'How far now?' she asked, getting her breath back.

'Nearly there,' Bridget said, one hand pressed to her side. 'Ooof, stitch.'

Mercy laughed. Bridget looked quite the picture in one of Mrs Stephens's old hats, complete with a giant bow and a spray of flowers on one side.

'She used to give me all her cast-offs,' she had told Mercy with a rueful grin, 'until you showed up, that is.'

Mercy had lost all her bearings by the time they arrived, panting and breathless, at the foot of some steps next to a church. She could see the huge dome of St Paul's not far away so they must be somewhere in the City.

'Come on,' said Bridget. 'We're here.'

She set off up the steps and for a moment, Mercy hung back. What were they doing? If Mrs Stephens found out about this night-time excursion, she would be furious. They could both lose their positions. Perhaps she should go back.

But then she thought of Mrs Stephens hauling her onto the stage at the Grocers' Hall, of Daniel Hazelwood and his hot, pawing hands, and of Dr Stephens. Dr Stephens who had spoken to her like a common servant. She thought of all this and then, a moment later, she followed Bridget up the steps.

Once at the top she could see Bridget waiting for her beneath a sign that was shaped like a large bell. Amber light flooded onto the cobbles from the windows of what she now saw was a tavern; the sounds of music and laughter could be heard even with the door closed fast.

'Ready?' said Bridget, and without waiting for a response, she pulled open the door.

They were greeted by a cacophony of noise, by light, by the warmth of a great fire that blazed in the hearth, by the smell of smoke and beer and meat, and by bodies – so many bodies.

'I can't,' Mercy said. It was too much. Too many people. Too loud.

'Yes, you can. And I need a drink after that journey.' Bridget hooked her arm into Mercy's and led her through the crowd. It was only then that Mercy noticed.

'Oh!' she gasped. And Bridget smiled at her broadly.

For almost everyone in the tavern was a varying shade of brown or black, and as Mercy walked by, no one stared, no one muttered or smirked. In fact, if anything, it was Bridget who drew some disapproving glances. Since coming to London she had seen some other black people – street-sweepers and beggars mostly – but here there were people of all kinds, young and old, well dressed, happy, laughing. It was as though they had stepped into another world.

The music they had heard was coming from a trio of musicians in one corner of the room: an elderly man with a fiddle, one ankle encircled with bells which shivered and jingled as he stamped his foot, and two other men, one with a French horn and the other with a pipe. As they passed by, the man with the pipe paused to blow a kiss to Bridget, who laughed and waved at him before leading Mercy to the back of the room where they found an empty table.

'You wait here and I'll fetch us some drinks,' Bridget said, and she was swallowed up by the crowd once more.

Mercy sat on one of the small stools and leaned back against the wall, her foot tapping in time with the music. She became aware that she was being watched and looked up to see a young man staring at her. He was sitting alone at another table, several empty beer glasses in front of him, and he looked away as she caught his eye. She looked instinctively for Bridget, wary after her encounter with Daniel Hazelwood. What if this man should speak to her? But there was Bridget, bearing two foaming glasses of beer.

'Here we are,' Bridget said, lifting her glass towards Mercy.

'Beer? I don't really drink beer—'

'Tonight you do! Sláinte!'

'Slawn-che!' Mercy repeated, and they clinked glasses and drank, laughing as the foam went up Mercy's nose.

'I think you have an admirer,' said Bridget, nodding towards the man who kept glancing over at Mercy.

'Stop it!'

'Ah, he's not bad-looking. You could do worse!'

'Bridget!' They laughed again. He wasn't her sort at all; far too scruffy.

'And how about your young man?' said Mercy. 'How is he?'

This was the first time she had referred to that night in the garden and she wondered for a moment if she had gone too far, but Bridget only smiled and leaned forward.

'Well, I'll tell you my secret. But not a word to anyone!' She waited for Mercy to nod her agreement before she went on. 'That's him over there.'

Mercy followed her pointed finger but there were so many people, it was impossible to tell who she meant.

'Who? Which one?' she asked.

'The fella with the pipe. That's him. That's my Joe.'

The musician looked up at her now and waved, and she waved back.

'But he's—'

'Black. Yes, I know. I had noticed!'

He was handsome, that was for certain. Tall and slender with a kind face and a wide smile. Mercy had pictured some gangly Irish butcher's boy, or one of the stocky young lads who delivered coal to the house and who always seemed to have time to flirt with Bridget before they went on their way. She had never expected this dark-skinned musician.

'But I thought…' She wasn't sure how to go on. 'I thought… well, I thought you didn't like me because—'

'Because you're black? No, I didn't like you because you were a stuck-up wee madam who thought she was better'n the rest of us.'

Mercy was speechless for a moment then couldn't help but laugh. Bridget was right.

'Ooh, here he comes, you can meet him.'

The other two musicians were still playing but Joe was making his way across to them, and Mercy turned away as the couple kissed and embraced. The man who had been looking at her turned out to be a friend of Joe's called Matthew. Joe led them over to him and he and Bridget made the introductions.

'Joe, this is Mercy,' Bridget said. 'She's had a hard day so we need to cheer her up.'

'Well, I'm sure we can do that, can't we, Matthew?' Joe said with a grin.

Matthew took her hand in greeting and she sneaked a look at him. He was a little short and not very well dressed but he had a nice face, she supposed. He was probably a few years older than her. Twenty-three or -four, perhaps. His skin was of the same dark hue as hers and, like her, he had dimples in both cheeks when he smiled.

Joe and Bridget started to dance, their eyes locked on each other as they spun and twirled. Other couples joined them and after an awkward moment, Joe's friend offered Mercy his hand and led her into the centre of the room, which had been cleared of chairs and tables to make room.

Mercy had learned some dances as a child, had attended some barn dances and parties before, but she'd never been anywhere like this. The dancers flung themselves about and stamped their feet as the fiddle grew faster and louder. The faces around her glistened with sweat, eyes bright and mouths open with laughter. Beer was spilled, elbows were bumped, toes were trodden on but no one seemed to mind.

She didn't really know how to begin but Matthew held on to her, one arm around her waist, and there was something comforting in his firm grip. He led the way and she let herself follow, holding tight to his other hand with hers, feeling the roughness of his palm, the calluses on his fingers. As they spun and turned, she felt a joyous sense of freedom and she tipped back her head and laughed, enjoying the dizzy sensation this gave her as the lamplight was transformed into streaks of light and the faces of the other dancers became a blur.

The music came to a stop then and so did she, breathless and hot. She could feel that some of the pins had escaped from her hair and was sure she must look frightful, but she couldn't stop smiling. Matthew was smiling too, still holding on to her, his face very close to hers. She thought briefly of Dr Stephens but blinked the thought away and moved towards him so that their lips might meet.

But the kiss didn't come. She opened her eyes to see that he had stepped back and was regarding her with an odd expression.

'What's the matter?' she asked.

She saw now that he was shaking, actually shaking, and she became afraid.

'What is it?'

'Malundama,' he said, and a strange tingling feeling crept down her spine.

'What did you say?' she asked him. She didn't know what the word meant but, like some half-remembered poem or prayer, she felt sure she had heard it before.

'Malundama,' he said again.

As she looked into his dark brown eyes, wide now with unconcealed emotion, she had the same sensation that she'd experienced in the doctor's study; as though she had been here before. As though in some previous life she had looked into these same eyes, held these same hands.

But she'd never met this man before. She tore her hands away from his and, overwhelmed now by the press of dancers all around her, who began to move as the fiddle took up once more, she turned to make her way back to the table. She grabbed her glass and drained the rest of her beer. Was she losing her mind? Was she, like the doctor's strange patient, destined to end up raving in some asylum? It was as though she couldn't trust her own thoughts, her own memories.

'Are you all right?'

It was Matthew; he had followed her and looked at her now with concern.

'What was it you said to me just then? What was that word?'

'Malundama,' he said for a third time, and he seemed to take such pleasure in the word. Then, with a smile, 'I believe it really is you.'

'I don't understand.' Mercy felt as though she were in a dream. Was it the heat, the beer, the music?

'I'm Matondo,' he said, looking at her expectantly.

There it was again, a distant bell that rang somewhere in her mind. Matondo. Malundama. Where had she heard these words before?

'I thought you were dead,' he was saying now. 'I thought I'd never see you again and here you are. I can't believe it.'

He went to embrace her but she pulled away from his touch. Who was this man? What was he talking about?

'I don't know who you think I am but you are mistaken,' she said.

'It must be you,' he said. 'The eyes, the nose, your little hands, your dimples. The other children used to tease us for our dimples. Do you remember?'

She shook her head. *No.* She felt her chest growing tight. Felt as though a hand had taken hold of her heart in a vice-like grip.

'You must remember, Malu. You must remember me? I'm your brother. I'm Matondo.'

No. No. No.

She couldn't hear any more. Wouldn't hear any more. She pushed past him, forced her way through the crowds, oblivious to the cries of protest as she pushed people aside. She flung open the doors and, with no idea of where she was going, she began to run, into the freezing night, with no one to watch over her but the silver moon above.

Time passed. How much time, he couldn't be sure. The boy had tried to keep a record, scratching a small mark each night onto a stone that he carried in his pocket. But then he ran out of space and couldn't find a new stone and he lost track. It was weeks, certainly. Months? Perhaps.

Mostly they walked. Walked and walked. Tied with ropes around their wrists to one of the men to make sure they didn't run away. Other times, when they were too tired and slow, they were carried, slung over a shoulder so that the ground seemed to bounce and shift around them as they were bumped along. At night, they slept on the floor side by side, clutching one another for comfort.

'Matondo… Matondo. Are you awake?' the girl whispered one night, pressing her face up against him.

The men were outside. He could hear the low hum of their voices. The odd bark of laughter. The children had been thrown into a small hut and given a piece of cloth to cover them, though it was barely big enough for one.

'Yes, I'm awake,' her brother said. 'What is it?' He rolled over towards her, taking hold of her two small hands in his.

'I can't sleep. I'm hungry.'

Matondo reached into his pocket and took out a small bone with a few shreds of meat still clinging to it.

'Here. Have this.' He passed it to his sister and she sucked on it, her little teeth tearing at the meat.

For days now they'd eaten nothing but a sort of grainy paste. Matondo had found himself dreaming of yams. Of juicy pineapples. Of meat. He'd managed to snatch the bone when their captors weren't looking, grabbing it from the floor near the fire earlier that evening. He watched his sister eat and tried to ignore the twisting pangs of hunger in his own stomach.

The children had been bought and sold several times by now; exchanged for food or weapons, rolls of cloth or a bag of salt. They had watched as men shouted, laughed and clapped each other on the back, handing the children over without a backward glance. At first they had tried to speak to their captors, find out where they were going, and why. But the men merely laughed, or ignored them. Or worse.

Some of them were not so bad. They let the children play and didn't tie them too tightly. Others were cruel, beating the children if they walked too slowly. They had learned to stay quiet and keep walking. They had learned not to let themselves think about home.

As they travelled west – Matondo knew this from the position of the sun and proudly told his sister so – the people changed from the small, dark men and women of their homeland to stouter, reddish-skinned people. Some of them covered their faces and bodies with small scars, which both terrified and fascinated the children. Matondo wondered how it would feel to make these tiny cuts and why anyone would want to. The landscape changed too; the plants and trees, the birds that soared overhead, the very colour and texture of the ground – all becoming unrecognisable as they travelled ever onwards.

Sometimes, as they passed from hand to hand, they were kept with other prisoners, and one day they found themselves with two girls from their own village. The girls were sisters, older than them but not quite grown up. They had been taken on that same night but had become separated from the others, exchanged by their captors for a gaggle of chickens.

The children hugged and kissed them, so happy to see familiar faces, to hear familiar voices. But before they knew it, the girls were gone – taken away by a fat, dark-skinned man, his fingers pressed deeply into the flesh *of their upper arms. The girls smiled weakly at the children as they were led quickly away.*

'Matondo, where are they going?' the girl asked, looking up at her brother.

'To work. Probably,' he said, with an uncomfortable twisting feeling in the pit of his stomach.

'Are we going to work too?'

'Maybe.'

'Papa will come and get us,' she said solemnly, and he smiled and squeezed her hand.

'Yes, Malundama, I'm sure Papa will come soon.'

But he knew that Papa wouldn't come. Even if he were still alive, he would have no way of knowing where they were. They didn't even know where they were. No, they were on their own now. And it was up to him to keep them both safe.

His sister was asleep now. Still clutching the bone in one hand. Greasy smears around her mouth. Gently, Matondo took the edge of their cloth cover and wiped her face. She whimpered a little and then fell still. He put his arm around her and held her close. He could feel the warmth of her breath against his neck and soon he too was asleep. Dreaming of Papa and Mama, dreaming of home. Until the morning came and a sharp kick in his side woke him, and the horror of it all washed over him once more.

Part Two

September 1820

Chapter 10

As the stagecoach finally rolled into London, Mat's first impression was of fog. Fog, fog and more fog. And not the cool damp of a sea fog, white and soft like the salty tears of a thousand mermaids, but a foul yellow fog that caught at the back of your throat and stung your eyes. Peering out of the open window, he could only see a few feet in front of him. Damned miserable city, this.

They eventually drew to a halt and he staggered out with the other passengers, his legs and arse numb from hours of sitting, his guts stirred up like milk in a churn. Give him the high seas any day over being cramped up in that godforsaken vehicle. He coughed, spat out a sizeable lump of mucus and ran the back of his hand over his mouth. He needed a drink. But first he needed to get his bearings, and with the unerring sense of direction that came from his years at sea, he turned and made his way towards the river. Once he was there he could make a plan. And find a pub.

The air cleared a little as he neared the river. The autumn sun sat low in the sky and the water glowed pinkish-gold. To one side he could see the huge dome of some church, dominating the skyline like a brig at full sail. On the river, boats of all sizes were ferrying bundles and crates of who-knew-what to and from the warehouses that lined the riverside.

He watched the water, fast-flowing and criss-crossed with waves from the wakes of all those boats, saw a cormorant gobbling up a fish in one huge gulp, and felt himself settle. This city might not be so bad after all. Not that it mattered. He wouldn't be here long. Just long enough to do what he needed to do and then he'd be on his way. Back to Bristol, or Liverpool, or maybe further afield. Maybe the further the better.

For the hundredth time his hand moved to his pocket, checking again that the paper was still there. Not that he needed it. *Duca Buclee.* Those two words were carved into his memory as deeply as the scars he still bore on his back, as darkly as the tattoo that adorned his upper arm. He said the words softly to himself. Like a mantra. Like a curse. Then he took one last lungful of the pungent river air and, tipping his hat to the cormorant that bobbed and floated just a little way out, he turned and began to walk away.

He was soon seated in the warmth of a nearby inn, cradling a tankard of ale. He licked his finger and dabbed at the crumbs on the table, which were all that remained of his bread and cheese. His stomach growled, still hungry, but he needed to be careful with his money. It wouldn't last forever, and he couldn't spend it all in the tavern or the whorehouse. Much as he might like to. No, he had work to do. But for now he was glad to be sitting, warm and fed, and he stretched out his legs, leaning his head back against the worn leather of the armchair.

The place was pretty empty at this time of day and he had an unrestricted view of the barmaid, who returned his glances with a smile. He watched her plump, white forearms as she poured drinks, wiped down the bar, and cut great hunks of bread for the occasional hungry punter. She had large, mannish hands and the skin of her face was pitted and scarred, but if he half closed his eyes, she was pretty enough.

She was certainly an improvement on last night's conquest at the coaching inn. He grimaced as he remembered his shock this morning on waking up next to a woman over twice his age, her wig tossed onto the floor to reveal her balding scalp, and her greasy lipstick smeared across her face like a wound. He finished off his beer in one more gulp and glanced at the barmaid again. He could at least get a drink out of her, if nothing else, he thought, and putting on his most charming smile, he headed towards the bar.

He spent most of the rest of that day walking. Having discovered that the friendly barmaid was possessed of a rather *un*friendly husband – and one with arms like a stevedore and fists the size of hams – he'd made a pretty swift departure. Now he found himself wandering the city, getting lost in the maze-like alleyways and streets, gawping at the size and splendour of the buildings, marvelling at the sheer number of people.

And what people! They seemed to come from all corners of the globe; from Irish street-sellers hawking their wares at the tops of their voices, to the turbaned entertainer who claimed to be able to charm snakes – for the right price, of course – to the clothes merchants with their dark beards and broad-brimmed hats who spoke together in a low, thick tongue that he couldn't place. Greek, perhaps? Or Russian?

There were horses and carriages everywhere he looked, the clean, pink faces of the rich peeping out as they clattered past. He saw a flock of geese being driven through the busy streets by a boy with a stick, who cheerfully ignored the complaints of those forced to change course by this gang of feathered brutes, clacking and hissing their way along the cobbles. And most noticeably of all, he himself was barely given a second glance. There was the odd grumbled comment, but for the most part, amidst the chaos of the city, he was invisible, unremarkable, and for that he was grateful.

As he felt the chill of evening approaching and noticed the sky beginning to darken, he decided he'd better find somewhere to stay and instinctively headed east towards the docks. On the way, he bought a pie from a stall at the side of the road. He ate it as he walked, glad of the warmth of the pastry on his fingers, and hungry enough even to enjoy the grey, stringy meat and spongy potatoes inside.

Tomorrow he would start work proper. He should have done it today. Didn't know why he hadn't. He had thought about this for so long, dreamed about it, planned it, and yet, now he was here, he found himself hesitating. Was it fear? He couldn't be sure. There wasn't much that he was afraid of. He'd faced the lash more times than he cared to remember, suffered broken bones, fevers – nearly been drowned on several occasions – but none of those had made him afraid. It had even earned him his nickname, Mat the Cat.

'Mat the Cat and his nine lives!' his shipmates would say, or, 'My missus always said black cats was lucky!' And they'd laugh and playfully rub his arm or pat his head for good luck.

Thinking of his shipmates, he realised that this was the longest time he'd ever been alone. He'd been on shore leave before, of course, but not having any family of his own, he'd spent most of that time drinking, packed into the cheapest and nearest taverns with the rest of the crew. So many times, when he'd been cramped up in his hammock, one man's arse not two feet from his face, another man's feet stinking the whole place out, another snoring like a walrus, he'd wished so desperately to be alone. And now that he was – with the dark river stretching out to his right and the vastness of the city to his left – he felt, well, lonely. Untethered. Yes, tomorrow he would get to work, do what he came here to do and then find himself the next ship out of here.

The streets were getting quieter as he moved further away from the city, and when he heard footsteps behind him he was immediately on his guard. His hand moved instinctively towards his clasp knife. Better to be prepared, just in case. But before he had the chance to get hold of it, he was shoved hard in the back, and he tripped and fell to the ground.

He looked up to see two lads grinning down at him, one holding out a nasty-looking blade, the other an iron bar.

'Looks like we caught ourselves a monkey,' said the boy with the knife – they must have been all of fourteen or fifteen – and his mate laughed, thumping the bar heavily into the palm of his hand.

Mat considered fighting them – he'd certainly taken on fellows bigger and harder than these two in his time – but he was in unfamiliar territory, didn't know how many more of them there might be. Best to play safe.

'Here, take it. It's all I've got,' he said, and he chucked a purse of coins a little way beyond them so that they had to turn away to retrieve it. As they did, he bolted, running until his lungs were straining. He stopped and listened out in case they'd followed him but there was nothing. He had to admit to being slightly shaken. They may have been little more than kids but they'd looked pretty nifty with those weapons.

Thankfully he'd hidden most of his money in a series of secret pockets sewn inside his shirt and jacket – he wasn't a complete fool – but he was still annoyed with himself for letting his guard down. He had to be more careful. He couldn't afford any more mistakes. Keeping his wits about him now, he walked on in search of somewhere to rest his head.

*

Later that night he lay on the floor of his lodgings with his bag as a pillow – more for security than comfort. The man lying next to him rolled over and mumbled in his sleep. There were six or seven other sleeping bodies dotted about the room, each lost in his own world of dreams or nightmares. It was freezing by now, and the stench from the overflowing cesspit outside crept in through the broken windows along with the cold night air.

He'd found a boarding house for dock workers. Men too poor and too tired to complain about the state of the place. Men without options. It had probably been a grand old house at one time but now it was one step away from a ruin; stairs without bannisters, masonry crumbling off the walls, each room housing several men all paying a penny a night for the privilege. The old sod who ran the place must be raking it in.

'It'll be an extra penny for the blanket,' he'd said, handing over a thin bit of cloth, grey and frayed at the edges with a stale, musty smell and some questionable stains.

Mat turned onto his back, his right shoulder growing stiff and sore from the cold that seeped up through the floor. He crossed his arms and folded his hands inside his coat for warmth. There he felt the reassuring presence of the brooch, its enamel front and scalloped metal edges as familiar to him as his own hand.

He ran the brooch between his fingers as he'd done every night since he could remember. With his other hand he felt for the piece of paper. He could do without comfort, do without money, as long as he had these two things. *Duca Buclee*, he whispered to himself, *Duca Buclee. Dear God, let me find them.*

Chapter 11

The Register Office of Shipping loomed up before him. The windows with their canvas blinds were hooded eyes looking down on him with disdain. It had been easy enough to get hold of the address. There was a camaraderie amongst sailors; it didn't matter if you'd never laid eyes on each other before – after a glass of rum and an exchange of tall tales, you were the best of friends. He'd soon found out where he needed to go to get the information he was after.

He tugged at his jacket, trying to smooth out any remaining creases, glad that he'd bothered to buy some togs from a second-hand clothes stall. The sleeves were a bit short and the trousers a bit tight but he certainly looked smarter than he ever had before. *Come on, Mat the Cat*, he murmured to himself, *let's get this done*, and he forced himself up the steps before he could change his mind.

The shiny brass knocker was shaped like a galleon – a nice touch, he thought as he rat-tatted on the door. The clerk that opened it did little to hide his surprise and dismay upon seeing a black man on his doorstep, but Mat knew that he was within his rights to see the records, and put on his most humble expression. He'd soon learned that with skin the colour of his, the meeker you seemed, the better you were treated. Even if he burned with fury on the inside, on the outside, he was the very picture of politeness.

The clerk eventually showed him in and he was taken to a side room, sparsely furnished with a table and a few chairs, and asked to wait. A moment or so later, the young man returned, bearing a book bound in black leather.

'Here you are, *sir*,' he said, putting unnecessary emphasis on the word, as if it pained him to say it.

He placed the book down on the table in front of Mat and retreated to the corner of the room, clearly not trusting him to be left alone. The book was embossed with a gold border and the image of an anchor, with the number *1806* in large print in the centre. Mat glanced up at the clerk who watched him with a beady eye and opened the book. There were several columns on each page with numbers and words listed in each.

He ran his finger down the page, trying to make sense of it, but the figures seemed to swarm about like weevils in front of his eyes. He could make out a word here and there – *D. Wood... J. Cook... G. Jones* – were they names of people? And he saw *Bristol* a few times, and *Liverpl*, which must be Liverpool. But nowhere could he see the two words he was looking for. *Duca Buclee*. There were so many pages, so many words, he began to feel overwhelmed.

As he continued to turn the pages he felt a hot panic rising up in him. He shifted in his chair, tugged at his collar.

'Is sir all right?' the clerk said with a sneer.

'Very good, thank you,' he replied. *Snivelling little snot-rag.*

He returned his attention to the book but no matter how hard he tried, he just couldn't make sense of it. *Idiot*, he thought to himself, *stupid, stupid idiot*. He had waited so long for this. Had thought it would be so easy. *Duca Buclee*. He'd carried the name of that ship in his head for so long, it was all he had to hold on to. He closed the book with a thump and pushed it away, across the table.

'Finished, sir?'

The clerk sprang forward and retrieved the book, cradling it to his chest like a rescued infant. He showed Mat out in silence. The loud thud as the door closed seemed the death knell of all his hopes and plans. He had failed. Failed before he had even begun.

Mat walked. He didn't know where. He just had to walk. And to think. All he needed was the name of the captain of the *Duca Buclee* and he could figure out the rest from there, but how else was he supposed to find it other than in the shipping register?

He could have asked the clerk for help, he supposed, but the thought of admitting that he couldn't read beyond a few words to that snooty piece of bum fodder made him feel physically sick. He could just picture the look on his face. And how could he trust that he'd have given him the right information, anyway? He'd probably have said anything just to get Mat out of there quick smart.

So, if not in the register, where else? He could hardly go around London asking every old sailor if they remembered who was the captain of some ship from nearly fifteen years ago. Maybe he could try the dockmaster? They must keep records of all the ships coming in and out. Yes, he could try that. But he didn't know if the *Duca Buclee* had even set sail from London; it could have sailed from Plymouth or Glasgow or any port in between. No, the register was the only way.

He'd left the boarding house early that morning, hadn't eaten anything, and as his anger cooled and his pace slowed, he felt suddenly exhausted and very, very hungry. He looked around, taking in his surroundings for the first time since he'd left the Register Office in Birchin Lane. He was in a busy street, people toing and froing as if they hadn't a care in the world. A girl was selling flowers on one corner, calling out her wares in a sing-song voice. On another corner a man was playing the fiddle and Mat stopped to watch.

He was a black man, but that wasn't what caught Mat's attention. He was dressed in the most outlandish clothes – a sort of patchwork jacket and bright red trousers – and on his head was perched the model of a ship, complete with masts and sails. As he played his fiddle, he performed a sort of dance, bobbing his head so that the ship appeared to be in motion across the waves.

Mat wasn't the only one to have stopped. Quite a crowd had gathered, and Mat watched as passers-by dropped coins into an upturned hat which lay on the ground by the man's feet. As each coin fell, he grinned at the crowd, bowing his head in thanks, causing the ship to bob up and down even more vigorously.

Everyone had to earn a living, Mat supposed, but there was something in the man's simpering smile that put him in mind of a performing bear he'd seen at a fair years ago. The beast lifting its paws to the rhythm of a drum as the crowd clapped and laughed. But Mat had seen the pain in the poor creature's eyes, the blisters on its paws still visible from where it had been taught its 'dance'.

Still, it was a harsh world out there and if this fellow could make a penny or two from his playing and dancing, then so be it. Who was he to judge? He turned away and headed towards a mash shop he could see just along the street, its windows misted up from the heat inside.

It was a tiny place with a handful of tables and a counter along the window. Mat managed to find a stool at the counter and wiped a hole in the condensation so that he could look out on the street as he ate. The mash was lumpy and the eel stew overly salted for his liking, but with a slice of bread and butter and a hot cup of coffee, he started to feel a bit better. All was not lost. He just needed to use his noddle to come up with a plan.

A man sat down next to him, a well-to-do looking gent, wearing a smart coat with an impossibly white shirt poking out at the collar and sleeves. Mat tugged at his own sleeves, aware suddenly of the yellowing and not-so-fragrant shirt beneath his ill-fitting jacket. The man glanced at Mat before carefully moving his stool slightly further away. The gent had a steaming plate of mash topped with a slice of pie and surrounded by a pool of liquor. As it cooled, he took a newspaper from under his arm and opened it up, forming a barrier between him and Mat. The title of the newspaper was printed in an ornate script and Mat could only make out one or two letters; the rest was a blur of tiny print that might as well have been in French or Spanish for all that he could read it.

He cursed himself again for not paying more attention to learning to read and write when he'd had the chance. It had been the ship's chaplain on one of his first commissions who had tried to teach him. Wanted to make him a good little Christian, and had taken pains when Mat was still a brat of eleven or twelve to show him his alphabet and teach him the Lord's Prayer by heart. He could still say it now, if required, not that the words meant much to him. *Apart from the daily bread*, he thought with a smile as he took another bite – *oh yes, give us our daily bread!* He could just about write out his name and one or two other words and could read a bit. But if only he'd tried harder back then, he wouldn't be in this mess now.

The man turned a page and refolded his newspaper, holding it in one hand and continuing to read as he forked food into his mouth with the other hand. *That's what I need*, Mat thought: *someone who can read*. He imagined asking this man for his help and inadvertently let out a loud bark of laughter as he pictured his reaction. The man stared at him in disgust, held his paper higher up and inched further away down the counter.

Mat took another gulp of coffee. Of all the people he'd met in London so far – the whores and dockhands, the lumpers and barmaids – he doubted that any one of them would be able to read a word. No, he was well and truly stuffed.

The door of the shop opened, letting in an icy blast of air, and Mat looked up to see the black fiddler coming in. He carried his model ship under one arm and a sorry sight he was, shivering from the cold and slightly stooped, clutching his battered fiddle and bow. He made his way to the counter.

'How much for a plate of your finest pie and mash, miss?' he asked.

'Shilling,' she replied.

'Oh dear, oh dear,' he said, shaking his head. 'That's more than I have.' He began forlornly searching his pockets.

'How much you got?' the girl asked him, and he held out his hand to reveal a few pennies.

The girl looked over her shoulder and, seeing that no one was watching, she heaped a generous helping of pie and mash onto a plate and handed it to him. When he offered her his pennies, she shook her head and wouldn't take them.

'Not a word!' she said as she handed it over.

'God bless you, miss, God bless you!'

The fiddler made his way through the busy shop, searching for a free seat, and as he squeezed past Mat, something fell from his pocket. With his hands full he couldn't pick it up, so Mat reached down to grab it and pass it back to him. It was a purse of coins. Bulging with coins, in fact. Mat and the fiddler exchanged a look. A look of conspiracy.

A look that said, *Don't say a word; we've got to stick together, you and I.* Mat handed the purse over to him and with the slightest nod of thanks the man took it, sat down and began to eat.

Cheeky bugger. Mat watched him for a moment. He wasn't so frail after all and he was younger than Mat had first thought, tall and slight with large expressive eyes and a wide mouth that twitched at the corner as if always ready to break into a smile. He must have felt Mat watching him as just then he looked up and gave him a wink, before getting stuck back into his huge plate of food.

The gent sitting next to Mat had finished and got up to leave. Mat noticed he'd left his newspaper on the counter and was about to call after him – but no, sod him, why should he do that stuck-up snob a good turn? He'd also left a bit of mash and Mat quickly mopped it up with his remaining bread. Waste not, want not.

He drained the last of his coffee. What to do? What to do? He hadn't come all this way to turn back at the first hurdle. He felt a presence at his side and looked round to see the fiddler.

'May I?' he asked, indicating the now-vacant seat.

'Suit yourself,' Mat said.

'And could I trouble you to watch over *Albertina*?'

'Who's Albertina?'

'My pride and joy,' the man said, placing his model ship onto the counter. 'Won't be a moment. Just need to go and water my horse, as it were.'

He patted Mat on the shoulder and went outside, turning down the alleyway at the side of the shop. The model ship really was a marvel. It was carved out of wood with tiny canvas sails and was attached to a cylindrical cap covered with blue-green velvet – to reflect the colour of the sea, Mat realised. Each tiny detail, from the rudder to the bowsprit, was rendered to perfection. There were little figures positioned on the deck, some holding on to ropes, one high up on the crosstrees and even a captain at the helm. Incredible.

Peering closer, Mat saw that the captain had a tiny black face underneath his hat. The figure was so small that no one would notice. Mat touched the little captain gently with his fingertip and smiled to himself.

'A beauty, ain't she?' The man was back and took his seat next to Mat.

'Must have taken a lot of work,' Mat said. 'Did you make it yourself?'

'I did indeed, my friend. I did indeed. A man's got to have a whole lot of talents if he wants to get by in this world.'

'I suppose so.' Mat felt like he didn't have much talent for anything at the moment.

'I'm Joe,' the man said, holding out his hand.

'Mat.'

'Short for Matthew?'

'Yes. And no. Was Matthew for a long while. Was Matondo before that. Now it's just Mat.'

'I see. Can I buy you a cup of coffee, Mr Matondo? To thank you for your discretion – and for taking such good care of *Albertina*?'

Mat hesitated. He was wary of accepting anything from anyone. Didn't want to be in anyone's debt. But then again, he had nowhere else to go and didn't relish the prospect of the long walk back to the boarding house.

'Thank you,' he said simply.

'Thing is, you'll have to go to the counter and get it.' The man surreptitiously passed him a couple of pennies. 'Seeing as I'm destitute.'

He grinned as Mat got up to go to the counter. What a fellow. Ah, well. Another cup of coffee and then he'd be on his way. Maybe he could try the Register Office again tomorrow. Might be a different clerk on duty. He paid for the drinks and took the two cups of thick, black coffee back to their spot by the window.

'See they're showing one of those panoramas up at Leicester Square,' Joe said as Mat put the coffee down.

'What?'

'Panorama. Of the Battle of Waterloo. Should be quite a sight.'

When Mat still looked at him blankly, he picked up the newspaper that had been left behind on the counter, and tapped his finger at one of the chunks of text.

'"The interesting panoramic painting of the Battle of Waterloo will be reopened for a short time",' Joe read.

Mat stared at him, this young rapscallion with his patchwork coat and infectious grin, and saw the answer to his prayers.

'You can read?' he asked, needing to be completely sure.

'I sure can, Mr Matondo. I told you, a man needs many talents to get by in this cold, hard world. And I, my friend, have more than most.' He held up his coffee. 'Here's to us, Mr Matondo.' He chinked his cup against Mat's as if they were drinking the finest wine.

'Indeed, my friend,' Mat said. 'Here's to us!'

Chapter 12

Joe lodged in a room above a chemist's and, as they made their way up the narrow staircase, he paused and held a finger over his lips.

'Don't. Make. A peep.'

'Peeeep!'

'Shhh!' They both giggled silently, holding their hands over their mouths and leaning against the walls until they were able to resume their slow climb up the stairs. Mat was wearing Joe's ship on his head, which had somehow seemed a very good idea at the time but which now caused him to sway from side to side as he tried to keep it upright.

'Issa stormy sea tonight!' he whispered, bobbing his head, and they both fell about again.

'Come on,' said Joe, 'in here. And quiet! I don't think I'm allowed to have visitors.' He showed Mat through a door into a comfortable attic room.

What had started as one cup of coffee had turned into several beers, one or five glasses of rum, a fight with a Danish dockhand, and a close encounter with a large and quite terrifying dog. Mat had a great tear down one leg of his nearly new trousers and he felt like he'd been keelhauled, but he hadn't laughed so much since – well, since he couldn't remember when.

He took *Albertina* off his head and placed her down reverently. How they had managed to get her back in one piece, he had no idea.

'Here, you can have this.' Joe threw him a blanket and started to clear some space for him on the floor.

When he'd heard about the freezing boarding house he'd insisted Mat come back with him, and – after a long day's drinking and with no idea where he was – Mat had happily agreed. He kicked off his boots, wrapped himself up in the blanket and fell instantly asleep, unaware of the smile that spread itself across his face.

The morning brought a sharp and blinding pain behind his eyes and a mouth that felt like a badger's arse. Mat groaned and rolled over, discovering several bruises as he did so.

'Ow. I feel like I've been trampled by a carthorse.'

'You nearly were!'

Mat squinted one eye open. Joe was dressed and sat on the edge of his bed. He looked remarkably chipper.

'Come on, Mr Matondo. We've got work to do!'

Mat groaned again.

'Work?' he asked, gingerly sitting up.

'Yes! We have to pay a visit to your friends at the Register Office!'

Mat groped through his still blurry mind. What had they talked about? How much had he told Joe? He remembered that his plan had been to offer Joe a small fee for going back to the Register Office with him to find the ship's details, but he had been determined not to give too much away. Not to tell Joe why he wanted to know about the *Duca Buclee* and what he planned on doing with the information.

After the third beer he recalled that his resolve had weakened somewhat. In fact, he was fairly sure that the whole sorry story had poured out of him like water from a leaky vessel. He'd told Joe about his childhood in Africa, about him and his sister being kidnapped and sold, and about how they had been separated.

'I made a vow back then that I would find her,' he told Joe. 'But seeing as that's nigh on impossible, I made another vow. That I would find the men who took her and make them pay.'

'Do you know what happened to her, your sister?' Joe had asked gently. Mat had never spoken about her before. He'd thought about her. Every day. Wondered how she was, if she was alive on some West Indian plantation somewhere. He knew that most likely she'd be dead by now. Life was harsh out there, he'd heard. He'd been lucky. Managed to get himself work on the ships as a lad and avoided the dreadful fate of so many of his countrymen.

'No,' he simply said. 'All I know is it was 1806 and the ship that took her was called *Duca Buclee*. The register should give me the name of the captain and I'll take it from there.'

Joe had been happy to help. He had no family of his own but he seemed to understand Mat's need for revenge.

'This one's for your sister!' he'd said, raising yet another glass of rum into the air.

After that, Mat's memory was somewhat hazy. He rubbed his hands over his face. A hair of the dog might be in order, he thought. He looked up to see that Joe was rummaging through his wardrobe and Mat noticed now that Joe was dressed in a fine suit and a white shirt with a tall collar. Was he still dreaming?

'These ought to fit you.'

Joe held up a pair of dark woollen trousers and Mat recalled now how he'd ripped his own as they'd careered down an alleyway after their encounter with the Danish dockhand. He saw that, hanging inside the wardrobe, Joe had a whole row of clothes – coats and jackets, shirts, what looked like a cape – and on top were various hats, stacked one on top of the other.

'What the— Why do you have all this stuff?'

'You never know,' Joe said, tapping the side of his nose with one finger, 'when it will come in handy.'

And so, within the hour, Mat found himself once more before the doors of the Register Office of Shipping, dressed like quite the gent and accompanied by Joe in his Sunday best. The clerk gaped like a fish when he saw the two of them, and when Joe explained that he was an African man of business who needed to check the records of one or two of his 'business interests', the man was rendered completely speechless.

He showed them into the same small room and brought them the book, as before, and when Joe tipped him imperiously with a shiny coin, it was all Mat could do not to laugh out loud.

'Right, let's see.' Joe opened the book and began meticulously running through the lists. Mat sat opposite, watching him, his left leg anxiously jigging up and down.

'Is it there?'

'Shh.' Joe turned page after page, a slight frown on his face.

'Have you found it? Is it there?'

Joe said nothing. He kept reading, his long index finger moving down each page as his eyes skimmed from side to side.

'Are you sure you got the name right?' Joe asked. He'd come to the end of the book.

'Yes, yes, of course I'm sure. Look!' Mat unfolded his scrap of paper and showed Joe the two words again, *Duca Buclee*.

'Funny name for a ship,' said Joe. 'Spanish, is it?'

'I don't know!' Mat said, a little more vehemently than he had intended. 'I just know that's the name! Ships get called all sorts – I've sailed on the *Talavera*, the *Malabar*, the blimmin' *Aboukir* – why not *Duca Buclee*?'

'All right. Calm down, Mr Matondo. I'm just saying *Duca Buclee*'s not in there. I'm sorry.'

'It has to be. It has to be.'

Mat felt a chasm open up around him. This was all he had thought about for so long. It had to be there.

'I'll look again.' Joe turned back to the beginning of the book.

They could hear footsteps now coming down the corridor towards them. The muffled voice of the clerk.

'He said he was an African merchant. I wasn't sure…'

And then another deeper, older voice. 'And you believed him? Good God, Perkins.'

The footsteps were getting closer.

'Anything?' Mat realised he was gripping the edge of the table, his fingertips digging hard into the wood so that the skin beneath them turned pale.

'Wait,' Joe said. '*Duca Buclee, Duca Buclee*.' He began frantically turning the pages. 'Of course!'

'What?' asked Mat. He could hear the clerk approaching the door.

'Not *Duca Buclee* – Duke. Of. Buckleigh! The *Duke of Buckleigh*. I've got it!'

The door flew open to reveal the young clerk, cringing behind what must have been his employer, a robust middle-aged man with cheeks as puce as his cravat.

'Whoever you are, you've had your fun. Now, get out! We don't want your sort in here.' He pointed his finger theatrically towards the door.

'Your sort?' said Joe, then turning to Mat, 'I think he must mean incredibly handsome young bucks, eh? Don't worry, rusty-guts, we've got what we came for. Here.'

Joe tossed the book towards them and as the two men floundered to catch it, Joe walked calmly past them.

'Good day, gentlemen.' He bowed and doffed his hat before turning to run out of the door. Mat hesitated for just a second, then ran hotfoot behind him.

While that morning Mat would have sworn on all that was holy he'd never drink again, after a pell-mell dash through the streets away from the Register Office, a celebratory drink seemed to be very much in order.

'I can't believe it. I can't believe we found it!' Mat slapped Joe on the shoulder for the umpteenth time, barely able to stay in his seat. 'You're a genius! Tell me again what it said.'

'I've told you.' Joe took another swig of his beer.

'Tell me again.'

'The *Duke of Buckleigh*. 1806. Sailed from London. Owner, J. Hazelwood. Captain, R. Dudley.'

'That's the one. It has to be.'

'So, what next?'

'Next, I find Captain R. Dudley,' Mat said. 'I find Captain R. Dudley. And I kill him.' Mat downed what was left in his tankard, slammed it back down on the table and rose to his feet. 'And there's no time like the present.'

Chapter 13

If he wanted to track down Captain Dudley, Mat knew he needed to head back towards the docks, and so he said goodbye to Joe and began the walk east along the river. They arranged to meet again later that evening. Joe said he'd ask his landlord if Mat could stay for a night or two – and, in any case, he'd need to give Joe his suit back if nothing else.

As he walked, the elation that had buoyed him up since they left the Register Office began to fade. And, just as an ebbing tide leaves flotsam and jetsam on the shore, as his joy receded, his mind was left scattered with fragmentary thoughts.

Could he really kill a man in cold blood? How would he do it? The captain would be old by now. Old and weak. He pictured bashing this imagined old man around the head with a heavy wooden club, or stabbing him through the heart with his knife. Blood seeping through a crisp, white shirt. He could strangle him, he supposed. Or push him, hard, beneath the wheels of a carriage, or the pounding hooves of a horse.

But in all these imagined scenarios, he kept seeing the old man's pleading eyes, his outstretched hands, the 'No, please!' that issued from his blood-flecked lips, and heard the words of the ship's chaplain. *If ye forgive not men their trespasses, neither will your heavenly Father forgive your trespasses.*

Heavenly Father be damned, Mat thought, shaking his head as if to dislodge his unwelcome thoughts. When had this 'heavenly Father' ever done him any good? No. He could do this. He *would* do this. Captain R. Dudley was a dead man.

Even though he'd only been in the city for a few days, he'd already heard of the notorious tavern the Prospect of Whitby, which perched on the edge of the river out east. It had apparently been a watering hole for smugglers, pirates and sailors for well over a hundred years. If anyone knew Captain Dudley, he would surely find them in the Prospect, and after a forty-minute trudge, he arrived and made his way inside.

Instantly he wished he'd changed back into his own togs. This get-up of Joe's was far too fancy for a place like this. A few curious pairs of eyes watched him as he made his way between the tables towards the bar, but they soon turned back to their drinks and their games of cards, their arguments and their tall tales. In this city it was hard to shock, and these old sea dogs had probably seen stranger things in their time than a black man in a fancy suit.

'Evening, handsome.'

A woman had sidled up next to him, putting her hand on his arm and giving it a squeeze. Another consequence of the suit, he supposed. He batted her away and ordered a drink. He didn't have time for any of that. He needed to stay focused.

He sipped at his beer and looked around. It was pretty dingy; the windows were yellowed from years of tobacco smoke and let in barely a smudge of daylight, and the oil lamps dotted about the place gave off only a meagre light. The main room was dominated by the bar that ran all along one wall but, off to the sides of the room, Mat could spy alcoves where groups of men gathered, hunched over their drinks, deep in conversation. An unsavoury bunch, they were. Men with faces hard as a November wind. Some with knives visible at their belts, others with eye patches or missing fingers. No wonder this place had been nicknamed the Devil's Tavern. He'd need to keep his wits about him.

Just along the bar was another chap on his own. He had black hair and was pale as a corpse. Mat thought he might start with him, strike up a conversation and see where it went, but then he noticed that the man was muttering to himself and barely able to stay upright on his stool. Perhaps not. Wouldn't get much sense out of that one. He eyed a table of three fellows who seemed to be sharing a bottle of wine and a good laugh, and decided to try his luck with them.

'Gents,' he said, 'I'm after some information…'

Before he could get any further, one of them, a great bull of a man, stood up and put his face very close to Mat's.

'Bugger off, snowball.'

His tone was so reasonable, so matter-of-fact even, that Mat merely smiled and backed away, and the man sat down and carried on his conversation as before. This might be harder than he'd thought.

He returned to the relative safety of the bar, wishing now that he'd asked Joe to come with him. He'd know what to do. Then a thought struck him. What would Joe do? He wouldn't try to fit in, he'd play a part. And Mat could do the same. He ordered a bottle of wine and, taking a deep breath, he approached another table.

'Gents,' he said, putting on what he hoped was a well-to-do accent. 'Sorry to intrude, but I'm new to the place and I'm looking for a little assistance. For a price, of course!'

He held up his purse of money in one hand and the bottle of wine in the other. After a moment's hesitation the younger of the two men, a sandy-haired lad, drew up a chair for Mat and the two accepted a glass of wine. Mat saw them exchanging a glance as if to say, *Our luck's in, here*, and he silently thanked Joe for the lend of the suit that gave him an air of respectability, and for his purse of money – though how long that would last, he wasn't too sure.

Once they'd established that Mat wasn't a threat, and that he seemed willing to top up their glasses whenever they ran low, the two men became quite talkative. They turned out to be sailors from Bristol and Mat found the rounded burr of their speech oddly comforting – aside from the deck of a ship, Bristol was the closest place he'd ever had to a home. Mat made up some vague story of having come into an inheritance from a distant relative and having given up his life at sea. They seemed to swallow it. Or perhaps they just didn't care. As long as the wine kept flowing, they were happy to chat and it wasn't long before Mat manoeuvred the conversation round to Captain Dudley.

'Dunno,' said the older of the two men. 'Might've met him. Met a lot of captains in my time.'

'He captained a ship called the *Duke of Buckleigh* a while back,' Mat said. 'I'm trying to find him. Got a message for him from an old friend.'

'*Duke of Buckleigh*?' the man said. 'Weren't that the one that went down 'bout fifteen years ago? Was a big hoo-ha about it.'

'Went down? You mean...?'

'All the way to Davy Jones's locker.'

Mat sat back in his chair, took a mouthful of wine to try to stem the tremor that he felt in his hands and which threatened to take over his whole body. The ship had gone down. He'd always known it was likely his sister was dead. He knew that most didn't survive the voyage and those that did often didn't make it past a few months or years. Yet now, faced with this stark reality, he realised that in some hidden place in his heart, he had wanted to believe that she was still alive. But the ship had gone down. She was dead, and so were the men who took her.

The two sailors were still talking though he barely registered what they were saying. He made an effort to smile, nod, appear normal, though inside he felt as though the world were ending. He'd finish his drink and get out of here.

'Big fat fella he was,' the older sailor went on, gesturing with his hands to indicate a big belly. 'His men used to call him Henry the Eighth on account of how fat he was! Henry the Eighth, oh Lord!' The man chuckled and wiped away a tear from the corner of his eye. '"Here comes old King Henry", they'd say and they'd laugh – not when he was around, mind, 'cause he was a brutal bastard too.'

'Who's that?' Mat asked half-heartedly, his mind still reeling with shock.

'Him. Yer man Dudley.'

'Oh, I see. So you knew him before he died?'

'Died? Has he died?'

'You said his ship went down?'

'Oh yes, but he didn't die! Most o' the crew survived. Not the cargo, though, if you know what I mean. Here.' He leaned in close and Mat could smell the vinegary tang of red wine on his breath. 'There's one who could tell you a thing or two about Henry the Eighth.'

He nodded towards the bar and Mat turned to see he was looking at the pale-faced soak who'd been mumbling to himself.

'Him? Why?'

'He sailed with him. Was 'is first mate back in the day, like, on the *Duke o' Buckleigh*. But they had a falling-out. Oh!' He held the bottle of wine upside down and waggled it over the table. 'And not a drop to drink!' He chuckled again and the younger man joined in.

'Well, we must remedy that, mustn't we?' said Mat, jumping to his feet. He jostled his way through the crowds until he reached the man who had been Dudley's first mate.

'Excuse me, sir.'

The man didn't turn.

'Hey!'

Nothing.

'You sailed with Dudley?'

The man looked round and Mat saw his eyes widen.

'What do you want?' he asked. 'What do you want?'

'Captain Dudley.' Mat could see the man was visibly cowering; no need for tricks and games with this one. 'Where is he? Is he still in London? I need to find him.'

'You've come for him.' The man spoke quietly, his eyes dark pools in his white face. 'I knew you would. Life for life, eye for eye. Life for life, eye for eye.'

'Just tell me where he is.' Mat moved closer to the man, grabbed the front of his shirt with one hand. 'Tell me.'

'You shall not have me, spirit! You shall not!'

With a sudden movement, the man twisted away from Mat's grasp and, half falling, half jumping from his stool, he made his escape, pushing his way through the crowd and out into the street. Mat followed, elbowing his way past the drinkers who stood in his way, and flung open the door. He looked left, he looked right, but there was nothing, save for the dark cobbles and the patter of footsteps fading into the night.

Chapter 14

Joe's landlord was a chemist by the name of John Alford; a Yorkshireman and a Quaker. Mat wasn't entirely sure what a Quaker was, but Joe assured him it meant that Alford and his wife Bettina were good folk and that they were happy for him to stay for a night or two.

As Mat watched the Alfords and their four children, in the smallish room that served as both dining room and parlour in the cold winter months, he felt he could almost see this goodness radiating off them.

They had insisted he eat with them that morning and so he and Joe had been given stools at either end of the table, while the two younger girls were sitting one on her father's knee and the other on the knee of her elder sister. Mrs Alford poured the tea and her son, a bright little chap of seven or eight, proudly handed round slices of bread and butter, boiled eggs, and little scones made with cheese.

'Thank you,' Mat said, 'for allowing me to lodge here. I expect to be finished with my business in a day or two, so won't impose on your kindness for too long.'

He saw Joe smirk at him across the table and became aware that his manner was stilted, awkward. There was something about the soft grace of Mrs Alford and the neat, round-faced little children that made him feel clumsy and uncouth. He felt his hands were too big for the dainty plate, his voice too loud, and he was more aware than ever that he hadn't bathed for many months.

'You are very welcome, Matthew,' said Mrs Alford with a smile. 'Now, have another scone – Cook made them fresh this morning.'

Mat had prepared an elaborate story in case they asked what his business was and why he was in London, but neither Mr Alford nor his wife had enquired. They simply said that any friend of Joe's was a friend of theirs, and left it at that. Apparently Quakers saw all folk as equal so were kind to everyone – that seemed a damned strange idea to Mat, but he was glad to reap the benefits of it. Very glad indeed.

'I'd better go and open up,' said Mr Alford, glancing at the clock and getting to his feet. Without warning, he handed the infant he'd been dandling on his knee to Mat who had no choice but to grab hold of the little thing, though he'd never so much as come close to a baby before. Mr Alford kissed his wife on the cheek and went out into the hall where there was a door that led to the shop at the front of the house.

'I think she likes you,' said Mrs Alford.

The child was looking up at Mat with her large blue eyes, each cheek so perfectly pink and smooth that she resembled a doll. He jiggled his knee up and down and she gurgled with delight.

'Her name is Charlotte.' Mrs Alford tickled the baby under her chin with one finger and the child giggled again.

'Charlotte,' Mat said softly, 'it's very nice to meet you.'

There was something unexpectedly pleasing about the solid weight of the child upon his knee, the warmth of her chubby body in his arms. He thought then of his sister, how he had held her when she was small. He had resented her at first, seen her as a threat, but he had come to love her more than he thought was possible.

He didn't think of those days often – had learned not to, in fact. Memories of his childhood, of his mother and father, of those days of endless sunshine, were too painful to dwell on and so he kept them shut away, like precious jewels in a padlocked box. Now he would need to add the death of his sister to that box, lock it away with everything else, or he would go mad.

On the walk back from the Prospect last night, he had tortured himself with thoughts of Malu drowning. He could see her disappearing beneath the dark waves, hands clutching at the air. He had cried then. Cried long and loud, howling into the night for his sister, for his parents – for himself. For all the things that had been taken from him and which he could never get back. And when he had no more tears left and his throat ached and his eyes burned, he had vowed again to kill Dudley, no matter how old or weak he had become, and if he hanged for it, then so be it. What did he have to lose?

'Isn't that right, Mat?' Joe's voice roused him from his thoughts and he looked up, like a man coming to from a deep sleep.

'What's that?' he asked.

'We should get going. Lots to do.' Joe looked at him expectantly.

'Oh, yes. Yes, lots to do. Business. You know.' He awkwardly held out the little girl and Mrs Alford gathered her up and kissed the top of her head. 'Thank you very much for breakfast, Mrs Alford.'

'You're very welcome, Matthew. Now say goodbye, children.'

The two older children dutifully stood and said goodbye, the little boy solemnly shaking Mat's hand. He wished then that he could stay and forget all about the horrors of the past and the horrors still to come. Wished he could stay and drink another cup of tea and listen to the chatter of the children. And yet. And yet, things were as they were and he didn't belong here. With a heavy heart, he turned and followed Joe, closing the door softly behind him.

They walked in silence for the most part, through the grey city streets, collars turned up against the wind. Joe must have noticed Mat's swollen eyes and hoarse voice last night but he had said nothing. When Mat had been ready to talk, he listened and nodded, his long fingers steepled under his chin, elbows on knees. After he'd lost track of the man who had been Captain Dudley's first mate, Mat had gone back to the inn and managed to find out that his name was Booth and he lived east of the City of London, near Spitalfields.

'I have to talk to him. He's my only way of getting to Dudley. He got away from me last night but I won't let him get away from me again.'

'I'm coming with you,' Joe had said then, and when Mat tried to dissuade him, he insisted. 'I know this city better than you, my friend,' he said, his hand on Mat's shoulder. 'And besides, I like an adventure!'

As they made their way into the narrow and uneven streets around Smithfield Market, the air became thick with the stench of blood from the butchers and abattoirs that clogged this part of the city.

'Watch out!'

Joe pulled him roughly out of the way as a man in a greasy leather apron poured a bucket of entrails and offcuts out onto the street, narrowly avoiding their feet.

'Oy, careful!' Joe said but the man merely shrugged, spat, and turned back into his shop, his feet squelching through the pink and pulpy mess.

On they went, leaving the stench of animals – both the living and the recently slaughtered – behind them as they headed further east.

Now they were surrounded by the sounds of weavers' looms and the woody, yeasty aroma of nearby breweries.

'Look,' said Mat, 'that's Eagle Street. I think we're nearly there.'

They picked their way through the filthy streets until they came to a row of old houses, which leaned together unevenly like a bunch of drunks. The glass was missing from most of the windows, replaced by greying bits of material pinned up over the window frames. Here and there chunks of plaster had fallen off, leaving the houses looking pockmarked, diseased.

'Well, he's certainly down on his luck,' Joe said, letting out a whistle between his teeth.

The sailors had told Mat last night that both Dudley and this chap, Booth, had once had a packet of money. They'd been paid handsomely after their voyage on the *Duke of Buckleigh* – but whereas Dudley had gone on to retire in comfort, Booth had descended into drink and debt, and this slum was where he now called home. There were two bare-legged children on the doorstep who moved away as they approached, their faces gaunt and their eyes dulled with hunger and cold. Joe flipped a small coin at them.

'Go on. Get some bread or something.'

The children scarpered, the older one's fingers wrapped tightly around the coin.

Mat knocked, lightly at first, then more loudly when no one answered. After a moment they heard a slow, heavy tread as someone approached.

'Who issit?' A gravelly voice from the other side of the door.

'Sorry to trouble you, we're looking for someone.' Mat did his best to sound well-to-do, unthreatening.

A pause, then the metal slip of a bolt and the door opened to reveal a craggy face.

'We're looking for a man by the name of Booth,' Mat said, but the face remained unmoved. Did he understand? 'Do you know him? Pale chap. Black hair. I'm told he lives here.'

The man blinked slowly.

'Booth,' Mat repeated. He was about to give up, simply push past him and be done with it. He'd search the whole building if he had to, but then the man sniffed and spoke.

'Strange chap? Hair all o'er the place?'

'Yes, yes, that's him. Do you know where he lives?'

'Upstairs. At the end on the left.'

The old man let them in, then wandered off down the hallway. Inside it was cold. Colder in than out. And dark. As their eyes adjusted to the gloom, they could see a staircase leading up off to one side. They hesitated for a moment, then Mat led the way, rats skittering away from them as they went.

The stairs groaned as they made their way up. The wood was riddled with wormholes. Here and there a tread was missing and the bannister rails had long since rotted away. At the top they were met with a landing and they could hear the hum of conversations from behind the many doors, a shriek of laughter, a cry – though whether of pleasure or of pain, it was hard to tell.

Mat knocked on the last door on the left but there was no response. He put his ear against it and strained to listen but there was nothing. He knocked again with the side of his fist and the door shivered in its frame. They waited but there was no response.

'Looks like he's not here,' Joe said. 'We can come back. Come on, Mr Matondo, let's go.'

Joe touched him lightly on the shoulder but Mat shrugged him off.

'Come out, you little bastard. Come out.' He pounded at the door with both fists now. Rhythmically punching out his anger and frustration.

'Keep it down, will you? It's enough to raise the dead!'

A head was peering out from one of the other rooms.

'Sorry to disturb you, sir, sorry, madam,' Joe said. 'My friend here—' But before he could finish, the figure disappeared with the slam of a door.

'Come on, Mat. He's not here.'

Mat stopped. He was breathing hard and could feel pain now spreading through his hands as he unclenched his fists.

'Very well,' he said and, as Joe turned to go, he gave the door one last furious kick. The wood splintered where his booted foot made contact and, to Mat's surprise, the door swung open. He let out a laugh and Joe turned back.

'Well, Mr Matondo, I'd say that's as good as an invitation!'

The room was tiny. A messy heap of blankets under the window was all that passed for a bed, and a table and stool were the only furniture. A full chamber pot sat fermenting in one corner, and they wrinkled their noses at the smell.

'What now?' asked Joe, and Mat shrugged.

He kicked through a pile of clothes that lay on the floor, though what he was looking for, he wasn't sure. He opened the drawers of the table: a tinderbox, a battered old bible, some papers, a few coins, nothing more.

'God, it stinks in here,' he said. 'I'll see if that window opens.'

Mat lifted the cloth that served as a curtain and pushed at the window but it seemed to be stuck fast. Looking down onto the street he saw the two children they'd met outside, sitting on the wall opposite, carefully sharing out a piece of bread between them. Poor little sods. Further down the street a scraggy-looking dog scratched at itself before loping off around the corner. And then he saw him.

'Joe. Look!'

Joe joined him at the window and they both looked down at the figure of Booth heading towards the house. He had his arms wrapped around himself against the cold, his body slightly hunched. He stopped suddenly and, surely sensing he was being watched, looked directly up at the window. They froze. Perhaps he wouldn't be able to make them out in the gloom – perhaps if they just stayed perfectly still he wouldn't notice them. Then Booth's eyes widened and he staggered backwards, almost falling into the road.

'Damn it. He's spotted us,' Mat said and raced out of the room. He clattered down the stairs and out into the street but Booth was gone.

'Which way did he go? That man? Which way did he go?' he demanded of the two children but they didn't answer, merely stared at him then walked away hand in hand, away from this strange man shouting at them in the street.

Joe was there now and Mat grabbed hold of him.

'Which way did he go? Did you see?'

'Hey, calm down. He went that way.' Joe nodded his head to one side.

'I have to find him!' said Mat, starting to run. He wasn't about to give up now. He had at least twenty years on Booth; there was no way that runt could outrun him.

'I don't know what you did to him last time,' Joe said as he caught up to Mat and jogged alongside him, 'but that man looked terrified. His face when he saw us. It was like he'd seen a ghost.'

*

They darted through the cramped and crumbling streets of Spitalfields, eyes darting here and there for a glimpse of their prey.

'Mat, he could be anywhere by now,' Joe protested, breathing heavily. 'This place is like a rabbit warren. We'll never find him.'

Just as Mat was about to agree, he saw him: the greasy, unkempt hair, the tattered coat. Booth. He was walking hurriedly along on the opposite side of the street, glancing nervously from side to side. Mat signalled to Joe and the two of them silently crossed the street and padded along behind the unsuspecting man. He turned into an alleyway and they followed. This was it, Mat thought. This was his chance. Before Booth was even aware of his presence, Mat had his hands on him, pinning his arms to his sides. Joe held back, ready to pounce if Booth slipped away.

'I have nothing!' Booth wailed. 'Nothing but a few coppers. Take them, take them.'

'I don't want your money.' Mat roughly twisted Booth round to face him, still holding on tight. The poor wretch was actually shaking.

'Oh Lord, preserve me,' he whispered when he saw Mat's face. 'I knew you would come for me.'

'It's not you I'm after. It's him. Dudley. Tell me where he is.'

Booth hesitated but Mat shook him, hard, and he stuttered out an address in Pimlico, wherever that was. Joe would know. Mat fixed the words in his memory.

'He made me do it. Dudley made me. You have to believe me.' Booth was gibbering. Their faces were so close that Mat could see the broken blood vessels that ran like rivulets across his nose and cheeks.

'Do what? What did Dudley make you do? Is this something to do with the ship? With the *Duke of Buckleigh*?'

Mat shook him again but Booth was crying now, sobbing so hard that his face was wet with tears and snot and spit. The man was insane.

Mat let go of him in disgust and Booth slumped to the floor, a puppet without its strings, and held his head to his knees as he rocked from side to side.

'He made me do it. He made me. Lord have mercy. Lord have mercy. Lord have mercy.'

Mat turned and walked back down the alleyway where Joe waited for him. He had Dudley's address and that was what he had come for. He should have felt triumphant – happy at least – and yet the encounter with Booth had left him uneasy, and he was glad to return to the busy city streets and away from the sound of those sobs that seemed to come from the very depths of Booth's soul.

Chapter 15

Pimlico was a good hour and a half's walk away and neither Mat nor Joe had the energy for another pursuit today. Once they were away from the foetid streets of Spitalfields, they found a decent inn where Mat insisted on treating Joe to some lunch, to thank him for all his help. As he handed over some pennies from his dwindling supply, Mat half regretted his impulsive generosity.

Later that day, back in Joe's room, he counted out what he had left. What with food and drink, plus the token amount he'd agreed to pay the Alfords for bed and board, he was certain to run out in a few days. This city sure was expensive. He needed to find some quids – and quickly.

'Can you sing?' Joe asked. 'You can come out with me if you can hold a tune.'

Mat shook his head. 'One of my old shipmates used to say I couldn't carry a tune with a bucket.'

'That bad?'

'That bad.'

'Play anything? I've got a pipe here somewhere.' Joe rummaged through a bag before producing a tin whistle. 'Here we are!' He trilled a pretty tune on the pipe before passing it to Mat. 'Give it a go.'

'How hard can it be?' Mat said, placing his fingers over the holes and blowing. The shrill squeak that he produced was not likely to cause anyone to part with their precious chink. He tried again, but the grimace on Joe's face told him that he was probably a lost cause when it came to the entertainment business.

'I know a chap could maybe help you out,' said Joe. 'Down at the docks. They're always looking for men to unload stuff into the warehouses. It's not much fun but it's a wage – and having seen how you beat down that door, you're certainly strong enough for it!'

'Very funny.'

Mat punched Joe playfully on the arm and Joe held his hands up as if in surrender.

'Please don't hurt me!'

They both laughed and lapsed back into a thoughtful silence.

'Or there's always begging. We could dress you up – give you a wound or a blind man's cane? I'm sure I've got one here somewhere.'

'No,' Mat said as Joe got up to look in his wardrobe. 'Not begging. I'll try the docks.'

'Suit yourself. Begging's a whole lot easier – and you can do it on your backside – but it's up to you.'

Mat had seen countless beggars since he'd been in London. Old men and women. Children as young as three or four. He'd seen them shouted at, spat on – even seen one man pissed on by a passer-by. He might be desperate but he wasn't that desperate. The docks would suit him just fine. And it wouldn't be for long. Just until he got his hands on Dudley and finished what he'd come here for.

It wasn't the best time of year to be working outdoors. Autumn was fast turning into winter and despite the layers that Joe and Mr Alford had lent him, after a couple of hours the cold nipped and pinched at him like a hungry dog, his fingers numb, his feet like blocks of wood inside his boots. The work itself wasn't too bad, though. Shifting and carrying. Lugging sacks or crates from the dockside and trucking them into the warehouse to be weighed.

His day started at seven thirty, when he'd gather with all the other chaps and wait for the foremen to come along and divide them up into gangs. There were all sorts – some great hulks of men who seemed born for this kind of work, others more respectable types, men who were down on their luck and needed a job, any job. Joe had been right about them always needing men. There were hundreds and hundreds of ships – some had been waiting months to unload.

The money wasn't great but it was something, and he'd heard there were all sorts of ways you could make a bit more. It seemed like everyone had some kind of scam going on. There were the river pirates – nasty characters, that lot – who raided any unprotected ships. Then there were the gangs of watermen who turned their small craft to nefarious undertakings under cover of night. They were known as night plunderers.

Others, including some of the men working alongside Mat, would pilfer a bit of sugar, coffee, cocoa – whatever they could get their hands on. Half the night watchmen were bent as well so there was a good chance of getting away with it. There were the river police, of course, but they had their hands full given the size of the river and the sheer number of ships and warehouses. Mat was tempted himself, truth be told, but for now he was content to get on with the job.

If you could cope with the cold, he found there was something almost soothing in the monotony of the work, in the sheer physicality of it. Mat was glad simply to be doing something – anything – that would keep his thoughts from spiralling round and round. Thoughts of his sister and how she must have suffered, of the men who took her and what he would do when he found them.

He hadn't been to Pimlico yet. He told himself it was because he hadn't had a day off yet, hadn't had time. He told himself it was because he was just too busy. But, if he was honest, he also felt an odd reluctance to go. Did he really want to confront what had happened to Malu? Did he really want to come face to face with the man who was responsible for her death? He'd go tomorrow, he told himself. Definitely tomorrow.

'Come on, lazybones, get moving! We're not paying you to stand around.'

The foreman prodded him with a finger and Mat saw that the man was wearing thick gloves and a muffler. He wouldn't be feeling the cold, lucky sod.

'I've got my eye on you, boy,' the foreman said. 'I know what your sort are. Liars and thieves, the lot of you.'

Mat bit the inside of his cheek to keep himself from responding. 'Sorry, sir,' he mumbled, and he bent down to pick up the next crate.

Come on, Mat the Cat, he told himself, *just keep your head down and think of the chink.*

After a few days of this indecision, he decided enough was enough. He needed to get this done. He had to go to Pimlico and find Dudley, though he didn't know yet what he would do when he got there. Part of him now just wanted to talk to Dudley, to find out what had happened when the ship sank, to find out if his sister had suffered. The other part of him was still set on revenge, determined to kill Dudley, as though by hurting him he could somehow heal his own pain.

Joe insisted on going with him.

'Someone needs to keep an eye on you,' he said. 'You can't just go whacking a man in broad daylight.'

'I'm not going to – whack him,' Mat had countered. 'I just need to see him for myself. Then I'll figure out what to do.'

But when Joe wasn't looking he had slipped his clasp knife into his pocket. Just in case.

It was cold and foggy the next day – when wasn't it in this god-forsaken city? – and they walked quickly, trying to warm up as they went. Joe began to whistle but there was something mournful in the way the fog deadened the sound and he soon stopped. They trudged on in silence. It wasn't a part of London that Joe knew well, but after asking an old street-sweeper they soon found the address.

'Somebody's doing all right for themselves,' Joe said as he took in the double-fronted house with slender columns either side of the front door. The contrast with Booth's place was on both their minds. 'Now what?'

'I don't know.'

Mat gazed at the house as if he might see right through the walls. Somewhere in there was the man who took his sister. The house stood on a square that had an elegant garden at its centre, with a fountain in the middle surrounded by stone benches. Joe led him towards one and they sat down, Mat breathing deeply to try to stem the emotion that coursed through him. Was it anger? Fear? He wasn't sure.

They had a good view through the spindly birch trees that bordered the garden and Mat continued to stare at the house, trying to catch a glimpse of movement behind the windows but seeing nothing. The solid door and blank windows were impassive, impenetrable. The size of his task dawned on him now. How was he supposed to get to

Dudley? He must have an army of servants in there and they'd never open the door to the likes of him.

'Hey, look!'

He felt Joe tense up beside him and Mat saw that the front door was opening. He swallowed hard and steeled himself to catch his first sight of the man he had hated for so long. Instead, a young girl stepped out, no more than eleven or twelve, neat in her white apron and cap. She held a cloth and began to rub vigorously at the doorknob and letterbox, her hands bright pink from the cold. After a moment she went back inside.

'Well, at least you know where he lives now,' said Joe, idly tossing a few crumbs from his pocket to a robin that hopped about on the ground near the bench.

'Yes, I suppose.'

Mat kicked at the ground with the toe of his boot. It had all seemed so clear to him before. He would find the captain, kill him, and be back off to sea before anyone had even noticed. And yet he'd been in London a full two weeks now and here he was, no nearer to getting it done. That house might as well have been a fortress for all that he could get in there.

'We could pose as piano tuners,' Joe was saying, 'I bet he's got a pianoforte in there. Take a bag for our piano-tuning tools and then, when he's not looking, whip out an iron bar or something and sock him over the head. And if anyone hears him screaming, we can say it's your singing!'

Mat smiled, despite himself. But Joe might be on to something – not piano-tuners but something like that – delivery men or furniture repairers or... Well, they'd think of something. Just then the door of the house flew open and a large man appeared, wearing an overcoat and hat, and went down the steps as fast as his bulk would allow him.

'Come on. That must be him!' Joe was up and heading out of the square before Mat had fully registered what was happening.

It was him. It was Dudley. It was really him. He jumped up from the bench, causing the robin to flutter up onto a branch, its red chest puffed out, indignant. Joe signalled at Mat to stay still, and they watched as Dudley began to make his way down the street away from them. A moment later they followed, glad now of the fog, which swallowed them up and muffled the sound of their footsteps.

Dudley turned a corner and headed towards a row of hackney coaches. Surely a man like him could afford his own carriage? They watched him speak to the driver before climbing up and hauling himself inside. The driver flicked his whip and the two horses began to slowly draw the carriage away.

Mat and Joe raced to the next cab and jumped in, Joe silencing the protests of the driver at seeing two black faces with a wave of some cash.

'Follow them. Quick. Follow them!' Mat urged, and they both fell back into the seat as the carriage jolted forward in pursuit.

The city flashed past them through the small window of the carriage. They seemed to be heading north-east and Mat glimpsed the green expanse of a park, the outlines of trees, then a mass of shops and houses, the shadowy figures of people and horses just visible through the fog. After about twenty minutes, the carriage drew to a halt and they paid and got out, just in time to see Dudley making his way up a narrow side street. They followed and watched him as he went inside a large building on the corner. There was a sign above the door but Mat couldn't work out what it said.

'What is this place?' said Mat.

'Garraway's. It's a coffee house,' Joe replied. 'We're not far from the shipping office.'

Mat looked around and realised that the streets were somewhat familiar.

'The coffee houses all cater to a certain type,' Joe went on. 'You've got Button's for your writers, Giles's for your Scotsmen, Old Slaughter's for your artists, and so on.'

'So what's this one?'

'Well, merchants, usually, and seamen. Not so long ago, the likes of you and me would have been bought and sold in here.'

'Will they let us in?'

'If we flash the cash, they'll let us in. Follow me.'

Mat stuck close to Joe as they went in. It was busy, with twenty or more tables of men playing cards and chess, smoking, doing business. There were a few raised eyebrows as they passed by but Joe, undeterred as ever, strode confidently towards the bar.

'There he is,' Mat said, nodding towards a table in one corner where he could see Dudley standing talking to two men who were sitting down. One had his back to them and Mat couldn't make him out but the other man – the other man was Booth.

'Come on, let's get a bit closer.'

Joe bought them each a cup of coffee and they made their way over to an empty table from where they could just about see the three men. Dudley had sat down now, his huge belly pushing against the table and his hand wrapped around a glass of sherry. Booth was talking but the place was too loud for Mat to make out what he was saying, though he strained to hear. Booth looked upset, desperate even, and he seemed to be pleading with the other two men, who weren't saying much at all.

'Why are they meeting now, today?' Mat said. 'It must be to do with the ship. It's too much of a coincidence that days after I collar Booth for Dudley's address, he's here with the man himself.'

'Maybe they often meet for a drink,' said Joe. 'It's not that strange for old shipmates to keep in touch, is it?'

'But I was told they'd fallen out. And why would a man like Dudley want to be mates with a cod's head like Booth? You saw where they both live – it's like me being friends with King George! Anyway, it doesn't look like they're mates. See.'

Dudley had stood up and was leaning over the table, speaking very closely into Booth's frightened face and prodding him hard in the chest with a fat finger. Mat pushed away an image of his sister, of her perfect skin being pulled and prodded by this huge, white hand. Dudley was leaving now and Mat leapt out of his seat to follow him.

'You stay here,' he said to Joe. 'Keep an eye on those two. Something's going on and I want to know what it is. I'll follow Dudley.'

'Don't do anything stupid,' Joe said, fixing him with a serious stare.

'I won't. I just need to… I don't know. I won't do anything. I promise.'

In his pocket, he could feel the reassuring weight of the knife.

Outside, Mat saw Dudley turning left at the bottom of the street and he made after him, keen not to let him get too far ahead, for he knew that if he lost sight of him in this fog he'd struggle to find him again. Dudley moved through the crowds like a galleon through the waves, never pausing or shifting his course to let others through but forcing all to pass in his wake. Mat, in turn, bobbed and weaved his way through, touching his hat by way of apology to the tutting and grumbling passers-by.

Suddenly, Dudley stopped and Mat was forced to do the same. The captain was looking in a shop window and Mat followed suit, a few doors down, forcing himself to feign interest in what turned out to be a ladies' hat shop. He glanced at Dudley out of the corner of his eye and as soon as the captain set off again, so did he.

This went on for some ten minutes or so, Mat ducking out of sight and holding his breath whenever Dudley stopped, and all the while his thoughts were churning round and round. When should he do it? How should he do it? Could he actually do it? They were in a square now, a small church on one side and not many people about.

This was it. He had to do it now. No time for questions and doubts. This was for his sister. He increased his pace, felt for the knife in his pocket. Three more steps and he'd be upon him. But Dudley suddenly spun round and before Mat could get his knife out, let alone unfold his blade, the captain had his hands around Mat's neck.

'Think you can rob me, do you, you little runt? I know what you're up to. I've seen you tailing me.'

Mat coughed as Dudley squeezed his throat and felt tears burst from the corners of his eyes. He tried to speak but could only let out a gurgle. He tried desperately to pull Dudley's hands away but the man was strong, despite his age. Dudley's face was livid, his teeth bared like a wild animal.

'I'll teach you to try your tricks with me. I've whipped plenty of little black boys like you before, I can tell you.'

Flecks of spit landed on Mat's face and all at once he was a child again, hands holding him back as his sister was carried away from him forever. With a surge of rage he tore at Dudley's hands, kicking him sharply in the balls at the same time.

Dudley released him and staggered backwards, his hands flying to his crotch as he cried out in pain. Mat reached again for his knife but a voice stopped him.

'Leave that poor man alone, you brute!'

He turned to see a woman, middle-aged, plump, in bonnet and shawl, marching towards them from the churchyard. Oh God, he was going to be hauled up before the magistrate before he'd even done anything.

'Madam—' he began his apology but then realised it was Dudley that she was speaking to.

'I saw what happened and I think it's disgraceful,' she was saying. 'Attacking a man in broad daylight. And right outside a house of God, no less.' She waved what appeared to be her hymn sheet at Dudley who gaped at her, still bent over and gasping like a fish on deck. 'I'm not afraid of you,' she went on. 'I've met your sort before. Bullies. Now, get away, go on!'

A small group of ladies had gathered at the door of the church and a few of them joined in now with calls of 'disgraceful' and 'shame'. Dudley looked from Mat to them and back again. He pointed at Mat and fixed him with a stare.

'If I see you again, boy,' he said, 'I will kill you, so help me God.'

Then he limped slowly away.

Mat was torn between relief that he could still breathe and despair that Dudley had got away.

The women now formed a circle around him, clucked and purred over him, offered him tea, stroked his arm. Mat thanked them and assured them that he was fine, really he was, and they eventually let him alone, returning to the church with a 'God bless'. He made his way back to Garraway's but there was no sign of Joe or of Booth, and when he asked the man serving if he'd seen them leave, the man shrugged as if he didn't understand and walked away.

Mat soon found an inn that was less picky about its patronage and bought himself a beer. He sat and took the knife from his pocket, unfolding and refolding the blade. Then he stuck the tip of the blade lightly into the table, twisting it round and round, thinking all the while of the marbled flesh of Dudley's fat face.

It was late when Joe got back. Mat was still sitting up, the candle all but burned down and the fire gone out, when he heard Joe's footsteps bounding lightly up the stairs.

'Well?' Joe asked. 'What happened?'

'Nothing happened. He got away.'

Joe nodded and came to sit at the table.

'And you? Where did you get to?' asked Mat.

Joe smiled, a slow, wide smile, and the reflection of the candle seemed to dance in his eyes.

'I? I am in love!'

'What? What are you talking about?'

Mat watched as Joe retrieved a bottle of wine from his wardrobe and poured them both a glass, smiling all the while.

'I have met Venus herself! If Venus was Irish. And worked as a housemaid.'

'You were supposed to be watching Booth!' Mat stood up, his temper rising. 'You said you'd watch him. I nearly got myself killed today and you've been gallivanting with some piece you met in the pub?'

'Hey, Mr Matondo.' Joe held his hands up, shook his head. 'Hey, I did keep an eye on Booth – and that other fella. The "piece", as you call her, came after that. Now, sit down. Have a drink. Tell me what happened. Come on.'

Mat sat back down. He wasn't angry with Joe, not really. How could he be? He was angry with himself; he'd had the chance to get rid of Dudley and he'd messed it up. He drank some of his wine, glad of the instant warmth it provided, and told Joe what had happened.

'Saved by a bunch of do-gooding white women?' Joe said and chuckled. 'They do say God moves in mysterious ways.'

'So what happened to you? Did you find out anything about Booth? Why they were meeting?'

Joe told him how Booth and the other man had stayed at the coffee house for a short time after Dudley left. Booth had started crying and the other man had given him a handkerchief and sat with him for a bit. Then he had got up to leave and on a whim Joe had decided to tail him.

'We already know where Booth lives, where he goes. But who's this other chap? I thought to myself,' Joe said. 'Anyway, he walks down to the river and then all the way to Westminster. He was in a world of his own. Didn't notice me at all.'

'So, who is he?'

'Well, I followed him to a house and in he goes. I wasn't really sure what to do next when out of the front door steps a vision of beauty.'

'Venus?'

'That's right, Mr Matondo! She starts scrubbing the steps and I was instantly transfixed! Arms white as lilies, hair red as... red as...'

'Roses?'

'No, not that red, sort of like – well, like the colour of a fox pelt, but that doesn't sound right. Anyway, she's quite a picture. So, I wandered over and we got to chatting and, long story short, we're going for a turn about the park on her afternoon off tomorrow.'

'Good for you, but what's all this got to do with Booth and Dudley? Who's this chap they were with?'

'His name's Stephens. Upstanding chap, according to Venus. He's a doctor and his missus is one of those do-gooders. Abolitionist. And they've even taken in some orphaned African, out of the goodness of his heart. My Venus ain't too keen on *her*, that's for sure.'

'Why's a man like that hanging around with Booth?'

'Dunno. Maybe Booth is his patient – maybe Booth and Dudley are both his patients. Or maybe… I don't know. Look, I know you think this is all to do with what happened – what happened to your sister.' He paused and they sat in silence for a minute or two. 'What was her name? You never told me.'

'Malundama.' Mat's voice caught as he said her name. He hadn't said it for a long time. 'Her name was Malundama. It means "that which is hidden".'

'Malundama,' Joe repeated softly. He put his hand on Mat's. 'I'm so sorry about what happened to her, Mat. And I know you want revenge but, well, we've all lost people. And the best thing we can do is to keep on living. Don't let the likes of Dudley ruin your life as well as your sister's. If you go after him, you'll hang. You know that, don't you?'

Mat nodded.

'And then he'll have won. He'll have murdered you and your sister.' He paused, patted Mat's hand gently. 'And I'd miss you, Mr Matondo. I'd miss you.'

They didn't say much after that. The candle had burned down and so they retreated to their beds, wrapped themselves up against the cold. Mat lay listening to Joe's breath deepening as he fell asleep – dreaming of his Venus, no doubt. Joe's words echoed in his head. *The best thing we can do is to keep on living… keep on living…*

But what if he couldn't? What if that just wasn't possible?

Chapter 16

He didn't see much of Joe in the days that followed. Most of the time, he was off seeing Venus – or Bridget as she turned out to be called. She was all he talked about these days, and his wide-eyed happiness was a bit much to take. The rest of the time he'd be out working and when it came to Joe, that meant he could be anywhere. As well as the performing, Joe worked as a street-sweeper, helped out with deliveries – the details of which he was always rather vague about – sat as an artist's model, and no doubt a whole host of other things that may or may not have been on the right side of the law. For his part, Mat took as much work as he could at the docks, labouring until he was so tired he could hardly stand, then coming back to eat and sleep before doing it all again the next day.

The Alfords were kind to him. Their cook, Mrs Bryson, had taken a bit of a shine to him and often gave him some extra titbits of food, saying he needed 'feeding up'. Some evenings, Mr and Mrs Alford would invite him to sit with them – they felt sorry for him, he supposed; they could surely see by now that he was a man down on his luck. He'd play with the children while Mrs Alford sewed or read and her husband sat by the fire, smoking or just sitting watching the flames.

Mostly those quiet, domestic evenings soothed him, were a comfort after a day toiling in the cold, grey sleet. At other times it was almost too much – like seeing another world through a glass that, no matter how hard you tried, you could never break through. Those times he'd retreat to his room, put his head under the covers and silently howl.

He'd given up all thoughts of murdering Dudley – for the time being at least. He couldn't think how he'd get near him now that he'd seen him face to face, and somehow he just couldn't muster the rage he'd felt before. Now he just felt numb. Often he found himself tortured with thoughts of his sister, of her final moments. Had she suffered? Had it been quick? He thought of sharks tearing her body apart – he'd seen that happen to more than one man and knew the horror of it, knew that death didn't always come straight away.

After several days of this, of thoughts of blood and bone and the dark, cold sea, he decided that the only way to put it out of his mind was to talk to Booth. He knew that Dudley would never speak to him and although Booth was a raving fool, he must have moments of lucidity. He must remember what had happened when the *Buckleigh* went down. However painful it might be, at least then he'd know.

Booth's place looked even more decrepit than before, if that were possible, with a large hole having appeared in the roof. It had rained all night; must be soaked inside. The place wasn't fit for pigs. He hammered on the front door until a woman eventually answered. Her hair was unpinned, falling in a tangled mess down to her shoulders, and she was dressed in only a nightgown. Mat kept his gaze firmly on her face, both repelled and aroused by the clear outline of her breasts and the dark mound of hair that showed through the thin fabric of her gown. Her eyes were vacant, and she looked right through him and let him in without a word before wandering back to her room. Gin? Opium? Whatever it was, she wasn't all there and Mat almost envied her.

The hole that Mat had kicked through Booth's door had been poorly repaired; one solitary plank was nailed across it, and Mat bent down to peer through the gap that remained. All was dark inside. No sign of him. Wherever he was, he was going to find a visitor waiting for him. Mat easily removed the plank from the door and twisted his arm up and round to open the door from the inside, before loosely replacing the plank and closing the door. He didn't want Booth to be spooked before he'd even got the chance to speak to him.

He wondered if there was somewhere he could conceal himself but there was no cupboard or wardrobe, and even if there had been, Mat had to admit that if there was one thing that gave him the sweats, it was the thought of being closed in somewhere. Aboard ship it hadn't bothered him too much: he'd be so exhausted after a day of tarring and greasing, scrubbing, pulling and hauling, that he'd fall into his hammock below decks and be dead to the world before he knew it. But when he had a choice, he'd far rather be up on deck, out in the open breeze, than cooped up inside. He'd just have to wait until he heard footsteps, then get himself behind the door, ready to jump out when Booth came in.

He waited and waited but there was no sign of the little wretch. It was starting to get dark and Mat groped to find the solitary candle that stood on the table. He remembered the tinderbox he'd seen in the drawer on his last visit and retrieved it now, lighting the candle, which was made of tallow and sent thin wisps of greasy, grey smoke into the air.

Booth's bible was still in the drawer and he took that out too, bereft of any other kind of amusement, and flicked through it, noting that passages were underlined here and there and that some pages had their corners turned down. A wretch, but a devout one, it seemed. The print was minuscule and Mat struggled to read more than a few words. He tossed it back into the drawer where he noticed another small book.

It was old and tattered, and handwritten rather than printed. As he turned the pages, which were yellowing and crisp to the touch, he noticed that the writing started out quite neat and uniform but got gradually messier. Some of it was set out in columns of words and numbers – a bit like the shipping register – and other bits were just writing. Booth's diary, perhaps?

Mat turned the pages, noticing that a page had been torn out, the edge of the paper all ragged. Inside the front cover was a date. *1806.* Then some words that he couldn't work out. *D-u-k-e. Duke.* He wasn't sure of the rest. The writing was fancy – all curls and squiggles. But it had to be. *Duke of Buckleigh.* It had to be.

He shoved the book into his pocket then blew out the candle and legged it along the hall and down the stairs. There was no need to wait for that little scrub Booth. If this was his diary from the ship then it could tell him everything he wanted to know. He'd just need to get Joe to read it for him.

Mat remembered that Joe had said he was performing tonight at the Old Bell near St Bride's. He knew St Bride's: it could be spotted a mile off with that tiered spire that towered over everything else nearby. Not too far. He could be there in under an hour if he didn't dawdle, and he set off with a lightness in his step that he hadn't felt for days.

It was a cold night and he walked briskly. It was almost November, he realised. Had he really been in London for over a month? He was almost a Londoner himself now, he thought with a smile. Perhaps he would stay here after all. Perhaps Joe was right; once he'd found out the facts about his sister's death, he could put it all behind him. Find himself a girl, like Joe had, get married even. He hummed as he walked, though at the same time a more cynical voice in his head seemed to mock him. *That life's not for the likes of you, Mat the Cat.* But he pushed that voice aside, hummed a little louder and increased his pace.

Chapter 17

The Old Bell was busy tonight; a mass of drinking, laughing, talking bodies. Mat pushed his way through towards the back where he could see Joe was in full swing and gave him a wave. Joe nodded back. He looked unusually serious but was probably just concentrating on the music. He would have to wait until Joe had a break to talk to him, so he got a beer and found a small table in one corner where he could be out of the way.

He tapped along to the music, buoyed up by the merriment all around him. Joe had taken him here a few times. Apparently a group called the Sons of Africa used to meet here. Mat had never heard of them before, but Joe said they were pretty influential some forty years back in helping to get the slave trade banned. And the Bell had also been a place for London's blacks to come when they were down on their luck. Joe's dad had been forced to come here for charity when times had been tough, and Joe loved being able to come back here now as an entertainer. He said he liked to think his da would be looking down on him, proud that his son was making decent money.

Joe never spoke much about his past, though come to think of it neither did Mat. It was best not to dwell on things you couldn't change. Best to look to the future. He knew Joe's father was dead, his mother too. She'd been white – had been ostracised by her family when she took up with Joe's dad. He told Mat once that he and his brothers had been in and out of the Foundling Hospital more than once. His ma would take them there when times got particularly tough, then collect them when she'd earned a bob or two. Then one day, not long after his father croaked, she took them there and never came back.

He appeared at Mat's side now, a sheen of sweat upon his face, and sat down next to him.

'Joe! Just the man. I need to talk to you.'

But before he could go on, Joe pulled out a page from a newspaper from his pocket and put it down on the table.

'And I need to talk to you,' he said, his voice low. 'Look!' He tapped at the newspaper before seeming to remember that Mat wouldn't be able to read it. 'Sorry, I forgot. Dudley's dead.'

'What?' Mat couldn't take it in.

'I'll only ask you this once, Matondo. And whatever your answer is, I'll stand by you. I want you to know that.' Joe gripped hard to his hand. 'Did you do it?'

'What?' Mat could only say again. Dudley was dead?

'If you did it, just tell me and we'll work out what to do. I've got friends who could help. Get you out of the country—'

'It wasn't me,' Mat said, some sense returning to him. 'I swear to you, Joe, it wasn't me.'

'Very well.' Joe released his hand. 'I believe you.'

'What happened? What does it say?' Mat grabbed the paper as though if he looked hard enough he'd be able to read it.

'He was done in. Yesterday. Bludgeoned round the bonce, it says. This doesn't look good for us, Mr Matondo.'

'What do you mean? We had nothing to do with it!'

'I know, but if we we was spotted outside his house – or anyone saw us following him? "Two darkies, killing a poor old man for his money". That's what they'll say. Or those women at the church! What if they see the papers and put two and two together?'

'But we didn't do it!' Mat insisted. 'This is all too strange. Why would someone have killed Dudley? Someone that isn't me, I mean. And why now? Listen, Joe, I think there's more going on here than we realise. I went back to Booth's today—'

'You did what?' Joe interrupted. 'Mat, you need to drop this. Whatever it is, you need to stay away from Booth, stay away from all of this.'

'But—' Mat felt for the notebook. If Joe could just read it, they might be able to make some sense of it all.

But just then, one of the other musicians whistled for Joe to come back and he got up. 'Stay here. We'll talk more when I finish,' he said.

'But, Joe, I need to show you something.'

'Afterwards. Won't be long.'

He strode back to the stage, leaving Mat to take in the news. Dudley was dead. He felt cheated. Some other bugger had got to see that frightened look in his eye as they bashed his head in. He hoped he'd suffered. But who had done it? It could just be a coincidence; a burglary gone wrong or some random madman. It couldn't be Booth – could it? He didn't have it in him, surely. Mat couldn't make head nor tail of it. Hopefully, Booth's notebook would shed some light on it all. In the meantime, Dudley was dead and he might as well celebrate. Mat drained his beer and went for another.

It was a while before Joe had another break and while he waited, Mat sat watching the crowds and getting steadily more drunk. Two lasses came past his table, one fair and the other as dark as him, all prinked up in fancy togs. *Probably a couple of strumpets*, he thought, and absent-mindedly felt for his purse. Maybe later he might fancy a bit. But first, another beer. He got up and made his way back to the bar.

The black girl was sitting on her own at a nearby table when he got back and he sneaked a look at her. Pretty enough. She caught his eye and looked away. A moment later she was joined by her friend and the two of them set to talking and laughing. There was something about the way she rested her head on one hand, the way she pursed her lips ever so slightly, the way her hands moved as she talked that was so familiar. She was probably about the same age Malu would have been now. The girl noticed him staring and turned her head away before collapsing into giggles with her friend.

He passed his hand over his face. What was he thinking? His mind had been so much on his sister that now he imagined he was seeing her. *Idiot.* He slapped himself on both cheeks then lifted his glass, silently toasting his sister. *Here's to you, Malu, rest in peace.*

A few minutes later he saw Joe coming back, but rather than heading straight to Mat, he wandered over to the two girls. *Ho-ho, he's had the same idea.* But then he greeted the redhead with a kiss and an embrace and led her over, the other girl following shyly behind.

'May I present to you, Mistress Venus!' Joe ushered her forward theatrically and the girl took Mat's hand and curtsied deeply.

'Pleasure to meet you, sir.' She smiled. 'It's actually Bridget but you can call me Venus, if you like.'

She had a lilt to her voice and Mat remembered now that she was Irish. He'd worked with a fair few bog-landers in his time. Good men for the most part. And she was definitely a well-rigged frigate and pretty with it. Bridget was now introducing her friend.

'Joe, this is Mercy. She's had a hard day so we need to cheer her up.'

'Well, I'm sure we can do that, can't we, Mat?' Joe said with a grin.

Mat stepped forward and took the girl's hand in greeting. So this was the African orphan Joe had mentioned before. She smiled shyly, two dimples forming in her cheeks. She really did look like Malu. It was incredible.

The other two musicians had carried on playing and Joe now grabbed his girl's hand and twirled her under his arm.

'Come on,' she cried, her skirts sweeping round. 'Let's have a dance!'

They hooted and laughed as they began to dance, and other couples soon followed until the floor was a sea of spinning bodies.

There would be no chance of getting Joe to look at Booth's book now and somehow, with several beers coursing through him, it didn't seem quite so urgent. They could read it tomorrow. He glanced at Bridget's friend who was nervously watching the dancers, and he offered her his hand.

'Shall we?'

She hesitated for a moment. With the look of someone about to dive into deep water, she took his hand with the tips of her fingers and together they stepped into the melee.

They were awkward at first – this girl had about as much rhythm as a three-legged cow – but as the music grew faster, and the stamping of the dancers' feet grew louder, she tipped back her head and laughed as he spun her around. He laughed too and felt all the pain and the worry of the last few weeks, months, years even, melt away, and as he held tight to her hand he felt somehow both bound and free.

The music stopped and the dancers drew to a halt, clapping and cheering and panting for breath. He was very close to the girl. Her face was shining and he moved towards her for a kiss. But all he could see was Malu. In her eyes, in the arch of her brow, the spread of her nose, the bow of her lip, and those two perfect dimples. He stood back, dazed. Could it really be her?

'Malundama,' he said. He was shaking now, actually shaking.

'What did you say?' she asked, a tiny furrow now between her brows.

'Malundama,' he said again. He felt his heart swell within his chest like an ocean wave as he looked into her dark brown eyes. Eyes he thought he'd never see again.

With a start, she pulled her hands from his and darted away. He rushed to follow her before the crowd could swallow her up.

'Are you all right?' he asked her. She must be in shock. Not surprising, really; he could hardly believe it himself.

'What was it you said to me just then? What was that word?' She looked confused.

'Malundama,' he said. 'I believe it really is you.'

But she still looked bewildered. Frightened, even. Surely she must remember her own name?

'I'm Matondo.' Was there a flicker of recognition in her eye? 'I thought you were dead,' he went on. 'I thought I'd never see you again and here you are. I can't believe it.'

He went to embrace her but she pulled away. How could she not remember him?

'I'm your brother. I'm Matondo,' he said again.

He had dreamed so often of being reunited with her, had pictured their smiles, their joy at being together again. He had never imagined that his sister would look at him with such – such horror.

With a cry she pushed past him, and before he knew it she had fled through the crowds and disappeared. Had he dreamed the whole thing? Was she a figment of his imagination, conjured up because he so desperately wanted to see his sister again? But no, she was real; her hat lay discarded on the table and he could still feel the touch of her soft hands in his. All around him, the music thumped on, the dancers danced and the drinkers drank. And Mat had never been more alone.

The children had been walking through woodland for some time, tied to the two men who had bought them a few days ago. They noticed the land around them was flattening out, and they could taste a sharp tang in the air. They looked ahead through the trees and saw that the land simply – stopped.

There was the earth; dark yellow-brown with patches of scrubby bush, and there was the sky; bright blue, smudged with cloud. And in between there was – something else. Instinctively, the children stopped, causing their captors to stumble as the rope between them tautened. Seeing their frightened faces, the men laughed and tugged at the rope to urge them on.

As they neared the edge of the woods, the men stopped and spoke to one another. The children couldn't understand what they said. Then the men tied them to a tree and moved away. Matondo and Malundama watched them as they made their way out through the trees to open ground, where many other people – men, women and children – were gathered. Some of the people were tied to each other; others were tied in groups to huge logs that weighed them down, causing them to stoop and stumble. There were men guarding them, with clubs and sticks held aloft or balanced over a shoulder, ready for use.

The children had never seen so many people in one place before and they became frightened. With their captors gone, Matondo tried to break free. He struggled and pulled and rubbed the rope against the rough bark of the tree, though he'd tried it a hundred times before and knew deep down that it was hopeless.

The men were coming back now, talking intently to one another. Matondo let his hands fall. Escape was impossible. The men untied them and stood back to look them over. Then they started to pull at their clothes, straightening them out, making them neat. They tugged Matondo's tunic *down so that it covered a dark bruise on his leg. They wiped off any smudges of dirt from their faces and when they seemed satisfied, they began to lead them out through the woods. At this, Malundama started to wail, pulling backwards, desperate to return to the shelter of the trees and away from whatever waited for them ahead. One of the men smacked her once, hard, around the face and she gulped back her tears, shocked into silence. Her brother could do nothing but whisper to her.*

'Everything will be all right, Malu. I'll look after you, I promise. I won't leave you.'

They arrived at the crowd of people and they could see now that the strange space between land and sky was water. So much water. It went on and on until it met the sky. It made Matondo feel dizzy just to look at it. Small boats, like the kind they had sometimes seen in the rivers near their home, bobbed about at the water's edge and further out they could see a large, dark shape with poles and flags. Like a house with wings, walking on the water.

There were men shouting and calling, pushing and shoving all the tied-up people. There was an odd sense of excitement in the air, like on a feast day or a holy day. Matondo wondered what was going to happen. The children found themselves being herded with the other prisoners into a long line, their captors standing behind them with hands placed firmly upon their shoulders. Bewildered, they looked from side to side and they were horrified to see men – or spirits, for surely no men could look like this – with pale skin and long red hair approaching the line of people. The sunlight flashed off the weapons they wore at their sides and their long leather boots sent sand flying up with every step. The children squeezed each other's hands and watched as these awful figures began to inspect the prisoners, prodding and poking them as if they were fruit in the market.

They were getting closer. The children fidgeted from side to side, earning a knuckle in the back to force them to stand up straight. One of the men – they

definitely were men, however strange their appearance – approached Matondo.
The boy could see the thick dark hairs that sprouted from the man's hands and
face, the blue veins that showed through the white skin at his wrists and temples.
Repulsed, he tried to take a step back, but his captor shoved him forward.

The man began to touch and prod the boy, encircling his scrawny
upper arm with a huge white hand. He bent down to inspect his mouth
and teeth, and a wave of his stinking breath hit Matondo's face. The other
man, taller and slighter than the first, gestured to him to turn around,
then lifted each foot to inspect it, the way Matondo had seen people do
when checking a mule or a horse. Now the first man turned his attention
to Malundama, smiling widely at her and patting her plump arms and
legs, squeezing her cheek between finger and thumb.

Once the two men had made their way along the whole line, they stepped
aside, talking together in their harsh, stilted tongue. Then they began pointing
at some of the prisoners. Those they had chosen were prised away from their
fellows, some crying out as they were pulled away from friends and family;
others, resigned to their fate, stepped forward without hesitation. The children
watched, drawing closer together, and fleetingly the boy wondered if they
should try to run – amidst all the commotion they might not be noticed – but
as he turned to look behind him, he felt his sister's hand slip from his and,
turning back, saw that she was being carried away, arms and legs wriggling
as she tried to break free. He made to run to her but was stopped by one
of their captors who held him firmly by the shoulders. He struggled and
fought to get away, but a sharp knee in the back made him wince with
pain and he could do nothing but cry out his sister's name. She had been
taken so suddenly. How had it happened? He had promised to protect her.

'Malundama! Malu! I'm coming! Malu!'

His cries drew the attention of the two men and they turned to look at
him. They laughed briefly and said a few words to one another before starting

to walk away. Then one of them stopped and turned back. He beckoned to Matondo and the boy's heart lifted – they had changed their minds; they would take him too. He ran eagerly towards the man and looked up at him. His eyes were the colour of the sky; his skin was tinged with pink and seemed to be coming off in flakes across his cheeks and nose. His hair, so fine and straight, stood out from his head in tufts, like fiery grass.

The man touched Matondo's face, which was wet with tears, and said something the boy could not understand. The man patted his clothes as if he were looking for something. He hesitated for a moment before unpinning a small brooch from his coat and holding it out. Matondo didn't move. The man gently took Matondo's hand and wrapped his small fingers around the metal brooch as if to hide it. He nodded, said something and smiled. And then he turned and walked away.

Matondo made to run after him but was stopped by a heavy hand upon his shoulder.

'Not you, little one. Not this time,' said his captor, laughing as the boy struggled and kicked.

He watched, horrified, as his sister was carried out through the shallow water to one of the small boats, followed by the men.

'Malundama! I will find you! I promise!' His voice was hoarse, his throat swollen with tears.

The distance between them seemed to stretch out and out. He had stopped struggling now. There was nothing he could do. He simply watched as his sister was flung into the boat, as the oars lifted and the boat began, slowly, slowly, to bob away. He clenched his fist around the brooch and was only vaguely aware of its metal edges biting into his palm, of the blood that trickled slowly down his hand, staining the soft white sand below.

Part Three

November 1820

Chapter 18

She emerged from the darkness slowly, ever so slowly. She could feel nothing. *Perhaps I am dead. Perhaps this is what it is to be dead.* The thought didn't bring panic, rather a sense of resignation. She became aware of a bird singing, knew with certainty that it was a blackbird, and this sound – familiar, beautiful – became an anchor for her drifting mind. Inch by inch, she felt herself become solid; limbs, stomach, fingers, shoulders, face. She fluttered her eyelids open.

There was the washstand, there the wardrobe, the table and chair. Tiny motes of dust hung in the air, illuminated by the winter sun that crept in through the window, and she watched them for several minutes. Turning her head, she saw there was a glass on the table next to her bed and she pulled herself up to a seated position. Her lips were cracked and her throat dry, and the liquid – some sort of fruit tonic – was the most delicious thing she had ever tasted. She drank it all and then lay back, exhausted.

Memories started to return to her now. Mrs Stephens standing over her bed, her face in darkness. Bridget holding a cool, damp cloth to her face. Dr Stephens with a device like a small telescope, one end pressed to his ear, the other against her chest. And other memories too; of a host of bodies crowded into her room, their faces without features, their limbs grotesquely extended. Of a voice calling her name from somewhere far away.

She closed her eyes and willed herself to go back to sleep, but now a sudden memory flashed into her mind of Bridget holding her as she used the pot, her head heavy against Bridget's shoulder, Bridget's hands gripping her arms. Her face burned with the shame of it.

She knew there was something else, too, a sort of darkness on the edge of her consciousness. Slowly, as one touches the edges of a wound to see how painful it is, she groped her way towards it. There had been that awful dinner, she remembered that. She flinched as she recalled Daniel Hazelwood and how she had hit him with a candlestick – yes, that must be it, the thing she didn't want to remember.

But no: her memories, with their own momentum now, continued to unroll like cotton from a reel. The flight through the London streets with Bridget, the inn with the music and the dancing and the— And there it was, the thing she was trying to avoid. That repulsive little man and what he had said to her. *I'm your brother.* The thought of it made her physically uncomfortable and she fidgeted beneath the covers like a dog with fleas.

She remembered running from the tavern. It had started raining and she hadn't known where she was. She had run and run. She remembered her feet had been wet and sore. She remembered crying. And then – she didn't remember anything else.

Just then there was a knock at the door.

She tried to speak but nothing more than a whisper came out. She tried again, managed a croaky, 'Yes?'

'You're awake! May I come in?'

It was Dr Stephens. Mercy pulled her nightgown closed at the neck and smoothed her hair as best she could. She must look a fright.

'Yes,' she said again.

He looked genuinely relieved to see her. He felt her forehead with the back of his hand, then took her pulse, frowning at first as he looked at his pocket watch, his finger on her wrist, then smiling as he put the watch away.

'You had us all very worried, Mercy. How are you feeling?'

'I'm not sure.'

'May I?'

He sat on the edge of the bed and regarded her. The skin under his eyes was grey and he looked tired.

'What day is it?' she asked.

'It's Wednesday. You've been ill for four days.'

'Four days?' How could it be so long?

'You've had a fever. A severe one. You must rest a little longer but you're through the worst of it now.'

He patted her hand and she thought back to that night with him in the kitchen.

'Could you get Bridget?' she asked, withdrawing her hand. 'I would like to wash and dress. I think I may need some help.'

'I'm afraid she's not here. Mrs Stephens has gone to her mother's for a few days and taken Bridget with her. They'll be back at the end of the week.'

'Oh.'

'She would have taken you, of course, had you been well,' he added, thinking perhaps that she was disappointed. 'It couldn't be avoided, you see – Catherine's mother was taken ill so she has gone to visit her.'

'I see.'

'I can ask Mrs Dowers to come up, I'm sure she wouldn't mind helping you wash.'

'No, no,' Mercy said quickly. She didn't want that woman touching her. 'Please don't. I'll manage. I'm feeling much better, really.'

'Very well. I shall ask her to bring you some food and some hot water in a little while, and I will light this fire for you myself.'

'Please don't trouble yourself—'

'It's no trouble.' Dr Stephens got up and knelt before the grate. 'Now, let's see.'

He fumbled to strike the flint, crying out as he caught his knuckles before eventually getting the kindling lit.

'There!'

He stood back as the fire took hold, then realised his hands and shirtsleeves were streaked with coal dust.

'Oh dear. Perhaps we need Bridget more than I realised!'

He smiled and she couldn't help but laugh, as she looked at him with a coal smudge on one side of his nose and dusty patches on each knee.

'I do feel much better, sir,' she said. 'I can help out with the house and so on, while Bridget's away.'

'Very well. But first you must get thoroughly better. I prescribe a bit more rest, and then perhaps you would care to join me for dinner this evening – if you are feeling well enough?'

'Oh yes, that would be very nice.'

'Well, I will see you later. Try to get some more sleep.'

He left and Mercy lay back, listening to the pop and crackle of the fire, and to the blackbird which continued to repeat its song just outside her window. Now fully awake, she allowed her thoughts to return to that night. *Malundama. Matondo.* Mercy rolled the words around her mouth like bonbons. There was something vaguely familiar about them, wasn't there?

But how could *he* be her brother? She remembered his rough hands, the skin chapped and scarred, his scuffed boots and his clothes that didn't quite fit. She was the daughter of a prince; if she did have a brother – and Mrs Whitworth had said nothing of that – then surely he would be, well, different.

It made no sense.

And yet there had been something about him. And she *had* felt that she had met him before – although she had thought the same of Dr Stephens. Perhaps she was a lunatic, after all, and should be locked up in Bedlam with all the other madmen and -women. She closed her eyes and willed herself to go back to sleep.

That evening she went down to the dining room and saw that the table had been laid with the best china, just two places, one for her and one for Dr Stephens. There were new candles lit, a fire blazing, and the doctor himself in a fine wool jacket and turquoise cravat, which brought out the blue of his eyes. She was determined to enjoy herself and to put all thoughts of Matthew – or Matondo or whatever his name was – out of her mind. He was probably just some chancer, thinking he could get money out of her by claiming to be her brother.

She had also been racking her brains as to how she could prove who she really was. If she could just find out her father's name or where he came from then that would be something. With Mrs Whitworth no longer here, there was only one person she could think of who might know something: Old Sarah.

'Dr Stephens? I was wondering if you might do me a favour?' she said, holding out the letter she had written.

'Of course! What is it?'

Mercy explained, without mentioning her disturbing encounter with Matthew, that she wanted to know if Old Sarah remembered anything more about where Mercy had come from.

'I know she went to work for the local vicar after she left Mrs Whitworth's. Sarah can't read but I thought the vicar might read my letter to her? I would so love to know something of my father, of my family. She might remember some small thing that will help me to find out.'

Dr Stephens smiled and slipped the letter into his inside pocket.

'Of course, Mercy, I will post it first thing tomorrow. You have my word.'

'Thank you,' she said. 'And I have been meaning to ask you about my inheritance – about my father's money? Mrs Whitworth never really told me how much it was and I have no idea if there's any left, or when I will inherit it.'

'Well,' said Dr Stephens, 'the funds were transferred to me for safekeeping when Tabitha – Mrs Whitworth – died. Whatever is left will come to you when you are twenty-one. But we can go through all this when you're feeling better. Now, have a seat. Let me pour you some wine.'

Mercy was glad to sit down. She felt as though her head was floating somewhere above her body, the remnants of the fever still tangible.

'I would advise just a little, at first,' Dr Stephens said, as though he could read her mind. 'You will still be weak from the fever. Some proper food will do you the world of good.'

In Bridget's absence Martin was serving them, and his sullen face betrayed all too clearly how he felt about that. Mercy couldn't help but smile as he placed the dishes down onto the table in front of her, as though she were the mistress of the house.

'That will be all for tonight, thank you, Martin,' Dr Stephens said once he was finished.

Martin's eyes flicked between the two of them. 'But—'

'But?'

'You won't need me to clear the table? Or bring up dessert?'

'I think we'll be able to manage, won't we, Mercy? Thank you, Martin.'

He held the doctor's gaze for a moment and then nodded and left, unable to resist one sly look at Mercy as he went.

'Now, pass me your plate,' Dr Stephens said, and he dished out generous helpings of sautéed carrots and boiled potatoes. 'And now for the main event!' He took the lid off the main serving dish to reveal a fragrant stew. Chicken fricassee, her favourite. How did he know that?

'Here's to your recovery,' said Dr Stephens and they touched glasses.

They began to eat, talking politely about how delicious the chicken was, how fresh the carrots, how the weather had been over the past few days. Then he put down his cutlery and looked at her.

'Mercy, I know what happened that night,' he said.

She sipped her wine. How much did he know? For a moment she thought he was referring to Matthew but then he went on.

'Bridget told us about the Hazelwood boy. That he tried to – well, you know. It must have been very unpleasant for you. And I'm deeply sorry that a guest of ours should have treated you in that way.'

'It was nothing, really,' she said. She didn't want to think of that ever again. Wanted to wipe the memory from her mind.

'The whole night was a bit of a shambles, if you ask me,' he went on. 'It was Catherine's idea, of course. She always likes to put on a show and—' He stopped himself from whatever he was going to say about his wife. 'In any case, I am sorry for the way you were treated that night. And not just by Hazelwood. I am afraid that I was a little harsh in how I spoke to you, and I should like to apologise.'

He looked at her gravely and she recalled how he had glared at her that night when she had interrupted him and Sir Jonathan. It seemed such a long time ago. 'There's no need, sir, really.'

'I feel we were partly responsible,' he went on. 'For you becoming sick, I mean. Bridget explained that you were upset and decided to go for a walk and lost your way. Getting caught in that rain is probably what brought on the fever.'

Bridget hadn't told him everything, then.

'It wasn't your fault, sir,' she said. 'I should never have gone out at that time of night. It was silly of me.'

'Well, let that be an end to it,' he said, and he poured more wine for her with a smile.

They continued to talk and eat and sip their wine, and Mercy felt a warm and fuzzy contentment spreading through her. How much more fun it was without Mrs Stephens. The two of them could finally talk properly without her constant interruptions or demands for attention.

'Sir, I hope you don't mind me asking, but I've been longing to know more about your time in Sierra Leone. You spoke of it that night at dinner. Would you tell me about it? I've never met anyone who has been to Africa.'

Dr Stephens smiled. 'Ah, yes,' he said. 'Well, I suppose I don't think of Sierra Leone as being Africa with a capital A, if you see what I mean.'

She didn't really see, but somehow she found herself nodding in agreement.

'It's so very British there, you see. Freetown was established by the British thirty years ago, you know. It's full of Englishmen! My time there was mostly spent cooped up in a hospital dealing with sunstroke and upset stomachs. There's not very much I can tell you, I'm afraid. Right, I believe it is time for some dessert!' He flung down his napkin. 'No, you stay there,' he protested as Mercy made to get up. 'This evening, I will be waiter. I won't be a moment.'

Mercy sensed that he didn't want to talk about his time in Sierra Leone. Perhaps it hadn't been a happy experience. In any case, Mercy had no idea whereabouts in Africa she was from – it was such a vast continent. And this was her home now, so what did it matter? She drank the last of her wine and sat back in her chair, her eyes half closed so that the candlelight became a dancing amber glow between her lids. All her sorrow and anger at how Dr Stephens had spoken to her on the night of the dinner had melted away like an early-morning frost under the warmth of the sun. And all her anxiety about Matthew had likewise faded.

Dr Stephens was soon back with baked apples for each of them, which they ate with cold custard – another of her favourites. He poured them both a glass of sherry from the decanter on the sideboard, sweet and delicious.

'This is all such a treat, thank you,' she said, and they lightly touched their glasses together again.

As they talked and laughed, Mercy found herself thinking, *This must be what it feels like to have a husband*. She thought of Bridget and Joe, of how happy they'd looked when they were dancing, how easy and natural they were with each other. She had never felt that comfortable with anyone in her whole life. Until now.

'Penny for your thoughts?' Dr Stephens asked, but she simply shook her head.

'Oh, it's nothing. I'm just having such a lovely time.'

'One more sherry, and then I think it will be time for bed,' he said and went to fetch the decanter.

He stood behind her and topped up her glass, one hand resting lightly on her shoulder.

'There you are,' he said. 'The best medicine there is.'

He kept his hand on her shoulder and she was acutely aware of his thumb, warm against the back of her neck, his fingers which lightly touched her collarbone. She was aware too of her heartbeat, which seemed to have increased to the pounding of a drum. Surely he must feel the blood pulsing in her veins against his fingertips.

'My patient has a healthy pulse, I see,' he said, their thoughts again in tune.

Mercy turned her face up towards him as he leaned down and kissed her, full on the mouth, as if it was the most natural thing in the world. Then he drew her up from the chair, held her tightly to him and kissed her again. She felt her body turn to liquid.

Then just as suddenly, he stopped, held her at arm's length. 'Oh God, Mercy, I am sorry.'

'There's no need—'

'I'm sorry.'

He pushed her gently away and walked out of the room, leaving her there, alone and bewildered in the candlelight.

Mercy could hear him pacing around in his room. She cleared away most of the dinner things, blew out the candles and made her way upstairs. She paused at his door, touched it with her palm but didn't knock, then went up to her room.

She undressed and put on her best nightgown, undid the ribbon at the neck with nervous fingers. Then she rubbed a little soap at her wrists and her neck, the way she'd seen Mrs Stephens do with her perfume, and she lay down to wait for him. She was sure he would come. How could he not?

Then she heard his foot upon the stair and held her breath, heart racing. He was coming. But then she heard nothing more and she realised it must have been the wind or that perhaps she had imagined it.

Once she went out onto the landing, straining to listen, but the house was silent. He wasn't coming. She went back to her bed and drew the covers up to her chin. She left the candle burning, just in case. But in the morning she was woken by the grey light to find the candle completely burned out. He hadn't come.

Chapter 19

It was cold in the church but Mat calculated that it was still warmer than outside, and at least in here he could have a sit-down. There was even a little leather cushion to rest his weary arse on. He gazed up at the huge effigy of Christ on the cross that hung above the altar, blood dripping from its marble head and hands and feet. *There's always someone worse off than yourself*, he thought to himself with a flicker of a smile.

And things could be worse. Yes, he had nowhere to live, and yes, his sister – if it really was his sister and he wasn't just going completely mad – had denied all knowledge of him, and yes, the only friend he had in the world wasn't speaking to him, but. But. He was alive. He still had a job. He still had Booth's notebook. And while he still had breath in his body, he was going to work this thing out.

Joe was firmly of the 'going completely mad' opinion. After Malu – he was sure it was Malu – had run off that night, Joe had been pretty decent, at first, had clapped his arm around Mat and sat him down with a beer. Once Bridget got wind of what was going on, though, that was it. They'd gone off into the corner and Mat could see they were having a row. Then off she flounced and Joe came back with a face like a thundercloud.

'She thinks I'm only with her because of you,' he'd said.

'What do you mean?'

'I told her about you and Booth and Dudley—'

'You told her about Dudley?'

'Not that he's dead but about the ship and why you wanted to find him. Anyway, she thinks that the only reason I've been courting her is so you could get close to Mercy—'

'Her name's Malundama.'

'Matondo, listen to me. She is not Malundama. Your sister is dead. I'm sorry to say it, but it's the truth.'

'But—'

'Mat, I don't want to hear it. Bridget never wants to see me again. She says that neither of us is to go near her or Mercy, or she'll have us up in front of the magistrate.'

'On what charge?'

'God knows! But she'd think of something, that one. Damn it, Mat, I wasn't just piddling around with her, you know. She's one of a kind. A force of nature. And now I've lost her.'

Mat had said he was sorry a hundred times but Joe was stern as a quartermaster. He'd said he thought it best if he not get involved in any more of Mat's 'schemes'. That he thought Mat should probably be moving on. The way he'd looked at him, it was as though he thought that maybe Mat had killed Dudley, after all.

And so here he was, friendless, homeless and – once he'd paid Joe and the Alfords what he owed them – practically penniless. He was trying to keep his spirits up but he had to admit, things were looking pretty bleak. He put his head in his hands and let out a sigh.

'Can I help you, son?' A voice at his side. That was all he needed, a man of the cloth.

'No, thank you,' Mat said. 'Just having a pray.' He put his palms together and nodded towards the crucifix.

'I see,' said the man. He was young with floppy blond hair and a nervous manner. 'It's just that, well, if you need somewhere to go...'

Oh, here we go, thought Mat, *another do-gooder.*

'If you need somewhere to go,' he stuttered, 'then I am sure the workhouse will take you.'

'The workhouse?'

'This is a house of God, not a place for vagrants and idlers to take refuge. Now, get on your way.'

Mat wasn't in the mood for a fight with a priest and so, shaking his head, he slowly got up and walked down the aisle and out of the church. Christian charity was only for the white and the wealthy in this place, it seemed.

Evening was drawing on now and he'd got nowhere to stay. The boarding houses of the docks were an hour's trudge away. He was exhausted, his legs heavy as lead weights. Maybe a drink for the road. He felt in his pocket and found a few coins. *Come on, Mat the Cat, let's see how many of your nine lives you have left.* Turning his back on the church, he made for the swinging sign of the nearest inn, the light from the windows like a beacon, guiding him home.

He woke up cold and stiff on a bench in some park or other, with no memory of how he'd got there. He checked his pockets. Thank the Lord. He still had some money and the notebook. He'd pinned his precious brooch onto his shirt so that was safe, and so too was his knife. He might need it now. There were villains and crooks at every corner in this miserable city.

He stamped his feet to try to bring some blood back into them and put his hand to his head To check he still had his hat. His fingers met a sticky mess and he realised a bird had shat on his head while he was asleep. He cursed and kicked out at the few scrawny pigeons who were pecking around his feet. They flapped and hopped out of his reach, before returning towards him, hopeful no doubt for a meal.

'You and me both,' he said, kicking out at them again.

He wiped the worst of the mess off his hat and onto the bench, then he stood and straightened out his clothes as best he could. Wandering out onto the street, he found a crossing-sweeper and asked where he was. The sweeper, freezing in his threadbare trousers and thin jacket, told him and asked Mat if he was all right. He must be in a bad way if this scraggy lad was pitying him. He was too far away to get to the docks for any work today. It must be gone seven o'clock already. Instead he found a stall and got himself a cup of scalding coffee and a bun, feeling life slowly returning to him as he ate and drank.

He had the whole day ahead of him, then. Later he could go to the boarding house, secure himself a spot on that maggot-infested floor and tomorrow be up with the sun to earn some more chink. But for today, well, what to do? He remembered how last night – before he'd got so far gone that he couldn't remember his own name, that is – he'd been mulling over what Joe had said. *She is not Malundama. Your sister is dead.* Was he right? He needed to see her again, to talk to her. Bridget might have warned him off but he didn't exactly have a lot to lose. He finished up his breakfast and headed west.

It was a fine-looking house. He watched for a moment, but seeing no sign of life he knocked on the door and waited. If it was Bridget he would turn on the charm and see if he could sweet-talk his way in. If it was Malu, well, there was no saying what she might do. He'd have to wait and see. He knocked again and heard footsteps approaching the door. A young chap answered, with dark hair and an oily look. He peered down his nose at Mat.

'Yes?' he said.

'I'd like to see Malu— Mercy. I'm here to talk to Mercy. Sir. Thank you, sir.' Mat held his hat in both hands and tried to look as unassuming as it was possible to look after a night spent in the open air and with a gutful of cheap brandy.

'Her Majesty's not taking visitors,' the man said. 'She's not well, apparently.' He made to close the door but Mat got a foot in just before he could.

'What do you mean?'

'I mean, and it's really not hard to understand, even for an ape like you, that she is not well.' He spoke slowly and emphasised each word as if he was talking to an imbecile.

Mat bit down on his anger.

'I'm sorry to hear that, sir. Could I leave a message for her?'

'No, you could not.'

Before Mat knew what was happening, the chap was shoving him hard in the chest so that he almost fell backwards down the stairs. The door slammed shut and Mat heard the whisper of a lock being slid into place from the other side. He stepped into the street, looked up at the blank windows. She was in there somewhere.

'Malu!' he shouted. 'Malundama! I need to talk to you! Malu!'

But there was no reply. He stood there for a moment, impotent, before turning to go. He walked until he came to a park, away from the bustle of the city, and he sat for a while beneath a gnarly old hornbeam. There weren't many people about on such a cold day but there was something about the still, icy air that gave clarity to his thoughts.

He needed to clean himself up before he tried talking to Mercy again. Or maybe he could find someone to help him write her a letter? Yes, that might work. And he still had Booth's notebook. That might tell him what had happened on the ship – how his sister could have survived.

First things first: he needed to try and have a night off the booze and get back to the docks at cockcrow tomorrow, earn some money. Maybe in a day or two, Joe would talk to him again. He had to keep hoping. Not get dragged down. Mat the Cat would find a way. He had to find a way.

The rhythm of work was soothing. The lifting, the hauling, the numb fingers and aching back, were familiar, uncomplicated. The few coins he got at the end of the day and the prospect of a hot meal and a stiff drink made it all the more bearable. And there was a camaraderie amongst the men that reminded him of being at sea.

He noticed that one of the younger lads he was used to seeing around was no longer there.

'What happened to Tommo?' he asked the others.

The men shifted uneasily, glanced at each other; one of them crossed himself.

'Accident,' one of them said.

'He was injured?' Mat asked. They all lived in fear of that. If you couldn't lift and carry, you couldn't earn.

'Dead,' the man said. 'One o' the pulleys failed. Crate fell right on top o' him.'

'Leaves his woman with three little ones,' said one of the other men. 'It's a terrible thing. A terrible thing.' The man shook his head and a silence fell over the group.

Tommo had been a strapping Welsh lad in his twenties with a back as broad as a Shire horse. Always with a smile on his face, no matter how cold it was. It was odd to think he was no longer around. Mat eyed the pulleys with a newfound suspicion after that. Danger was always just around the corner, it seemed, but there was no way to make money that didn't involve a bit of danger, and money was what he needed.

That afternoon he spotted some of the men in a huddle round the fire, deep in conversation, and needing a break to try to get the feeling back into his freezing hands after several hours of lugging sacks around the dockyard, he wandered over to join them. They hushed up when he approached and he spotted one fellow hastily hiding something inside his jacket.

'Is this a game anyone can join?' he said, looking from one to another as they avoided his eye. 'What? What's going on, lads?'

One chap, Spanish or Portuguese or something, answered him. 'Just doing a little private business.' He emphasised the word *private*.

'Ah, well, don't want to interrupt. But if this "business" puts more chink in the purse, as it were, then perhaps you could deal me in?' He'd played it straight so far but everyone else seemed to be at it, so why shouldn't he?

The man hesitated for a moment but he must have calculated that Mat didn't look the sort to go tattling to the foreman, because then he held open his jacket to reveal a row of pockets that went all the way around the inside. From one of these he drew out a packet.

'Tobacco,' the man said. 'Can fetch a very good price if you know the right people. Which I do.'

Mat hesitated, instinctively looked round to make sure the foreman was nowhere to be seen. He knew that if you were caught thieving, at best you'd be flogged or beaten, and at worst, hanged or transported on a prison ship.

'We take only a little from each consignment,' the man went on. 'Just a very little. Not so much to affect the weight. Then they're none the wiser.'

Mat thought about how much you could get for a wedge of tobacco like that. With some extra money, he could really clean himself up – get some new togs, have a proper shave at the barber's. Maybe Malu would be more inclined to speak to him if he turned up looking more presentable and without a pile of pigeon crap on his hat. It was too good a chance to pass up.

'You got room for a new recruit?' he asked. 'I'm in need of some additional funds, shall we say. This would suit me nicely.'

The man turned away with the rest of the gang and they spoke together in low voices. Eventually, the Spaniard turned back to Mat and held out his hand. Mat took it and they shook, no words needed.

Later, he found himself working alongside the same chap, who told him his name was The Greek.

'I thought you were Spanish,' said Mat.

'I am,' the man said with a smile. 'Real name's Miguel. It's a long story.'

He explained that it wasn't just tobacco they were into. Whatever the consignment they were unloading, be it sugar or cloth or rum, they would find a way to cream some off the top and sell it on. His jacket with all the pockets was what they called a Jemie, he said, although he wasn't sure where the name came from. Some of the chaps also made long bags or pouches which they tied to their legs underneath their trousers. Mat was handy with a needle – he'd had to be when mending sails and the like – so he was confident he could knock something up for himself.

Even some of the foremen were involved, The Greek told Mat – with so much wealth all around them, how could anyone be expected to resist such temptation? The Greek and his mates had some contacts Mat could sell on to, once he got his hands on some goods.

'What is it you English say? It is a pleasure doing business with you!' The Greek grinned as he shook Mat's hand again.

'Oh, I'm not English,' Mat said.

'Of course,' said The Greek quickly, not wanting to offend. 'Where are you from, amigo?'

Mat hesitated. He thought of a hundred ports, the decks of a hundred ships, and somewhere, very far back, he thought of a neat, round house where he had played with his sister.

'That's a good question, my friend. A very good question.'

'Oi, stop the chitter-chatter and get on with some work, you pair!' It was the foreman. The same one who had given Mat an earful before. He seemed to have something against him, was always watching and ready to pounce if Mat so much as paused to scratch his arse.

'Yes, sir, sorry, sir,' Mat muttered, and he and The Greek turned back to the stack of boxes they were unloading. He wouldn't be here forever, and it would all be worth it once he got his hands on some baccy and a bit more money in his pocket.

Chapter 20

Mercy felt an odd mixture of embarrassment and excitement when she woke up. Had she dreamed the whole thing? No – she could still feel his lips on hers, his arms around her, holding her close against his body. But then she thought of how he had pushed her away and she felt ashamed. He was a married man. It was wrong. And yet she couldn't help but imagine what it would be like if they could be together.

Maybe Mrs Stephens wouldn't come back, she thought. Maybe she would have some tragic accident and die – quickly and painlessly, of course. It happened all the time, after all. And then Dr Stephens would be a widower and, in time, he could marry again, couldn't he? Mercy forced herself to rein in her unruly thoughts. How could she even think such things?

The house was cold and quiet when she eventually got up and went downstairs. She sensed, as she went past his door, that Dr Stephens – Edwin, surely she could call him Edwin now? – was out. In the kitchen, she could hear Martin and Mrs Dowers talking. They stopped when she appeared at the door and both stared at her. Mrs Dowers was making quince paste, a row of jars in front of her, flecks of pink on her fingers.

'Her Highness is up and about then, is she?' Martin said. Always that sly smile. 'Enjoy your dinner last night, did you?'

Did he know? How could he know?

'The dinner was delicious,' Mercy said. 'Thank you, Mrs Dowers. The chicken was wonderful.'

Mrs Dowers gave a small, stiff nod.

'I shan't be cooking today,' she said. 'Not with the master and mistress out. There's some cold ham and a bit of bread. That will have to do us for today.'

'Dr Stephens has gone out?' Mercy tried to sound casual, bitterly aware that she didn't.

'That's right,' said Martin. 'He was off early this morning and in a right mood. Said he'll not be back until late tonight.'

'And he left me no message?'

'Message? Why should he leave you a message?'

Mercy felt her hands grow clammy. 'No reason. There was just a matter that we were discussing last night that I wished to – to continue with him.'

'Well, he didn't say a word. So your little matter will have to wait.' Martin paused, dipped a finger into the bowl of quince. Mrs Dowers slapped his hand half-heartedly. 'But you did have a visitor the other day.' He sucked the paste from his finger with a slurp.

'A visitor?' Who could it be? She knew no one outside these four walls.

'Didn't know you were courting, Mercy, you dark horse.' Martin emphasised the word 'dark' with a raise of his eyebrow.

'I'm not!' she said. Mrs Dowers glanced sharply at her. Clearly they had been discussing this already. 'Who was it?'

'You tell me.' Martin grinned. 'But I would have thought you had higher standards, Your Majesty. Quite the picture he was. Looked like he'd been dragged through the mangle a few times.'

The two of them sniggered.

'Maybe our African princess isn't quite the lady we thought, eh, Mrs D?'

'He was black,' Mercy said, a statement, not a question.

'As the devil himself,' said Martin.

Matthew. He knew where she lived. Of course he did. *Bridget*. She should never have gone with her that night. How dare he come here? How dare he try to inveigle his way into her life?

'I don't know who that could be,' she said. 'Perhaps he is something to do with Mrs Stephens's work.' Her voice sounded strange, like the voice of someone else.

'Whatever you say,' Martin said and they stared at her again.

As she went upstairs, she heard the low hum of Martin's voice and the sound of Mrs Dowers laughing. Laughing at her, she was sure of that.

The day wore on and on. No fires had been lit in the parlour or dining room, since both master and mistress were away. Mercy spent the morning in her room where she kindled a small blaze and sat in bed, reading, a blanket tucked around her legs. Yet the words seemed to slide right off the page, and when she got to the end of the chapter she realised she had no idea what she had just read.

She tried to draw. Took the art set that Dr Stephens had given her and carefully unpacked it, cradling each pencil as if it was made of gold. But her mind wouldn't rest, wouldn't stop drifting back to the events of the night before. She wanted to see him. To speak to him. Just to be near him. Was this how it felt to be in love?

Mercy got out of bed and went to the landing, peering down over the bannister rails to the stairway below. All was quiet. She tiptoed down the stairs to his room, Edwin's room. She hesitated for a moment then turned the handle and slipped inside. It would be hours before he was back.

His jacket was hanging on the back of his chair, and she went over and lifted it up and held it to her face, breathing in his scent. Then she put it on and wrapped her arms around herself. How silly she was. She carefully took it off and placed it back on the chair, just the way it had been. She wondered if he had taken her letter to be posted and slipped her hand into the pocket, relieved to find it empty. He had remembered.

She traced her fingers over the desk and picked up his pen, rolling it between her fingers. She tried to open one of the drawers but it was locked, so she turned her attention to the bookshelf; medical manuals mostly, a book on the birds of the British Isles, and at the end, a ceramic head with all sorts of lines and numbers and words painted on it.

She was about to take it down from the shelf for a proper look when she heard the squeak of a floorboard from out on the landing. Someone was coming. In a panic, she flung herself down and crawled under the daybed, her face pressed against the floor. The door opened and she saw Martin's legs and feet as he came into the room. She held her breath, willed every part of her to be perfectly still.

Martin walked over to the bookshelf and she heard him moving one of the books. Then he went to the desk and unlocked it, placing some letters inside before relocking it and returning the key to its hiding place on the bookshelf. He took the jacket off the chair and stood in the centre of the room. Mercy could feel the tickle of dust in her nostrils, and she wrinkled her nose to hold back a sneeze. Was her dress peeking out from beneath the daybed? She didn't dare check; any movement might give her away.

'What's this?' said Martin, and she felt her blood freeze in her veins.

He bent down and she saw his hand, the dirt beneath his nails, the chapped skin across his knuckles, and she prepared herself to be grabbed hold of, dragged out from beneath the bed. What could she possibly say to explain herself? But then she saw his fingers close around a glass that sat on the floor next to the bed.

'Someone's been having a tipple, have they?' Martin said to himself.

He walked across the room and Mercy could no longer see him. *Just leave*, she willed. But then she heard more movement and the sound of liquid being poured.

'Just a small one,' Martin said and he drank, smacking his lips together with an 'Ah!'

After replacing the bottle he left the room, taking the doctor's jacket with him, and Mercy lay there for several more minutes, anxious that he could come back. When there was no sign of him, and with pins and needles pricking at her legs, she slowly pulled herself out from under the bed. She knew she should leave but she couldn't resist having a peek into his desk; she'd seen where Martin had hidden the key and she retrieved it now and opened the drawer.

She rifled through the letters, finding nothing of interest. What was she doing? She went to close the drawer, realising now how reckless, how ridiculous she was being. But then she spotted an envelope at the bottom of the pile, an envelope with her own handwriting on it. It was her letter to Old Sarah, the letter he had promised he would post. He must have forgotten. But why would he have locked it away in his desk? There was bound to be a good reason why he had kept it.

He'd probably just mixed it up with his own correspondence – yes, that must be it. He would find it later and post it then. She hurriedly put everything back where she'd found it and darted back to her room, barely able to believe what she had done. *This must be love*, she thought, *it must be.*

Chapter 21

It turned out to be easier than Mat thought to pilfer a few odds and ends from the consignments on the docks. He opened up the lining of his jacket and made a sort of hidden compartment where he could stow the tobacco. Like The Greek had told him, he just scraped off a tiny bit here and there, not so much that anyone would really notice. Once he'd got a sizeable chunk, he handed it on to The Greek or one of his contacts in exchange for the chink. There'd been a few close shaves where he thought the foreman had spotted him, but so far his luck had held out and he'd got away with it.

He figured that with the extra money he'd get, he could probably find better lodgings in a day or so. He wasn't getting much shut-eye in the boarding house, what with the cold and the stench and the blasted rats. As he lay on the floor that night, he thought of Joe and their warm room and all the laughs they had shared. He wondered if Joe missed him at all. Maybe he should pay him a visit? See if his temper had cooled.

And what about his sister? Had she given him a second thought? It seemed crazy that they were in the same city, that she was lying in bed not more than a few miles from him, and yet he couldn't see her. He racked his brains to work out how she could have come to be alive and here in London.

If the *Duke of Buckleigh* went down, how had she survived? With Dudley dead and his sister refusing to see him, the only person who could possibly tell him was Booth. He still had Booth's notebook but that was a fat lot of use to a man who couldn't read. There was only one thing for it; he'd have to go and talk to him in person.

He made the journey back to Spitalfields the next day. As he got to Booth's place, a man barged out of the front door, going at some speed and knocking into Mat as he went past.

'Watch it!' Mat shouted, but the man didn't respond. He just stared at him for a moment, then raced off down the street.

There was something familiar about him but Mat couldn't think where he'd seen him before. Looked a well-to-do type, not the sort you'd expect to see round here. *Probably why he was moving so fast*, Mat thought; *he'll have been poking some trollop and now he's off for lunch with the wife.* In fact, that's probably where he'd seen him, at some bawdy house or other.

The house was quiet, all the doors closed, and there was no sign of any of the other residents. Mat made his way down the landing and when he saw that Booth's door was ajar, he felt a creeping sense of unease. He slowly pushed the door open and peered in.

At first he couldn't make sense of what he was looking at. Booth was lying on his front, dressed in his usual worn suit and scruffy shirt. His arms were flung out to either side and his head – or the pulpy mess that was what remained of his head – was turned away from the door. The blanket and the floor were soaked with blood, and there were gobbets and spatters of it all over the walls. Mat fought back the urge to vomit as he looked at the mulch of hair and bone and brain and blood.

He scanned the room with a sudden lurch of fear that whoever had done – *that* – to Booth might still be in the room. But there was no one there, and nowhere to hide in this hovel. He saw that the desk drawer was open, the contents thrown out onto the floor. The bible lay open, face down on the floor, and for some reason Mat found himself picking it up and placing it next to Booth's body. Whatever he'd done, he didn't deserve this. There was a sound from one of the rooms across the hall and Mat suddenly saw how bad it would look if he were found in here. He left, as quickly and soundlessly as possible.

It was only as he was walking hurriedly away down the street that he thought of the man he'd seen on his way in. The man who had been in such a rush. The man who had looked so out of place. *My God*, thought Mat, *was it him?* Had he murdered Booth? He tried to picture the man again. Short reddish hair. Tall. Why had he seemed familiar?

Mat felt for the notebook in his pocket. He had to know what was written inside. Whatever had happened on the *Duke of Buckleigh* all those years ago, it wasn't over, that was for sure.

Joe was his only hope. And surely once he'd heard what had happened to Booth, once he saw Booth's notebook, he would have to listen. He would make him listen. Mat had even brought him a gift of a pouch of tobacco – pilfered from the docks, but still a gift. If he could just get Joe to read the notebook then he might be able to understand what was going on.

He spent so long practising what he was going to say when he got to the Alfords' that he never considered that Joe might not be there. He went around to the back door and the maid, Lucy, answered. She was clearly surprised to see him and he wondered what Joe had told them all about his sudden disappearance.

'Is that you, Matthew?'

Mrs Bryson appeared behind the maid, her whole face stretched into a smile when she saw him. 'It is you! Where on earth have you been? You look half starved. Come in, I've a pot of mutton stew here. You must have a bowl. Come on, sweetheart, in you come.'

The warm welcome and the offer of food was too much to resist, and he let himself be drawn into the kitchen and seated at the table.

'I mustn't stay long,' he said, through a mouthful of stew and bread.

'How about a little beer to wash it down?' she said, ignoring him and sending Lucy off to the pantry to fetch a bottle.

'I just wanted to see Joe. I'll leave him a message, if I may?'

'Of course, of course. Your jacket's seen better days, if you don't mind me saying, Matthew, dear.' Mrs Bryson brushed and picked at his arm, her mouth turned down with disapproval. 'Let me give it a proper brush for you, won't take a moment.' And she wrestled him out of it before he could stop her.

She marched off to the scullery with a determined look and Mat felt such a pang of, well, a pang of homesickness, he supposed, that it physically jarred him. Though he'd not stayed here long, it had become a home. The first real home he'd ever had.

'Lucy?' It was Mrs Alford. She stopped when she saw him, but the initial flash of fear as she saw a man at her kitchen table was quickly replaced with a genuine smile. 'Matthew! How lovely to see you! Joe said you had been called away. He said you wouldn't be coming back.'

'Yes,' Mat said, avoiding her eye. 'My plans changed somewhat.'

Mrs Alford sat opposite him at the table and looked at him with her clear grey eyes.

'You don't look very well, Matthew,' she said simply.

Mat put down his spoon. A piece of gristle in the stew had called vividly to mind the battered head of poor Booth and he pushed the bowl away, unable to stomach another bite.

Lucy appeared just then with his bottle of beer.

'Thank you, Lucy,' Mrs Alford said. 'Watch the children, will you? I'd like to speak with Matthew.'

Lucy gave a small nod and left. Mat drank deeply from the bottle, felt his nerves settle a little.

'You don't have to tell me anything if you don't want to,' Mrs Alford said. 'But if you do need anything, anything at all, then I am your friend. Mr Alford and I are both your friends. And we will help you, if we can.'

She spoke gently, as though coaxing a frightened animal from its hole, and this gentleness, this kindness, was so pure, so unexpected, that Mat felt himself begin to weep. Huge, hot tears welled and dropped from his eyes and his whole body shook. When the tears stopped, and with Mrs Alford's cool hand placed over his own, he told her everything. The whole dreadful story poured out of him like water from a bilge pump. About his sister, his plans for revenge, about Dudley, and finally about what he had seen that morning: the murdered body of Booth.

Mrs Alford said nothing throughout, merely nodded from time to time. Did she believe him? Saying it all out loud, he was aware how ridiculous it sounded. How could his sister have survived? And even if she had, how had she ended up in London dressed like a lady and so hoity-toity? And if he hadn't killed Dudley and Booth, then who had?

'I think we need to take a look at that notebook,' she said finally. 'Do you have it with you?'

'My jacket!' Mat jumped up from the table. 'Mrs Bryson took it to clean it.'

'I'll go.' Mrs Alford went out to the scullery and returned a moment later, holding the book. She sat down and opened it.

'It says the *Duke of Buckleigh*, doesn't it? Just there?' Mat pointed and she nodded.

'Yes, yes it does.'

Mat held his breath as he watched her read, her forehead drawn into a frown.

'It seems to be some kind of log book,' she said as she turned the page. 'There's information about the crew – how many they are, their names and ages and so on.'

'Is that it?'

'Wait a moment.' She continued to read. 'Here he's talking about the weather. The food on board.'

'Anything else?'

She turned the pages, her eyes skimming over the writing which became more untidy, harder to read as the book went on.

'Oh dear, yes,' she said. 'The *Duke of Buckleigh* was definitely a slave ship. There's a passage here where he describes them anchoring off the west coast of Africa, unloading all the goods and making the ship ready for its next cargo. A cargo of human beings.'

She shook her head, turned the page. 'Oh, there's a page missing here, looks like it's been torn out. There are notes about the various illnesses of the crew and the slaves – different treatments he's trying. Records of deaths. Those poor souls.' She flicked through the pages until the writing suddenly stopped. 'It ends rather abruptly. The rest of the pages are blank.'

'Does it say anything about the ship going down? How they escaped? Anything about what happened?'

'No. I'm sorry, Matthew, it just stops.'

That was it then. He was no closer to finding out what had happened than he was before. Then a thought struck him. 'Mrs Alford, you said it mentions the different treatments he's trying?'

'Yes, that's right.' She flicked back through the pages.

'But Booth was the first mate – why would he be treating people?' Mat went on. 'That makes no sense.'

'Then I don't think this is Booth's book. This looks like it belonged to the ship's doctor. Though how they can call themselves that when they turn their hand to such work is beyond me.'

'The ship's doctor?' Mat thought back to that day in the coffee house. There had been three men: Dudley, Booth and the other one. What had Joe said his name was? Dr Stephens. Mat had only seen him from behind; short reddish hair, tall. *Oh God.*

'I need to see my sister.'

Mat leapt from the table and ran, calling his thanks to Mrs Alford as he went. His sister was living with a murderer and he had to save her. He had failed last time, but this was a second chance and he wouldn't fail her again.

Chapter 22

Mercy didn't see Dr Stephens again until the next day. She was in her room drawing a pencil sketch of the view, trying to capture the sense of distance as she looked out over the roofs, when she heard the distant slam of the front door followed by the thunder of his footsteps up the stairs. It was funny how she could recognise immediately that they were his and no one else's.

She waited, breath held – was he coming to see her? – but the footsteps stopped on the floor below and she heard him go into his room. He shut his door with such force that she jumped a little. He must be in turmoil, just as she was. She would go to him.

Mercy went downstairs and stood outside his door. She could hear him moving about inside, the rustle of papers, the thud of a cabinet door and a grating sound which she realised was the poker being thrust into the fire. With a boldness she didn't know she possessed, Mercy knocked but then opened the door without waiting for an answer. She needed to talk to him before Mrs Stephens came home.

The sight that met her was unexpected, shocking. Dr Stephens was bent over the fire, naked from the waist up. His jacket lay crumpled on the floor, and his shirt, on which dark patches were visible, was burning in the grate. On hearing Mercy's gasp of shock, he turned and she saw such raw fear on his face that she immediately backed away, mumbling, 'Sorry, sorry, sir,' and left the room.

Mercy half ran, half stumbled down the stairs into the parlour. How could she ever face him again? She closed her eyes but could still see his bare back, his chest, moon-white save for the patch of dark hair that curled across it. She grabbed a cushion from the chair and held it to her face as though she could blot out the memory somehow.

'Mercy? Are you in there?'

At the sound of his voice she clutched the cushion more tightly to herself. 'Yes, sir,' she replied.

Dressed in a clean shirt and jacket, he looked neat and calm. 'You gave me quite a shock,' he said with a smile.

'I'm sorry, sir,' Mercy said. 'I shouldn't have— Well, I should have knocked. Should have waited. I'm very sorry.' She couldn't bring herself to look at him.

'You're probably wondering what on earth I was doing?' he asked, but before she could answer he continued. 'I'm afraid I had to see a very sick patient this morning. Stomach trouble. And, well, without going into too much detail, my shirt was stained beyond repair. I thought I'd save Martin the trouble of getting rid of it by burning it. You see.'

Mercy looked at him then. He seemed to be waiting for a response. She had been so startled at seeing him without his shirt that she hadn't really questioned what he had been doing. It was rather odd, now that she thought about it. 'Yes. Yes, I see,' she said.

They held each other's gaze and thoughts of their kiss swirled through Mercy's mind. She felt a hot, giddy rush of emotion twisting through her. Could this be it? The moment he declared his love for her? She looked up at him expectantly.

'Very good,' he said. 'Well, I must be off.'

'Sir?' She stopped him as he turned to go. 'I just wondered if you had managed to post my letter? The one to Old Sarah?'

'Oh, yes,' he said with a smile. 'I posted that first thing yesterday, as I promised. Now, I really must go.'

He left the room and Mercy heard him talking to Martin in the hall before going back out. Why was he lying? She couldn't make sense of it. And why was he acting as if nothing had happened between them? Did she mean nothing to him after all? But no – she knew he felt the same as she did. She just knew it. Ever since they had first met, there had been something – some undefinable intimacy. The business with her letter must just be a mistake.

Mrs Stephens would be back tomorrow. How was she to spend any time alone with him, with *her* in the house? Mercy didn't think she could bear her loud voice, her briskness, all the questions she was bound to have about what had happened on the night of the dinner party with Daniel Hazelwood. She would probably be more concerned that Mercy hadn't damaged her relationship with the Hazelwoods than with how Mercy was feeling. The 'great campaign' came before all else.

Her thoughts were interrupted by a knock at the front door, and she dragged herself up from the chair and went to open it. When she saw Matthew standing there, she gasped. When they'd met that night at the inn, it had all been so strange – the music and the beer, her giddy mood after the dinner party – that she had almost managed to convince herself it had been a dream. But now here he was, on her doorstep, and though he was scruffy and scarred she couldn't deny that for a moment – a brief moment – she felt an odd spark of pleasure to see him.

'What do you want?' she said, noticing now that he was out of breath, panting as though he had run across all of London to get here.

'I need to talk to you,' he said, catching his breath. 'It's very important.'

She hesitated. She considered closing the door on him, closing the door on whatever he had to say. Why should she entertain his crazy notion that he was her brother? And yet she had to admit that part of her was curious.

'It's about Dr Stephens,' he said, seeing her hesitation.

'What?' What on earth could he be talking about? How did he even know who Edwin was?

'What about him?'

'Not here,' he said, looking anxiously past her down the hall. 'Please.'

Mercy hesitated still. Mrs Stephens would frown on her taking a walk with some unknown man, especially such a dishevelled one. And how did she know she could trust him? He might turn out to be a madman or a murderer. But there was something in his look, so serious and so without guile, that she felt compelled to hear him out.

'Very well,' she said, 'meet me at the corner in five minutes. I need to get my coat.'

He looked relieved when she arrived at the corner a few minutes later and she realised that he must have thought she wouldn't come.

'I tried to see you before,' he said as they began to walk. 'They told me you were ill.'

'I was. After that night, I… I became unwell.'

'I'm sorry if I was the cause,' he said. Mercy could sense him looking at her but she kept her gaze straight ahead. 'I shouldn't have just blurted it out,' he continued. 'About who I am. Who you are. I should have known it would be a shock.'

She stopped walking then, looked straight at him.

'Look, Matthew – or Matondo, or whatever your name is – I don't know who you are or why you think you know me, but I am not who you think I am. My name is Mercy Whitworth. I grew up in Worcestershire. My father was a prince. I do not have a brother. And if I did, then I am quite certain he would not look like you!'

To her surprise he laughed. Her voice had risen in anger and she felt her hands clench inside her gloves. And he just laughed.

'You always had a temper,' he said. 'If you didn't get your own way, all hell would break loose.'

'This is ridiculous.' She turned to go back but he stopped her with a hand on her arm.

'No, wait, Malu. Sorry, I mean Mercy. Wait. I do need to talk to you. Whether you believe me or not. I think you are in danger. I think Dr Stephens is dangerous.'

She hesitated. What could he possibly mean? She thought about her letter and Dr Stephens's lie, about his strange behaviour today. Then she nodded and they continued walking in silence. If he had something to tell her about Dr Stephens, then she wanted to know what it was. When they reached the park, they found a solitary bench at the edge of the lake and sat.

'Go on, then,' Mercy said. 'Say whatever it is that you have to say.'

He fidgeted, as if unsure where to start, then began to speak. Mercy stared straight ahead, watching the gulls that wheeled and swooped across the water as she listened. He told her how he had been born in a small village in Africa – he didn't know whereabouts or even what the name of the village was – how he had lived with his mother and father, and his sister, Malundama. Mercy heard his voice break as he described the night their village had been raided and how he and his sister had been kidnapped. He described it all so vividly that Mercy felt she could hear the shouts and smell the smoke as the huts were set on fire. She shivered, drew her mind back to the here and now, to the frosty grass and the still lake in front of her.

Mat was leaning forward, elbows on his knees. He was talking now about how he and his sister had been separated, she carried away to one ship, he to another a short time later. He described watching her getting further and further away from him, knowing he could do absolutely nothing.

'At that moment, I vowed I would find you,' he said, looking at her with a face raw with grief.

Mercy looked away, rubbed at some imaginary mark on her skirt.

'I'm sorry,' she said, 'I really am. It sounds terrible, what happened to you. But I am not her.'

'But you are, you are,' he said with absolute certainty. 'The way you purse your lips – yes, like that! The way you laugh. Those dimples you get when you smile. It's you, Malu, I know it.'

'No,' she said. 'I came to England with my father. He was a prince.' It was the truth, wasn't it?

'Are you sure?' He was pleading with her now.

'Of course I'm sure. I know who I am!' She said it emphatically, but a seed of doubt had planted itself in her mind. Did she really know? She couldn't actually remember her father, only knew what Mrs Whitworth had told her, but why would she have lied? And it was impossible that she could be related to this man. If she did have a brother – and indeed she had often daydreamed that she might – he would be tall, handsome, accomplished. He would like reading and speak softly. He wouldn't be some filthy old sailor with missing teeth and an ill-fitting suit.

'Anyway,' she went on, 'what does all this have to do with Dr Stephens? You said he was dangerous.'

He told her that he'd found out the name of the ship his sister was taken on from one of the men on the beach that day. They were black men but could speak the same language as the white men on the ships. Some of them were even wearing the same sort of clothes, he said, parading around in their breeches and woollen coats, despite the sweltering heat. He'd seared those two words, *Duca Buclee*, into his mind and later, when he'd learned to read and write a little, had committed them to paper.

'When Joe and I went to the Register Office we realised the ship was called the *Duke of Buckleigh* and we found the records, found the name of the captain – R. Dudley – and that's how we got to your Dr Stephens.'

'What do you mean?'

'We followed Dudley, and another fellow called Booth who was first mate on the ship, and they met up with Dr Stephens. We saw them together.'

Dudley. The name echoed in her mind. Where had she heard it before?

'And?' she asked, aware she sounded defensive. 'He meets a lot of people – he's a doctor.'

'And now Dudley and Booth are both dead, and this all happened after I started asking questions about the *Duke of Buckleigh*. The ship was wrecked, you see. Only the crew survived. The slaves all drowned and I thought you... I thought my sister had been killed too.'

'There was a shipwreck?' She thought of the painting at the Géricault exhibition, of her own violent reaction to it. Was it possible he was telling the truth? She would have been young, too young to remember perhaps.

'That's right. This morning, I went to Booth's to ask him some questions and I'm sure I saw him – Dr Stephens. Outside Booth's. Just before I found Booth's body. He was leaving just as I got there.'

Mercy remembered how she had seen the doctor burning his shirt, the look on his face when she'd walked in.

'He said he was with a patient,' she said. 'Are you sure it was him?'

'I can't be completely sure. I only caught a glimpse of him, but—'

'Then it wasn't him,' she interrupted, holding up a hand as though she could stop his words. If she accepted one tiny part of this story then the whole fabric of her life would unravel.

'You should have seen what he did to Booth,' Matthew said, turning towards her. 'It wasn't a pretty sight.' He took her hand in his. 'Whether you're my sister or not, that man could be a murderer. You're not safe with him. Look, I have this notebook, just read it and you'll see.'

He took out a tattered old book from his pocket and pressed it into her hands.

'How dare you?' she said, flinging the book back at him, angry now. How could he suggest that Edwin could kill someone? 'You don't know anything about him, anything about me. This is all just some silly story. Dr Stephens is a good man. He saved me, he took me in when I had nowhere else to go. He loves me!'

Her words rang out in the cold air. She was close to tears and she turned away from him. His whole story was nonsense. Dr Stephens wasn't a murderer and she wasn't some poor slave.

'I have to go,' she said. 'I don't want to hear any more. Don't come near me again.'

'Mercy,' he said. 'I know this all sounds crazy. And I don't understand it myself, but I'm sure it was him I saw this morning. The man's head had been staved in. Stephens could be capable of anything. Just take the notebook.'

She continued walking, increased her pace, leaving him holding the book in one outstretched hand.

'If you change your mind,' he called after her, 'go to 36 Dolphin Street. The chemist's there. Mr and Mrs Alford. They can get a message to me. Be careful! Please!'

She turned the corner and didn't look back.

When Mercy left the park she found that she couldn't face returning to the house, not yet, and she continued walking, unsure where she was going, unaware even of her surroundings. Her mind was a kaleidoscope of fragmented thoughts, ever-shifting and incoherent. She felt desperately alone.

Who was this Matthew? She had no doubt that his story about his childhood was true – he was so sincere – but he was mistaken in thinking that she was sister. How could she be? He was uncouth, ugly, dirty and stupid, she thought angrily; how dare he claim to be related to her? She was a princess; Mrs Whitworth had always told her so. And if she wasn't, then where had all the money come from to pay for her upbringing – her inheritance? Mercy pushed aside the nagging thought that a princess would have more than one good dress, would have no need for Mrs Stephens's cast-offs.

If only Edwin had posted her letter! Sarah must be able to confirm what Mrs Whitworth had always told her. Why hadn't he? Again and again she came back to that question. What was it that he didn't want her to know?

But she was certain that he was a good, decent man. A man who saved lives – who gave up his time to work with his wife on the campaign against slavery. There was no way that a man like him could be capable of what Matthew accused him of. It was unthinkable.

She remembered again that day in Dr Stephens's study when she'd cut her head, how for a moment she thought he had kicked her. But he hadn't, not really, it was an accident. Just an accident. And this morning, when she'd seen him burning his shirt, well, he'd explained all that. It was unusual, yes, but he'd told her the stains were from his ill patient.

A queer sick feeling came over her and she slowed her pace. It was impossible, ridiculous to think that Dr Stephens could beat someone to death. *Beaten to death*. She knew then where she had heard the name Dudley. The night of the dinner party, hadn't Mr Alderney said the man who had been murdered in Pimlico was called Dudley?

Nothing made sense, but she had an odd, heavy feeling in her gut. She had to find out. She had to know what Dr Stephens was hiding. She turned towards home, Matthew's voice echoing in her mind. *Be careful. Please.*

Chapter 23

Mat watched her as she walked away, her neat, small figure disappearing into the distance. She'd looked at him like he was something she'd stepped in and he couldn't help but notice how she'd inched along the bench so as not to sully her precious skirts by coming into contact with him. A right little madam, she was.

He wandered back to the park bench and sat.

'Well, I suppose that's that,' he said aloud.

What more could he do? If she wouldn't listen then that was her lookout. He'd tried to warn her. And maybe he was wrong about all of this; maybe the doctor wasn't the man he'd seen, maybe Booth and Dudley's deaths were just coincidence, and maybe she wasn't his sister at all. And yet, he knew that she was. He knew it in his bones. The more time he spent with her, the more convinced he was.

He looked out across the lake, the water shimmering silver in the winter sunlight. Ducks dipped their heads beneath the water, coots and moorhens scudded about as if they were late for a meeting, and the gulls screeched and circled, fighting over any morsel of food they spotted. There was an island in the middle of the lake and on the solitary tree that grew there, Mat could see a cormorant perched on the uppermost branch, its wings stretched out to dry.

'Good day, old friend,' he said.

A sharp pang of longing for the sea overwhelmed him then. A longing for the movement of the waves, for the salty spray, for the feel of the ropes and the smell of a freshly oiled deck. Even for the monotony of the food and the routine of work; four hours on, four hours off.

It was the only life he'd ever known, really. He wasn't cut out for a life on land. A life in one place. Not any more. How different his life might have been, if those raiders hadn't come that night. He would be married by now. He'd have children. His own little plot of land, his own animals. He'd feel the sun on his face every day and he'd sleep well at night in his own bed.

But there was no use thinking like that. If it hadn't been then, it would have been some other night. And maybe he was lucky that he'd been young when it happened; it meant he could adapt. He'd seen others – grown men and women – who refused to resign themselves to their fate, who had jumped overboard or starved themselves rather than submit.

From early on, Mat had made the decision to do whatever it took to survive. When he was first taken onto the ship, he'd kept his head down and his mouth shut. He'd been scared, of course, but he was determined not to let it show. He laughed to himself now as he remembered that he'd thought the white men were going to eat him. He hadn't even really believed they were human – how could they be, with their long red and yellow hair and those terrifying blue eyes?

As a child, he'd had the luxury of being allowed on deck for some of the day, unlike the other poor souls who'd been chained up below, confined in the hold with their own shit. He remembered how one of the older fellas, who had got sick not long after they set sail, had died and how he had remained chained to his neighbour for a full day before the crew removed the body. It made him feel sick to think of it. He'd never been able to stand being shut in anywhere since then.

When he was allowed up on deck, he had watched and he had listened. He had made himself useful, helping the crew to holystone the deck in the mornings – down on his knees, scrubbing away with the gravelly sand until his fingers bled. He'd started to learn a smattering of English and made the sailors laugh when he said a word or two. They took to having him run errands for them, and he learned how to repair a sail and how to do the various knots and splices needed for the rigging. He'd had a real knack for that, and it wasn't long before he could do rope-work as well as some of the most experienced hands.

When they'd finally docked – somewhere in the West Indies, he now knew – he'd wept like a baby at the thought of leaving the ship. He remembered how he'd clung to the leg of one of the fellas who had been kind to him and the captain had laughed so hard that he'd decided to keep him. And so began his life at sea.

When he had watched the men and women being dragged off the ship, some barely able to walk, many with visible wounds, some of the women clearly with child, Mat hadn't realised quite how lucky he was. He hadn't known then what would happen to them. It was only when he was a little older that he found out about the reality of the plantations, about what life was like there. The thought of his sister being treated like that was more than he could bear.

Never could he have imagined that his sister would end up in London, dressed like a fancy lady and talking as if she were a Queen of England. He shook his head in disbelief. None of it made any sense.

The cormorant had folded up its wings now. It stretched out its great neck and looked from side to side before taking flight and soaring away over the water. Mat watched it go with a twinge of envy. Perhaps it was time for him to go too. He could be out of here by tomorrow – there were always plenty of ships looking for men – and he could put all of this behind him.

Could he really leave his sister, now that he'd finally found her? She'd made it pretty clear that she didn't believe him and he couldn't see her changing her mind. He had no proof that she even was his sister, and what could he say or do to convince her? Twice now they'd met, and twice she'd rejected him. Why torture himself any more?

Yes, it would be better for everyone if he just disappeared. He could call in on the Alfords, hopefully say goodbye to Joe – maybe have one last beer with him – then get himself out of here. He put the notebook back in his pocket and his knuckles brushed against the brooch that he still had pinned to his shirt. He took it off and held it in his hand, remembering that day when Malu had been taken and how he had vowed to find her. He lifted his arm to throw it into the lake. Then he stopped himself, closed his fist around it. No, not yet. He wasn't ready for that just yet.

Chapter 24

Mercy stood in the hallway listening, but the house was quiet. She looked up towards the doctor's study then went down the stairs towards the kitchen. There she found Mrs Dowers buttoning up her coat.

'Been out, have you?' she said when she saw Mercy. Had she seen her with Matthew? Would she tell Mrs Stephens?

'Yes, I—'

'No need to explain yourself to me,' the cook said. 'I couldn't care less what you get up to.'

'Yes,' said Mercy. This everyday hostility was almost a comfort in its familiarity. 'Is Martin here?'

'Martin? No, he's off out,' Mrs Dowers said with a sniff. 'Taken advantage of the doctor going away and off to the pub, no doubt. Dr Stephens said he'd be out late, you see. And I'm off now too. I'll be back first thing in the morning to prepare for Madam's arrival. She'll want a good lunch after travelling, if I know her.' She put on her gloves then looked at Mercy. 'You'll be all right, on your own?'

'Oh yes, I'll be quite all right,' Mercy said. With the house empty she could do what she needed to do. She would be perfectly all right.

'Very well, there's some pie in there you can have. And I made a loaf yesterday so there's plenty of that and, well, you know where everything is.'

'Thank you, Mrs Dowers. I'll see you tomorrow.'

She bustled off out through the back door and Mercy locked it behind her.

This was the first time she had been completely alone in the house, she realised, as she listened to the gentle tick-tocking of the clock that was the only sound. It felt odd – both liberating and dangerous.

She went along the passage to Martin's room and opened the door, holding her breath against the fusty air that seeped out from within. On the wall by the door was a row of pegs, keys dangling from each of them. She found the key to the doctor's study and slipped it from its hook. If he had something to hide, then she was going to find it.

Inside the study, the fire had been tamped down and there was no trace of the doctor's shirt in the grate. The desk was tidy and the blanket that had been on the daybed was now folded neatly and placed to one side. She went to the bookcase and took the key to his desk from its hiding place.

Her letter to Sarah was nowhere to be seen – maybe he had posted it after all? Her gaze was drawn irresistibly to the fireplace. Or maybe he had burned it. Her heart quickened as she lifted out the pile of letters. Here, surely, there would be something. Something that would tell her what sort of a man the doctor really was.

They were mainly thank you letters from patients he had treated – nothing untoward there – an acknowledgment of a donation to the Foundling Hospital and another to a charity for the working poor. There was nothing to suggest that he was anything other than a decent Christian, and Mercy now felt a trickle of shame that she had ever suspected him. How could she have listened to a wretch like Matthew?

She put the letters back and, in her efforts to leave them exactly as she'd found them, her fingers pushed against the bottom of the drawer and a section of it clicked and lifted up. How odd. She tried to put it back, anxious that she had broken it, but as she did so, the entire bottom section came loose, revealing another shallow drawer beneath.

She glanced at the door, even though she knew she was alone, then slid out the papers that lay within. There were several documents, some yellowing with age, others clearly more recent. She picked up the one on the top, knowing that she shouldn't but unable to stop herself.

I received your note. We have nothing to worry about.
B is an imbecile. Nothing he says can hold any weight.
I do not wish to be contacted on this matter again.
I trust you understand.

Yours etc,
JH

She read it again. What could it mean? *B is an imbecile.* Matthew had said the dead man's name was Booth. Could he be B? And who was JH?

The next letter was older and she felt her heart contract as she recognised the ornate handwriting of Mrs Whitworth. It was as familiar to her as her own hand and Mercy traced her fingers over the paper, trying to call to mind Mrs Whitworth's face, her voice. She found that the memory was vague, insubstantial, as though she'd known her a lifetime ago, even though it was only a few short months. Mercy perched on the daybed and began to read.

3 September 1806
Hamblin, Worcs.

Dearest Edwin,

I do hope you are now rested from your travels. I was delighted to hear the good news about your forthcoming marriage. Please accept my heartfelt congratulations.

I am writing to let you know that the child is settling in well. We did have our concerns about her at first. She was quite the little savage! Only a few weeks ago she spent an entire day hiding beneath the dining room table and was only coaxed out by a bowl of custard proffered by the eminently sensible Sarah. The girl has taken to Sarah, in particular, and will now allow her to bathe her and dress her.

I'm afraid we are at a loss as to what to do with her hair – Sarah tried goose fat on it but the smell was too much to bear and so I'm sad to say we have had to cut it quite short. The experience was not unlike shearing a sheep, as Sarah remarked. (You will recall she is from a local farming family and has a most colourful turn of phrase.)

In any case, she is now looking more civilised and is beginning to speak a little. I hope that in time, she will prove to be a good-natured girl, if not an intelligent one, and that we may teach her Christian ways. She responds to her name very well. I would have preferred Hope, as you know, but am happy to indulge you in your desire to name her Mercy. In truth, it is a pretty name and suits her very well.

As you requested, I will not write again, unless in the case of some emergency. I simply wished to let you know that all is well and that you can rest easy about her. We will tell her only that which you instructed, you may be assured of that. I have absolute trust in you, Edwin, and your generosity regarding the poor child will no doubt be rewarded in heaven, where, God willing, we are all destined to reside one day.

The child is tugging at my skirts as I write this letter and, indulgent as I am, I will let her take the pen and draw you a picture on the reverse of this note.

I will end here, dear Edwin. Please rest happy that your little Mercy will be well cared for here in Hamblin.

Your ever-loving cousin,
Tabitha Whitworth

Stunned, Mercy turned the paper over and, sure enough, there were a child's lines and scrawls on the back. Had she drawn these with her very own hand? She read the letter again in disbelief. Dr Stephens had known her since she was a little girl – had given her the name of Mercy. Why had he never told her? The room seemed to contract around her as she struggled to understand. To remember.

Mrs Whitworth had told her that when she first came to live with her, Mercy had been so terrified that she would often hide and that custard was the only thing that would lure her out. 'Like a cat with a dishful of cream!' Mrs Whitworth used to joke.

She remembered that, sort of. Remembered Sarah, of course. She had straight, blonde hair that Mercy had liked to twist around her finger when she sat on Sarah's knee. Sarah used to let her eat cold custard with a wooden spoon, which somehow seemed to be the most wonderful treat.

Mercy knew she didn't speak when she first came to live in Hamblin. Would communicate only with signs and sounds. She would cling to Sarah's skirts in the day and was inconsolable at night.

'You kept the whole household awake with your howling, poor little thing. But it was only to be expected with you losing your father so young,' Mrs Whitworth had told her.

But Mercy could remember nothing of this. Could remember nothing of her father. Or could she? She no longer knew which were real memories and which were the stories told to her by Mrs Whitworth. The letter talked about Dr Stephens's generosity – what did that mean? If her father had left her so much money, why had Dr Stephens needed to be generous? *We will tell her only that which you instructed, you may be assured of that.* What had they kept from her? And why? She thought again of Matthew, his absolute certainty that she was his sister. Could he be right?

As she began to read the letter for a third time, she heard a noise from downstairs. It sounded like the front door. Who could it be? Not Dr Stephens, surely? Panic seized her and she quickly threw the letters back into the drawer, locked up the desk and replaced the key.

She could hear voices now, and she leapt from the room and closed the door behind her just in time to see the figure of Mrs Stephens coming up the stairs, closely followed by Bridget.

'Mercy!' Mrs Stephens declared. 'There you are. I thought the place was deserted! My, you do look queer. Are you still unwell?'

'No, ma'am, no, I'm quite better.' Mercy fought to speak normally. Had Mrs Stephens seen her coming out of the doctor's room?

'Good. I've never known anyone so prone to being indisposed. But I suppose we can't all be as hardy as this one.' She indicated Bridget. 'And your talents lie elsewhere, don't they, Mercy? Some have brawn and some have brains.'

It was almost impressive how she could insult them both in one fell swoop, thought Mercy. In the past this would have added to the rift between Bridget and herself, but since that night in the tavern things had shifted and she flashed a quick smile at Bridget, who responded in kind, rolling her eyes dramatically behind Mrs Stephens's back.

'Bridget, take my luggage through to my room, will you?' Mrs Stephens went on, stepping onto the landing so that Bridget could get past her with the two large bags.

'We weren't expecting you until tomorrow,' Mercy said.

'My mother being quite recovered, I decided to return early. Lots to do, lots to do. Now, be a dear and run down to Mrs Dowers, will you? Ask her to rustle up something delicious. I need it after that journey.'

'Oh, I'm afraid Mrs Dowers isn't here,' Mercy said. 'She went home. And Martin's out too.'

'Oh,' said Mrs Stephens, lips pursed in disappointment.

'There's some cold pie.'

'Cold pie?' It was as if Mercy had suggested she eat from the gutter. 'Where's my husband? Has he disappeared as well?'

'Dr Stephens has gone out, ma'am, yes. He won't be back until late.'

'Where's he gone?' Mrs Stephens eyed her sharply as though Mercy was somehow responsible for his absence.

'I don't know, ma'am.'

With a prolonged sigh, Mrs Stephens pushed past Mercy and went into her room, sending Bridget out and slamming the door. Bridget's eyes widened as she watched Mercy locking the door to the doctor's room with Martin's keys.

'What were you doing in there?' she whispered.

'Come on,' said Mercy, taking her hand, 'I need to talk to you.'

Sitting at the kitchen table, with Bridget piling up the fire, Mercy tried to explain everything she had learned since she'd seen Bridget just a few short days ago.

'I just can't make sense of it. Any of it. I think I need to talk to Matthew again. I was so rude to him earlier. But what if he's right? What if he really is my brother? He said I could get a message to him at the chemist's on Dolphin Street.'

'Dolphin Street?' said Bridget. 'That's where my Joe lives. Well, not "my" Joe any more. With the Alfords.'

'What do you mean, not your Joe any more?' Mercy was so wrapped up in her own affairs that she hadn't even thought to ask how Bridget was faring.

'I don't like to be taken for a fool,' Bridget said with a sniff. 'Seems I was just part of Matthew's plan to get to you.'

'Oh, Bridget, I'm sure that's not true! You seemed so happy together. And the way Joe looks at you – that can't be feigned.' She remembered watching the two of them dancing together, how perfect they had looked.

'Yes, well, there we are. Anyway, it sounds like you do need to talk to Matthew. You should go.'

'But what about her?' said Mercy, glancing up to indicate Mrs Stephens.

'Oh, I'll think of something,' said Bridget with a grin. 'I'll stuff her so full of food that she'll want a lie-down and she won't even notice you're gone. Go on, head out the back. You can borrow my coat, here.'

Bridget packed her off out of the back door, and Mercy dashed through the gate and into the street before she could change her mind.

The chemist was polishing the counter of his shop when she went in. He looked up as the bell above the door tinkled gently.

'How can I help you, madam?' he said.

'Mr Alford?'

'That's right.'

'It's about Matthew. I've come to see Matthew.'

He looked at her properly then. 'Ah,' he said. 'I think you'd better come through to the back.'

He lifted up part of the counter and ushered her through a door that led to the house. It was sparsely furnished – not at all like the Stephenses' – but it was neat and calm, everything in its place.

'Bettina?' Mr Alford called as he showed Mercy into the parlour.

Bettina was a slim woman with ash-brown hair swept back into a bun and large grey eyes. When she saw Mercy, she repeated her husband's 'Ah'.

'You're Mercy,' she said, gesturing for her to come into the room.

'Yes, how did you know?'

'Matthew told us about you. He didn't think you'd come.'

'I need to see him. Is he here? He said you would be able to get in touch with him.'

Mrs Alford looked at her husband then back to Mercy.

'I'm sorry, dear,' she said. 'You're too late. Matthew's gone.'

Chapter 25

Mat went back to the Alfords' after his encounter with Mercy, but there was no sign of Joe so he had to resign himself to leaving without saying goodbye. He was surprised by how much that bothered him. In a short time, he realised, Joe had come to be the closest friend he'd ever had. Ah well, there was no use dwelling on what couldn't be changed.

He told Mrs Alford what had happened with his sister. How she didn't believe him and that she'd looked at him as though he were a bit of shit on his shoe – he didn't use quite those words to Mrs Alford but she got the general idea.

'I'm so sorry, Matthew,' Mrs Alford said.

'Well, maybe I got it all wrong,' he said, more for his benefit than hers. 'Maybe I just wanted it to be her so badly that I convinced myself.' If he kept repeating that then he might come to believe it. If she wasn't his sister then it would make leaving her behind so much easier.

'I gave her your address,' he went on. 'Hope you don't mind. In case she wanted to speak to me. But it was pointless. I know she won't come. She looked as though she wanted to get as far away from me as possible.'

Mrs Alford was so kind. She held on to both his hands and told him he was always welcome to come back and visit. She made him take some bread and cheese wrapped up in a piece of waxed cloth, and kissed him on both cheeks. He didn't say goodbye to the children. Didn't want to cause a fuss. But just before he left, he unpinned the brooch from his shirt and handed it to Mrs Alford.

'I don't know if it's worth anything. Probably not. But I'd like you to have it – to pass on to little Charlotte when's she's older.'

Mrs Alford tried to protest but he insisted. He didn't want it any more, had no need of it now. Everything he had held on to was gone. His sister – if she really was his sister – didn't want to know him and the men who had taken her were in their graves. And so he shook hands with Mr Alford, thanked them both again and set out into the wet and windy streets, feeling more desolate than he ever had before.

How changed these city streets seemed to him now. Where once they'd held life and infinite possibility, they were now a labyrinth of misery and poverty. The passers-by, hunched against the cold wind, wore grim expressions. Somewhere a child cried – a harsh cry of hunger or of pain. Even the great dome of St Paul's, glimpsed through the drizzle, was indifferent to the suffering all around, turning its great face away towards the heavens.

The rain was getting heavier, each drop of water a tiny, cold needle. Mat cursed to himself. Even the weather was against him. He felt rainwater begin to seep in through the holes in his boots.

He was near the river now and he stopped for a moment and looked out across the water, letting the rain lash down on him. In the gloom of the late afternoon, with the rain clouds gathered above it, the river was black, the water moving in dangerous eddies and whirls. He found himself wondering what it would feel like to step out into that cold, dark water. To feel the chill embrace of the waves, to let that icy blackness enclose him and carry him away.

He'd seen a man drown. More than once. It was surprisingly silent and swift. Just a few moments of struggling and then – gone. All his worries would be over. And what did he really have to live for? No friends, no family, no life to speak of. Just wake, work, then drink to forget. Day after day. What was the point?

He edged nearer. The black water beckoned him in like a siren. He paused. Imagined the shock of the icy water and the irresistible pull of the current. He stepped back. No, he could never do it. Too much of a coward. And what was it they said, *While there's life, there's hope?* He turned his back on the river and continued to walk.

Come on, Mat the Cat. Tomorrow is another day. And who knew what tomorrow might bring? By first light he'd be on a ship out of here. He'd feel better then. He needed a change, needed to get away from the endless fog and rain. It would be good to feel the sun on his skin again. To not be permanently damp and cold. To have some food with a bit of spice. And women with a bit of spice, too. He began to whistle to himself and increased his pace. *This cat still has a few of his nine lives left, oh yes.*

The boarding house was of a slightly better class than the one he'd stayed in when he first arrived in London. It wasn't exactly luxurious but here he shared a room with just one other man and had a bed with clean sheets and blankets. The room was empty when he got back, and he closed the door behind him and knelt down to retrieve the baccy from where he'd hidden it beneath a loose floorboard under his bed.

There was a sizeable amount but he reckoned he could soon get rid of it. And with the funds he could treat himself to a hot meal and a bottle of something decent. Might as well enjoy his last night on dry land. He unwrapped the bread and cheese that Mrs Alford had given him and used the waxed cloth to wrap up the tobacco. He didn't want to risk it getting soaked in this rain. *Thank you, Mrs A.* Time to find a buyer.

In this city, there was a market to be found for whatever goods you were selling and tobacco was one of the easiest to get rid of. Plenty of folks wanted it and, even better, the evidence would be up in smoke in no time, making it a bit safer than nicking silver cutlery or fancy lace, say. And you could take a small amount without anyone really noticing. Mat had only taken a handful or two. It wasn't much of a crime.

The inns were all full at this time of day; men needing to warm up their freezing hands and faces with a gulp of gin, to numb themselves against their despair, their poverty, to have a laugh and a sing-song and maybe end the night in the arms of some pretty piece, if they were lucky – or if they had enough dosh. Mat shouldered his way through the drinkers, looking for a likely target. He spotted The Greek and some of the other lads and gave them a nod and a wave; he'd have a drink with them in a bit.

In one corner he saw the foreman who seemed to take such pleasure in making his life a misery. Mat tipped his hat to him with a grin. *Won't have to look at your ugly mug for much longer*, he thought. The man scowled at him, which only made his grin even wider. Mat continued on to the back of the room, out of sight of the foreman, and found a spot from where he could survey the place. He spotted some chaps that he'd sold to before and headed over to them, clapping one of them on the shoulder and opening up his jacket to reveal the pouch of rolled-up tobacco in his inside pocket.

Too late, he saw a man watching him through the crowd; too late, he spotted the uniform of the river constable who was now barging his way towards him. He prepared to talk his way out of it. The tobacco was a gift; he didn't know where it had come from. Someone had given it to him. But then he saw the constable wasn't alone. The foreman was at his side. And he was pointing at Mat, yelling, 'That's him! Filthy thief! I knew it.'

A space had cleared around him, the men instinctively drawing away from danger. Mat remembered how as a child, when he and his friends would be caught doing something they shouldn't, the same thing had happened; the other children formed into a circle around him as though to say, *There he is! He's the guilty one!*

He had no choice but to let the foreman hold him by the arms while the constable whipped the tobacco from his pocket and searched him. As the man patted him down, Mat suddenly remembered the notebook but just as quickly realised that he'd left it at the Alfords'. Probably for the best. He didn't want anything that linked him to Booth. In the current situation that would not be helpful, to say the least.

'Watch out, he's got a blade,' the constable said as he found the knife in Mat's pocket.

'Oh no,' he protested. 'That's not—'

'You keep your mouth shut,' the constable said, pocketing the knife.

Half the men had their own blade – at sea it was your most useful and treasured possession – but if they wanted to, they could make out that he'd tried to use it on them. It would be their word against his.

'I knew you were trouble,' the foreman said. 'Can't trust a darkie. I've always said it.'

Mat knew there was no use protesting – it would only make things worse for him – and so he allowed himself to be led quietly out of the inn. As he passed the lads from the docks, most looked away, not wanting to be associated with him. The Greek gave him the smallest of nods, a nod that seemed to indicate solidarity as well as a warning to say nothing. Not that he intended to. It was no use dragging any of the others into this. It was his own stupid fault. This would be a tricky one to get out of, he thought as the constable secured his hands behind his back, a very tricky one indeed.

Chapter 26

Mercy hadn't meant to start crying but once she'd started she found that it was hard to stop. She let herself be led to an armchair by Mrs Alford, as her husband quietly retreated from the room.

'I'm so sorry,' Mercy said through her tears.

'Not at all,' Mrs Alford said. 'I'll get Lucy to make you a hot drink. Tea with plenty of sugar.'

Left alone, Mercy breathed deeply and wiped her nose with her handkerchief. It was the same one that Mrs Stephens had given to her when she first arrived in London. How full of airs and graces she had been then. How impressed she had been with the Stephenses and their sophistication. What a stupid child she had been. They had been hiding her past from her all this time. She couldn't understand it. Why hadn't they told her that the doctor had known her since she was a child, had been involved in her upbringing?

Mrs Alford returned and sat down opposite her.

'Your tea will be ready in a moment.'

'I shouldn't impose.' Mercy made to stand up but Mrs Alford stopped her with a raised hand.

'Stay there. You're not imposing. And it's teeming with rain outside. You'd do better to stay here for a while until it stops.'

'Thank you,' Mercy said gratefully. 'So, you really don't know where Matthew has gone?'

'I'm afraid not. He said he would be taking a job on whichever ship would have him. Perhaps he'll change his mind. Perhaps he'll come back.' She patted Mercy's hand but didn't look her in the eye. They both knew that was unlikely.

'There's something I think you should see,' Mrs Alford said. She rose and went to the table, returning with a small book, bound in brown leather, slightly tatty. She handed it to Mercy.

'The notebook,' Mercy said. 'Matthew tried to show this to me but I refused.'

'I think he left it by mistake.'

There was a knock on the door and a maid came in bearing a tray.

'Thank you, Lucy. Put it down there,' Mrs Alford said.

Once the maid had left, she poured Mercy some tea and added three lumps of sugar. Mercy saw that she had one of the sugar bowls sold as part of Mrs Stephens's campaign. *East India Sugar* it declared in bold lettering. Was that all a lie too? Mercy felt she could no longer trust anything she knew. If the Stephenses had lied about her past, what else were they lying about?

'Here, drink this,' Mrs Alford said. 'I'll leave you for a little while to look at the book. I'll be just upstairs, and Lucy's through there in the kitchen if you need anything.'

She left soundlessly and closed the door. Mercy turned the book over and over in her hands. Did she want to know? That was the question. Did she really want to know?

She recognised his writing immediately; she'd seen it on countless notes and letters, on those little labels in his cabinet of curiosities. That neat, slanted hand. It was dated 3 April 1806 and on the front page was written, *Journal of Occurrences on board the Duke of Buckleigh, Slave Ship, during a voyage from London to the West Coast of Africa and thence to the West Indies.* She felt her heart contract as though someone had squeezed it in their fist, and she took a deep and steadying breath before she turned the page.

It began with the ship setting sail from London and the first few passages were uneventful, describing the early days of the voyage; the toothaches and stomach troubles of the crew, the weather, the food, and so on. Mercy flicked through the pages, seeing the weeks go by. It took them two months to reach Africa, and it was here that she began to read more closely, not wanting to go on but unable to stop herself.

6 June – The long boat came back at 11 p.m. with 12 casks of water and some traders. The captain and first mate talked with them some time before they returned to the shore.

8 June – Purchased 4 slaves. Tolerably good condition.

12 June – Sailed down along the coast.

13 June – Some canoes came on board with some slaves but none in any fit condition to buy. Will sail on tomorrow.

30 June – Went ashore and purchased 17 slaves. Brought them on board and washed them before sending them down below. Some crying most piteously. Pray God all will survive until we reach our destination.

On and on it went. Mercy felt sick but she continued to read as men, women and children were brought on board like cattle or sacks of grain.

There was a page missing and she remembered now the piece of paper given to her by the wild-eyed man. She hadn't understood it at the time but now she saw that it was from this notebook; the doctor's journal. *Tell him he must come or there'll be more of this.* That's what the man had said. So he'd had this notebook – how had Matthew got hold of it? Or Matondo, as she should really call him. She read on, hardly believing that this was written by the same man she had lived with for the past few months. The man she had laughed with, whose hand she had held, whose lips she had kissed. She shuddered and forced herself to read on.

4 September – Slaves is very indifferent with Colds and Purging.

5 September – Woman no. 32 died today.

7 September – Rotten weather so unable to allow slaves on deck for exercise.

9 September – Concerned food rations are too low. Captain is firm in his opinion to the contrary. Slaves complaining of Gripeing and Fluxes. Another three died today.

12 September – Washed and shaved slaves today. Girl no. 7 a most diverting little thing.

13 September – Parkins fell from the top-sail today and has broken both arms. Poor fellow in a great deal of pain.

14 September – Man no. 15 died today. Captain not concerned but I admit to being anxious for our Cargo.

Mercy closed the book. She felt that she might be sick and took a small sip of her tea. Then another. It was impossible to take it in, impossible to believe that this was her Dr Stephens. And what about Mrs Stephens? How could she go about campaigning on behalf of the enslaved when her own husband had been part of the slave trade?

A flood of feeling swept over her and Mercy felt as though her small frame could not withstand this storm. She stood and paced about the room as though by moving she could somehow release this awful dread that had hold of her. She had been on that ship. She knew it now. Knew it with a certainty that eclipsed everything else.

She remembered being carried. Over someone's shoulder. She was small. She was crying. She remembered the motion of a ship through water, the sounds of people shouting, singing, weeping. She remembered hurting her head, and a man, a kind man, leaning over her, dabbing her wound. And a smell, sickly and sweet, like sage.

Her stomach heaved and flipped and she leaned against the mantelpiece with both palms, head hanging down, fighting for breath as the old, familiar panic reared its head. She could hear a sound, faraway, like an animal howling in pain, and then she realised that the sound was coming from her.

She felt gentle hands on her back, the soothing voice of a woman, and she felt as though she were falling, falling, into a soft grey nothingness, and she allowed herself to fall. Welcomed the surrender, welcomed the oblivion.

She woke up in an unfamiliar bed in an unfamiliar room. Had it all been a dream? Please God, let it all have been a dream. Perhaps she was in Hamblin and could live out her life in peace and quiet. Alone, yes, but calm and content. Unquestioning.

'Mercy? Are you awake?'

As her vision came into focus, she saw a woman coming towards her and recognised Mrs Alford, her brow pinched with concern. The events of the day, of the last few days, came back to her now.

'Don't try to move, don't speak. Lie back.'

She felt a cool cloth pressed against her forehead, smelled the scent of lavender, and she closed her eyes and laid her head back on her pillow.

'You must rest for a while.'

In her delirium, the voice became the voice of her mother. The hands that so tenderly bathed her face were the hands of the woman who bore her. She could see those slender arms, encircled by beads and bracelets. Wanted so much to see her face, but where her face should be was just a blank.

'I should never have given you that book. I'm so sorry. Rest now, dear.'

The voice faded and the room melted away as Mercy felt herself drifting, drifting, drifting.

When she woke again the room was empty. She felt oddly energetic, her mind clear and her body loose and light. She often felt this way after one of her attacks, as though she needed these violent passages in order to renew herself. Like a butterfly that emerges from its dark slumber, breaking out through its chrysalis and stretching its new-found wings.

She had to speak to Dr Stephens. She had to face him and find out the truth – the entire truth of how she had come to be on that ship fifteen years ago, how she had come to be in England and what his role in it all really was. It was the only way she could begin to understand who she was. And she needed to try and find Matthew – Matondo – her brother. Yes, her brother. How strange and wonderful it felt to say it.

There was a gentle knock and Mrs Alford peered around the door.

'How are you feeling?' she said.

'Much better. I'm so sorry—'

'You don't need to apologise. If we can't care for our fellow creatures when they are in need, then of what use are we? I'll leave you to get up and then you must join us for dinner.'

'Dinner? What time is it?' She wondered if Mrs Stephens had noticed she was missing yet.

'It's almost seven. Come down when you're ready.'

She found Joe downstairs, and Mercy was glad to see him. He was her only link to Matthew.

'I don't know where he's staying, I'm afraid,' he said. 'It's one of the boarding houses out near the docks but there's tons of them. He could be in any one of them.'

Mercy bit her lip. Joe looked at her for a moment then said, 'I'll go out after dinner and look for him.'

'Would you really?' If she could, she would do it herself.

'Of course! I know a few places he might be. We'll find him. I'm sure of it.'

Mercy knew he was only saying it to make her feel better but she allowed herself to be comforted nonetheless. She pushed her food around the plate, trying to eat but unable to summon up any kind of appetite. She saw Mr and Mrs Alford look at one another. Mr Alford nodded at his wife.

'Mercy?' she said. 'Would you like to stay here tonight? It's getting late and you've had quite a day.'

'I…' She hesitated. She had to speak to Dr Stephens but she didn't know if she was ready, just yet. It would be better to do it in the morning. 'I don't want to put you to any more trouble.'

'It would be no trouble at all,' said Mr Alford and his wife agreed.

'You can have the girls' room. They can sleep in with us. They'll love it. They can pretend they're on holiday. I'll let Lucy know and we'll find you something to wear, and so on.'

As she went towards the door, Lucy herself appeared and announced that they had a visitor. Mercy's heart leapt; it must be Matthew, he must have sensed that she was here and come back to find her.

'It's a young lady. Says her name's Bridget,' said Lucy with a sniff, clearly not impressed.

'Bridget!' Joe jumped up from the table, nearly sending his dinner flying. *He loves her*, thought Mercy, *he really loves her*.

Lucy showed Bridget into the room and Bridget apologised for disturbing them all so late.

'I thought you might want your things,' she said, holding out Mercy's bag.

'Oh, thank you! How did you know?'

'Well, when you didn't come back, I just thought – well, I wasn't sure. But I was worried about you. I wanted to make sure you were all right.'

She looked embarrassed after this unusual expression of emotion, her cheeks pink, and Mercy stood and hugged her tight.

'Thank you, Bridget,' she said. 'Thank you. Oh, you're wearing my coat!'

'Because you took mine, remember?'

They both laughed and Mercy went to fetch Bridget's coat for her.

'I'd better get back,' Bridget said. 'Before the mistress realises I've gone and calls the night watchman.'

'I'll be back first thing tomorrow,' Mercy said. 'There's a few things I need to ask Dr Stephens.'

'Very well,' said Bridget. 'Good night, everyone.'

She nodded at the Alfords, then looked at Joe, who had been uncharacteristically quiet but who hadn't taken his eyes off Bridget since she arrived.

'Well, are you walking me home or not?' she said to him, and he practically ran to her side and grabbed hold of her hand.

'Of course, madam, of course. It would be a great pleasure. Then I'll go and look for Mr Matondo,' he said, turning to Mercy. 'Promise.'

He and Bridget left, hand in hand. Mercy was happy for them; they belonged together. Then she thought of Dr Stephens – how he had caressed her hand, had kissed her – and she felt the bile rise up in her throat.

'I'm sorry,' she said, pushing her plate away. 'I can't eat any more. I suddenly feel awfully sick.'

Chapter 27

The police office was a tall, thin building that sat on the riverbank not far from the inn where he'd been nicked. The constable dragged him along the street and down the dingy alleyway that led to the main entrance. It wasn't far from Execution Dock. Surely they wouldn't send him there, would they? That was usually reserved for the worst kinds of piracy, but he knew men had been hanged for less than what he'd done. He'd heard of lads, young as fourteen, who'd swung for no more than pinching a fancy watch or an umbrella.

Once inside, they registered him in their book and emptied out his pockets, making a note of the knife, the stolen baccy and his purse of coins. They missed a few coins he'd sewn into the hems of his trouser legs for safekeeping so he still had a bit of money on him – not that he had anywhere to spend it.

After that they took him through to a cell at the back of the building and chucked him inside, the door thudding shut with an air of finality. It was black as pitch. He fumbled his way across the room until he felt the wall beneath his fingertips and stood with his back against it until his eyes started to adjust to the gloom.

There was one window – thank the Lord – heavily barred, but at least it let in a little light. He grabbed the bars and shook them, but they were solid and unmoving. Even if they weren't, the window was so small that he doubted he'd be able to squeeze himself through.

His foot made contact with something that let out a clanging sound. *Ha*, 'kicking the bucket'; how appropriate for a condemned man. The sloshing sound and the foul smell indicated that it hadn't been emptied since the last occupant had made use of it. He backed away and sat down against the wall on the other side of the cell, drew his knees up to his chest and hugged his arms around them, trying to conserve a bit of warmth. From outside, he could hear the faint sounds of voices – revellers making their way home, he supposed. Somewhere a woman was singing, drunk, out of tune, shrieking like a dying gull. Someone shouted at her to shut up but she carried on, louder than before. *Go on, girl, you sing while you still can*, Mat thought. As tuneless as it was, her singing was a lifeline right now. A link to the living. And, in all honesty, he didn't know for how long he'd be able to count himself amongst them.

When Mat woke up the next morning, there were a few blessed moments when he couldn't remember where he was. Then, with all the crushing weight of a bad hangover, the memories of the night before came thudding down upon him and he opened his eyes to see the rough stone walls of the small cell he'd been thrown into. He groaned as he rolled over, then slowly sat up, aching and stiff with cold.

In the early-morning light, as he stretched and cracked his back and rubbed some life into his arms and legs, things didn't look much brighter. He couldn't escape, that much was clear. All he could hope for now was a lenient magistrate, though they were rare as hen's teeth. He wasn't the first, and he certainly wouldn't be the last, to be caught on the take, and with it being his first offence, well, he might be lucky.

He had to hold on to that hope, for it was the only hope he had.

His thoughts were interrupted by the sound of the bolt on the other side of the door drawing open, and a young constable peered cautiously into the cell.

'In you come,' Mat said, 'I'll be no danger to you.' He stood back, palms open as though to demonstrate that he posed no threat.

The chap came in and Mat saw the cutlass hanging from his belt. If only he could get hold of that. But then what? Slice his way through the entire Thames River Police and out into the street? No, it was useless to think of escape.

'Breakfast,' the constable said, holding out a bowl and spoon.

Mat took it with a nod of thanks. It was gruel, the colour and consistency of bilge water with some questionable lumps floating about in it, but he was ravenous and it was better than a poke in the eye with a sharp stick. He dug in.

'You'll be up before the magistrate tomorrow,' the constable said.

He couldn't be more than twenty, Mat thought, though he looked even younger. His cheeks reddened as he spoke and he looked mostly at the floor. A shy chap. Probably forced into the job by his ma and pa. Who would choose to become a river pig? The most hated men on the Thames as far as Mat and his fellow dock workers were concerned. But if he could get friendly with this chap, then perhaps he might help him. It was a long shot but worth a try.

'Good sort, is he? The magistrate?' Mat asked, and the young fellow squirmed and shuffled his feet. 'Don't worry, I'm only joking. What is it they say, a magistrate is like a restless man in bed.'

'What?' The constable looked confused.

'He lies on one side, then turns round and lies on the other!'

The constable looked bemused. Comprehension slowly dawned and he laughed before glancing nervously over his shoulder at the door.

'Well, until then, you'll be kept here,' he said, cheeks reddening even more. 'You'll get another meal later on.'

'Lucky me,' Mat said, letting some of the gruel dribble down from his spoon and back into his bowl. 'It reminds me of the last time I had the runs.'

Mat grinned and the chap laughed again; he was no more than a kid really.

'Any chance of getting a message out of here?' Mat asked, trying to sound as casual as he could.

'Oh no – I mean, that's not permitted, I'm afraid.'

'Righto.' Mat thought for a second; should he risk it? Nothing ventured, nothing gained. 'If you were to get a message out for me, it wouldn't go unrewarded.'

'I don't— What do you mean?' He glanced back at the door again but it was closed. No one could hear them.

Mat bent down and extracted a coin from the hem of his right trouser leg. He held it up for the constable to see. 'There's more where that came from,' he said and jiggled his leg.

'How did you…? You shouldn't have that.' The constable reached for it.

'Now, you could report this,' Mat said. 'But if you do, that's gonna get your mate who signed me in last night in trouble, isn't it? I mean, he shouldn't have missed this, should he?' The young man shifted uneasily and Mat continued. 'And I imagine he wouldn't take too kindly to you getting him in trouble. Looked a bit of a bully to me.'

The constable looked at the floor again; Mat seemed to have struck a nerve.

'All I need,' Mat went on, 'is for you to get a message delivered to a mate of mine. In return, you can have half of all I've got. And no one's any the wiser. What do you say?'

'I...' He hesitated, chewed his bottom lip. 'Very well. Just one message. You'd better be quick or they'll wonder what I'm doing in here so long.'

Mat thought for a moment, then leaned forward and whispered in the young chap's ear. The constable nodded and pocketed the coins Mat offered him before leaving, the bolt scraping into place once more. Mat scooped up the rest of his gruel and gulped it down, trying to taste it as little as possible.

He didn't know what anyone could do for him, didn't even know if the message would get through, but he did know that if anyone could help him now, that person was his old friend Joe. The constable had said he'd be sentenced tomorrow and, if the worst was to come, then he wanted to get a message to his sister. He wanted to say goodbye. He closed his eyes and prayed that the message would reach Joe in time.

Chapter 28

Mercy was glad when a soft knocking at the door indicated that it was morning at last. It was Lucy, come to light the fire. She lifted herself up to sit as Lucy began quietly to go about her work; kneeling to light the flint, then blowing into the grate until the kindling began to catch and burn. Then just as quietly she left.

Mercy had spent a restless night, unaware for most of it whether she was waking or dreaming. It had been a night of strange visions: rolling seas; hands reaching out to grab at her; Dr Stephens's face, floating, disembodied. As she tried to order her disordered mind, she remembered her brother – had Joe been able to find him?

Joe was in the kitchen. He'd been out until late looking for Mat, but there'd been no sign of him.

'I'm sorry,' he said. 'I'll try again today. Maybe it's not too late.'

But she felt sure that it was too late. Matthew could be anywhere by now. Sailing away across the world. Gone from her life before she'd had a chance to know him. And she'd been so cruel when they last met. She couldn't bear to think about it. She was so ashamed to think of how she'd left him in the park, how she'd despised him for being poor, for being badly dressed. How disgusted she was with herself now.

She had to speak to Dr Stephens. However hard it might be, she had to do it.

'Before you go,' Mrs Alford said when Mercy went to say goodbye, 'there's something that I think you should have.' She handed Mercy a brooch, quite old and battered. 'It was Matthew's. He gave it to me but I think you should have it.'

Mercy turned the brooch over in her hands. In the centre was an oval piece of enamel, decorated with an abstract design in jade green and gold, and around that were delicately wrought twists of metal, rather tarnished and bent in places. She rubbed her thumb over it, held it to her mouth as if to kiss it.

'Thank you,' she said, and Mrs Alford embraced her and wished her luck. 'You are welcome here any time,' she said. 'John and I will always be happy to see you.'

After saying her farewells, Mercy left out of the back door and as she opened the gate into the alley beyond, she almost collided with a young boy running in the other direction. A rough little thing, his trousers patched and ragged, and wearing only a thin shirt on what was a particularly chilly morning.

'Slow down! Where are you going in such a hurry?'

'Got a message,' the boy said.

Her heart leapt for a moment. Could it be from Matthew? 'Who for?'

'Joe,' said the boy. 'He live here?'

'Yes,' Mercy said, her brief hopes dashed. 'Yes, Joe lives here. Just knock on the back door there. And here, take this. Get yourself something to eat.' She handed him a coin, which he pocketed instantly and trotted across the yard to the back door.

Mercy sighed and continued on down the alley. Matthew wasn't coming back. She couldn't blame him after the way she had treated him. She could hardly believe that he had found her after all this time and she had turned him away. The guilt was almost overwhelming. She had pinned the brooch to her coat and she touched it lightly now. At least she had something to remember him by. She turned onto the main road, heading for Cowley Street. She owed it to Matthew – and to herself – to find out the truth about what had happened to them. And there was only one person who could tell her that.

She faced Mrs Stephens across the parlour, that very same room where months ago she had sat, shy as a field mouse, in awe of this dazzling woman. Now, they stood, Mercy in hat and coat, Mrs Stephens still in her dressing gown, her hair undone, a cup of chocolate in her hand.

'What is all this, Mercy? What is going on?'

'I need to speak to Dr Stephens. Is he here?'

'Mercy, where have you been? You've been out all night, without a word to anyone, and now you're demanding to speak to my husband?'

'I don't need your permission to stay out,' Mercy said. 'Is he here?'

'Young lady, I think you are forgetting yourself,' Mrs Stephens said. She put down her cup and drew her gown around herself. 'I think you are forgetting that you are—'

'That I am what?' Mercy demanded. 'Your servant? Your slave?'

Mrs Stephens looked at her as though Mercy had slapped her around the face. 'No,' she said, more softly now, 'no. That's not what I meant at all. Mercy, you are very dear to me, I hope you know that.'

Mercy looked away. Mrs Stephens had been good to her, mostly. She had given her so much, but that couldn't outweigh the fact that she had lied to her for all this time.

'I'll go and find him myself,' she said and turned to go; he would be in his study, no doubt.

'He's not here,' said Mrs Stephens. 'I assure you, he is not here. Now, what is all this about?'

Mercy turned back towards her. 'Why didn't you tell me?'

'Tell you what?'

'That you knew me from when I was a little girl.' Mercy heard her own voice breaking. 'That I'm not the daughter of a prince. That I was a slave. A poor, miserable slave.' Tears were falling fast now and she gulped for breath, wiped her face with her sleeve.

'What are you talking about?' Mrs Stephens came towards her but she backed away.

'Don't touch me. Don't touch me. And don't lie to me!'

'Mercy, I don't know what you're saying. I met you when you came here a few months ago, you know that. I'd never seen you before, never heard about you until my husband mentioned you.'

Was she acting? It was so hard to tell. Mercy had seen her in performance mode so many times; at events and parties, in meetings and on the doorstep. She was so good at saying just what people wanted to hear. Is that what she was doing now?

'You're lying,' she said, shaking her head. 'You and your husband. You've lied to me my whole life.'

'No, Mercy, no. Where's all this come from? Who's been telling you this?'

'I've read it with my own eyes.'

'Read what?' Mrs Stephens really did look confused – was it possible that she truly didn't know?

'The letter from Mrs Whitworth. The notebook from the ship.'

'Ship? What ship?'

'The ship that Dr Stephens was working on. The slave ship. The *Duke of Buckleigh*.'

'Now you really have lost me.' Mrs Stephens held up her hands as though in surrender and went back to her chair and her half-eaten breakfast. 'I think you're having another of your episodes, Mercy, dear. When Edwin comes back we'll have him make you a tincture. Something to calm you. Here, have some bread. It was baked fresh this morning.'

'You really don't know, do you?'

Mercy began to laugh despite herself. Mrs Catherine Stephens, the acclaimed abolitionist, the saintly heroine, so charitable that she had even taken a poor black girl into her own home, was married to a former slaver.

'Stop it, stop it!' Mrs Stephens cried, her eyes wide, colour rising on her neck and cheeks.

'Your husband' – Mercy spat the words out like apple pips – 'your kindly, caring, gentlemanly husband, worked on a slave ship.'

'You've gone quite mad.' Mrs Stephens looked afraid of her now. 'Why are you saying all this?'

'Because it's true! I've seen his diary. He was the ship's doctor. He chained and whipped and punished people – my people – as if we were nothing. Worse than nothing. He's a murderer. He's an evil murderer!'

Without warning, Mrs Stephens flew at her with a cry like a wild animal and Mercy jumped back in astonishment.

'How dare you! How dare you, you filthy little bitch!' Mrs Stephens's face was contorted with rage as she tried to grab and claw at Mercy.

She was almost unrecognisable in her anger and for a moment, Mercy was motionless with shock before she held up her arms to defend herself. They grappled for a moment, Mercy holding Mrs Stephens off with all her strength. As they fought, Mrs Stephens caught her hand on Matthew's brooch which Mercy had just that morning pinned to her coat, pulling it off and sending it flying through the air. Mrs Stephens sprang back with a cry of pain as she caught her finger on the pin. Mercy, desperate not to lose the one thing she had left of her brother, dashed to grab the brooch from the floor where it had fallen and the two women stood panting, staring at one another.

Mrs Stephens looked at the brooch in Mercy's hand and her expression changed quite suddenly.

'What is that?' she said, her voice low.

'It's nothing.'

'Let me see it.'

Mercy made to move away but, quick as a viper, Mrs Stephens grabbed hold of her wrist with one hand and took up the brooch with the other. 'Where did you get this?'

'It was my brother's. Give it back.'

'Brother?' Mrs Stephens let go of Mercy's wrist.

There was something so odd about her expression, as though the sight of this old, tatty piece of jewellery was more shocking than hearing that her husband was a slave trader. Mercy watched her as she turned the brooch over, and then she twisted or clicked some part of it and the back sprang open. Mrs Stephens let out a sound; half-sigh, half-moan.

'What is it?' Mercy asked.

Mrs Stephens looked at her then. Her eyes dark, her mouth half-open.

'Mercy, this is my brooch,' she said. 'I gave it to him. I gave this to Edwin.'

Mercy looked at the brooch in her open hand. Inside was a small coil of chestnut-brown hair. The very same hair that now hung loose around Mrs Stephens's shoulders.

Chapter 29

The hours passed slowly. From time to time Mat heard noises on the other side of the door, and his heart jumped into his mouth as he thought they were coming for him – had they changed their minds and were going to sentence him today? Or could it be Joe, come to visit him? But then he'd hear the footsteps passing on, the voices moving away, and he'd settle down again.

To the other side, he could hear the sounds of the outside world, now so distant, as people went about their business. The street-hawkers, the dock workers, the rattle of a carriage moving along the cobbles. The window was positioned high up on the wall – to discourage thoughts of escape, he supposed – and he could see only a small square of grey sky. He fixed his eyes on it, watching as clouds met and merged then melted away. Occasionally he would see a gull or a pigeon fly past, and once he saw a cormorant, that familiar silhouette with its long neck stretched out, and it gave him a tiny bit of hope.

He hated being cooped up. Hated it more than anything. He got up and paced around the cell, his nose now accustomed to the stink of the bucket. He probably didn't smell much better himself. It was a square room, no more than seven foot across, with bare brick walls and a small fireplace – empty, of course. If it got much colder they'd have to light a fire for him, surely? He'd freeze to death in here – though maybe that's what they wanted.

He patted his arms and jumped up and down a few times. If only he hadn't tried to sell that last package. He cursed himself for the hundredth time. How could he have been so stupid? And how was he going to get out of this one?

He must have nodded off at some point because the next thing he knew, he was woken by the sound of the bolt. Was it food? Or were they going to drag him off to the magistrate after all? He struggled to his feet as the door opened. It was the young officer who'd brought him his breakfast.

'You've got a visitor,' he said. 'I can't give you long.'

He stepped aside and Joe walked into the cell with a grin. Mat thought he had never been so happy to see anyone in his entire life.

The officer closed the door, leaving them alone, and they hugged each other tightly.

'You stink worse than usual,' Joe said, wrinkling his nose as he stepped back.

'And that's saying something!' Mat said, and they laughed and clapped each other on the back.

'I thought you might not come,' Mat said. 'Wasn't even sure if the message would get to you. Thank you.'

'Little lad turned up at the door,' said Joe. 'When he told me Mr Matondo was in trouble, well, I had to come and see for myself. And he was not wrong.' Joe looked around the room, let out a silent whistle. 'What happened?'

Mat explained and Joe slowly shook his head.

'I should never have left you unattended,' he said. 'Here's me, been getting away with every crime save rape and murder since I was knee-high to a grasshopper, and Mr Matondo goes and gets himself caught after nicking a bit of baccy!'

Mat wanted to smile but somehow having Joe here, knowing that Joe was going to turn around and walk out of here when Mat himself could not, brought home to him how serious his situation was.

'Hey,' said Joe, seeing his expression. 'I have some news that will cheer you up. Your sister came to see you.'

'What do you mean?'

'Mercy. Malundama. She turned up at the Alfords' looking for you.'

Mat could barely take this in.

'I can't believe it, Joe. Did she really come?' He could feel tears spring to his eyes and made no effort to wipe them away.

'She sure did. Seems she believes you now. Sent me out to look for you last night. And she read that notebook you left at the Alfords'. She's on the warpath. Said she's going to have it out with that doctor fella. Find out the truth.'

'But he's dangerous!' Mat said. 'Joe, I think he killed a man. She needs to stay away from him. I have to get out of here, Joe. I have to see her!' Mat hit the wall with the flat of his hand, let out a cry of frustration. How could he protect her from inside these four walls?

'Quiet, quiet,' said Joe. 'Let me think.'

Joe began to walk around the room checking the walls and the window, his expression one of absolute concentration. He tested the bars of the window, as Mat had done the night before, pressed his fingers into the edges of the bricks, feeling for any sort of weakness. Then he came to the fireplace and crouched down so he could try to look up into the chimney. He let out a breath and tapped his chin with one finger, then turned to Mat and looked him up and down.

'I think it's our only option,' he said.

'What?' Mat asked. He'd already ruled that out as a means of escape – it was tiny for one thing and even if he could get up it, which he couldn't, he would be on the roof of a police office with no way down.

'Ever heard of Jack Sheppard?' said Joe as he reached into the lining of his coat and pulled out a coil of rope, followed by a metal file.

'No,' said Mat.

'Well, you're about to do a Jack Sheppard, Mr Matondo. Here, hide these, we haven't got long.'

His plan was simple: once it started to get dark, Mat would climb up the chimney and out onto the roof, then he would climb across to the building next door, which was a boat-mender's workshop, and from there use the rope to get down onto the street and away. Joe would be outside and would give Mat a signal when it was safe to climb down.

'I'll whistle, like this.' Joe gave a low two-tone whistle and it reminded Mat of how his mother used to call him and his sister in after one of their games of hide-and-seek, or when she wanted them home for dinner. He wondered if she was looking down on him. He'd never much believed in that sort of thing, but now the thought was rather comforting.

'What if I get stuck?' he asked. He'd heard of sweeps getting lodged in the chimneys until someone came to free them, or even suffocating inside.

'You won't,' Joe said. 'You'll make a perfect little flue-faker! You're skinny enough.'

'Joe, I can't do it.' Mat hesitated. He hated to admit his fear. 'I'm not – good with small spaces. Give me anything else – give me sharks, give me lions, give me the devil himself and I'll fight him. But being cooped up gives me the terrors.'

'It's the only way, Mat. If you don't get out of here you could get locked up for a very long time – or worse. And don't you want to see your sister again?'

Mat knew then that he had to try. He had to do it for Malu.

'It won't take long,' Joe went on. 'It'll be over before you know it. And if it worked for old Jack Sheppard, it can work for you.'

'Did he get away then?'

'Sure did,' Joe said. 'Well, that time anyway.'

'What do you mean, that time?' Joe avoided his eye.

'Let's just say his luck ran out. Ended up meeting his maker at Tyburn.'

They heard the sound of footsteps then, approaching the door.

'Joe. I don't think I can—'

'Good luck, Mr Matondo,' Joe said. As the officer opened the door, he started to speak in a pompous kind of voice. 'You're in the hands of God now, Matthew. And I pray that you will find forgiveness for your sins.' He flashed a smile at Mat, then turned a serious face to the officer. 'Thank you, my man. Take good care of this reprobate, won't you?'

The officer blushed and nodded. He showed Joe out and the door slammed shut behind them. Mat squatted down and peered up inside the flue. It was dark as the devil's arse in there. Was he really going to do this? It looked like he had no choice but to try.

Chapter 30

Mercy told Mrs Stephens everything. She was worried that Mrs Stephens would be furious that Mercy had searched her husband's desk, but she barely even reacted. She simply sat and listened to the whole thing with an occasional nod of her head or a tightening of her lips. Then she asked Mercy to show her the papers and she glanced through the notebook, her face bloodless, her eyes darting across the words on the page. Mercy had never seen her so quiet, so withdrawn. It was as though a light had gone out, all her customary cheer and sparkle completely gone.

'You really didn't know any of this?' Mercy asked her.

'No.' She was still holding the brooch, staring at it as though it might bite her. 'He told me he was going to Sierra Leone. It was around the time that the English settlement there was being created. He said he wanted to help. He said he was going out to work as a doctor and to train others. We'd met not long before.'

She gazed out of the window, twisted a strand of hair around her finger as she talked.

'I was so in love with him. He asked me to marry him but I was so worried that he would leave and forget all about me, so I gave him this brooch. It had been my mother's but I wanted him to have it. I cut off some hair – I remember it so vividly – and I held it to my lips and kissed it and placed it inside. As though, if he had a part of me with him, he wouldn't forget me.'

As she talked, telling Mercy of how she had waited those long months for him to come back, how he had returned with money and an engagement ring in his pocket, how he had been so keen to get involved with her work campaigning against slavery, she began to pace about the room, her voice rising.

'We'd just achieved the great victory,' she said, thumping the top of the armchair. 'The end of the trade in slaves! We knew there was still a long way to go – to end slavery completely – but it was a huge step. He celebrated with me! He looked me in the eye and smiled at me and kissed me, and all the time – all the time he…'

Mercy nodded. He had betrayed them both, it seemed. And true to form, Mrs Stephens was far more concerned about the impact on herself than on how Mercy was affected. How had she ever looked up to this woman? Outwardly so concerned for others, but in reality barely able to see beyond her own nose. Mercy realised now what she had long suspected: that to Mrs Stephens, she had been nothing more than a useful prop – something to show the world how much she cared.

'I need to see him,' Mrs Stephens said. She rang the bell for Martin, who for once lost his smirk when he saw Mrs Stephens practically quivering with anger.

'He has a meeting,' Martin stammered.

'Who with?' Mrs Stephens replied.

'Sir Jonathan. He said he was going to see Sir Jonathan Hazelwood.'

'Very well. Organise a carriage to Sir Jonathan's offices. As quickly as you can.' Mrs Stephens snapped her fingers at him and he darted out of the room.

Jonathan Hazelwood. JH. Could it be? There was only one way to find out.

'I'm coming with you,' said Mercy.

'No,' Mrs Stephens said quickly. 'He is *my* husband and I will speak to him.'

But any power she had held over Mercy had gone, dissolved like sugar in hot tea, and she seemed to know it.

'I'm coming with you,' Mercy repeated. 'This is my life we're talking about. I deserve to know where I came from, to know what happened to me.'

Soon they sat opposite each other in a carriage, rocking gently from side to side as they made their way into the city, to the offices of Sir Jonathan Hazelwood MP. Mrs Stephens had been surprised at that. Why was Dr Stephens having a private meeting with Sir Jonathan? She was the one who was talking to him about supporting a Bill in Parliament to abolish slavery. Mercy said nothing of her own suspicions. She was sure Sir Jonathan was the JH from the note. *We have nothing to worry about*, it had said. Sir Jonathan was mixed up in this business too and Mercy needed to find out how.

They arrived at his offices and jumped out of the carriage. Mrs Stephens told the driver to wait, tipping him handsomely for his trouble. The doorman looked Mercy up and down with pursed lips, but Mrs Stephens swept past him and Mercy followed in her wake. Through the main hallway they went, past the front desk with a nod to the man behind it who barely had time to stand, let alone try to stop them, and up the great stairway to the offices above.

Sir Jonathan was alone. He was sitting behind a great desk and rose to his feet as they came in.

'Catherine, my dear, what a pleasure to see you!'

He ignored Mercy, didn't even register her presence. He came around the desk to greet Mrs Stephens and Mercy noticed how the curl of his lip when he smiled was just the same as his son's. *He probably behaves in exactly the same way*, Mercy thought, and she shuddered, thinking back to that night.

He explained that Dr Stephens had indeed been there a little earlier but that he had left and that, no, he hadn't said where he was going, and was there anything he could do to help?

'Oh, no,' said Mrs Stephens with her most charming smile, 'it's nothing at all.'

'Are you sure he didn't say where he was going?' Mercy said, and Sir Jonathan turned his gaze to her for the first time.

'I have just told you that he did not,' he said firmly.

'Come along, Mercy,' Mrs Stephens was saying. 'We don't want to waste any more of Sir Jonathan's time.'

But Mercy held Sir Jonathan's gaze. She was sure he knew more than he was letting on.

'Why did he come to see you today?' Mercy said, hearing Mrs Stephens tut at this impertinence.

'I'm afraid all matters of business are confidential, young lady.' Sir Jonathan's voice was velvet but his look was hard as iron.

'Of course,' she said meekly. She was certain there was more to it but she had to be careful. Sir Jonathan was a powerful man. Her gaze was drawn to a painting on the wall behind him. It was a seascape and she let out a gasp as the image became clear to her. It was a shipwreck. Several small boats, packed with people, tossed about in a foamy sea.

'Mercy?' Mrs Stephens's voice sounded very far away.

She remembered the Géricault painting, how it had troubled her and she hadn't realised why. It had troubled the doctor too. And yet he'd gone back to see it again and again. Of course. She knew then where the doctor had gone, knew with a certainty that she couldn't explain but couldn't deny either.

'Mercy!' said Mrs Stephens again. 'Are you quite all right?'

Mercy knew this was something she needed to do alone. Without a word, she dashed from the room, leaving a bewildered Mrs Stephens behind her. She flew down the stairs and out into the street where the carriage still waited. Climbing in, she explained that Mrs Stephens had been detained and that she would be continuing alone.

'You can come back for her once you've dropped me off,' she said to the driver as he urged the horses on and they began to move.

'Where to?' he asked.

'Piccadilly, please. To the Egyptian Hall.'

Chapter 31

At some point in the afternoon – he'd lost all track of time now – the officer appeared again, this time with a bowl of soup. It wasn't too bad, actually; a bit of meat, a few chunks of potato and a sliver or two of onion. He tried to make it last but he was starving and it was gone in no time. He licked the metal bowl until there was nothing left. It would soon be time. Once they'd come to collect his bowl, that would be it. His chance to escape. He just hoped he wasn't too late. Hoped that Malu wasn't in any danger from Dr Stephens.

He still wasn't at all sure that he could make it up the narrow chimney – for all he knew it would be blocked off further up. He tortured himself with thoughts of getting stuck, unable to go back, unable to go forward. The thought was unbearable.

The officer came back to take his bowl away. He had a blanket over his arm and he held it out now.

'Here. Thought you might need this.'

Mat grabbed it gratefully and wrapped it around his shoulders.

'Thank you,' he said, and the officer nodded and left him alone again. He almost felt sorry for the poor chap. He'd be bound to get the blame when they found out he'd scarpered.

This was it, then. If he was going to do it, he had to do it now. Outside the sky was darkening and somewhere out there, Joe would be waiting for him. He crossed himself, said a prayer to a god he didn't entirely believe in, and made a silent wish to the spirits of his mother and his father and all the ancestors before him, to help him now.

He took off his jacket. It would mean he'd get cold if – no, when – he did get outside, but he needed to be as streamlined as possible and the jacket was far too bulky. He arranged the blanket and the jacket so that, at a glance, it might look like he was lying down. It wouldn't fool anyone for long but it might buy him a few precious seconds if anyone did come in. He had the rope that Joe had given him circled around his waist – he'd need that to get down from the roof, if he made it that far – and the file was stashed down one trouser leg.

He had to crouch down to get into the opening of the chimney, but being pretty nimble from all those years clambering up masts and ropes, he managed to get down low enough that he could get his head up inside. It was dark and cold, and the walls were stained black from years of smoke and grime. There was just enough room to wedge himself up inside and, as it was made of brick, there were small ridges that served as fingerholds.

As he began to inch his way up, he kicked off his boots, letting them tumble back into the hearth below. He would be better off barefoot so that he could use his toes to grip and push himself up. There was no sign of daylight up above him and reaching in with his arm, he realised that there was a bend in the chimney that led to a sloping section. He slowly pushed himself up, feeling the skin on his knees and his elbows being grazed right off by the rough brick walls. All he could hear was his own breathing, ragged and unnaturally loud in this confined space.

Making his way along the sloping section, he came to another slight bend and found the chimney went straight up above him, though he could still see no sign of the night air above. Maybe it was blocked. Maybe they'd sealed it off because they didn't use that fireplace any more. Maybe it was bricked over and he'd be stuck in here and they wouldn't find him until it was too late. *Keep calm, Matty boy, keep calm.* He knew that if he began to panic, he'd be done for. He just had to take it one step at a time.

He was sweating now, sweating from every inch of his body, and as the perspiration mixed with the dust from the walls it made his skin itch and prickle. Sweat ran into his eyes and he could do nothing but try to blink it away. He stifled a cry as he gouged the side of his big toe on a rough bit of brick. He took a moment to rest – every muscle in his body was on fire and his toe was throbbing so that it felt three times its normal size. His fingers were beginning to go numb from the pressure of gripping and clawing his way up.

Take it steady, he told himself. He knew that the more he tensed up and the more he panicked, the harder it would be. He needed to conserve his energy, to control his fear. He thought about the open sea, pictured gently rolling waves and a great wide sky. If he ever wanted to see that sight again, he had to do this. He forced himself to breathe more slowly and began to push himself up higher, higher, inch by painful inch.

He had no idea how long he had been going. It was as though time had stopped and he was in some strange otherworld. He strained to listen for any sound below or above but could hear nothing. He must be passing the room above his cell by now, and he prayed that no one would hear him on the other side of the wall. Hopefully if they did, they'd think it was a pigeon or something fallen down into the chimney. Surely, surely, he must be nearly at the top.

There was another bend in the chimney now, shorter this time so that he had to contort himself to get round it, his back in agony, his clothing ripped and shredded. For a strange moment he felt like the world had been turned upside down and that he was actually burrowing down rather than climbing up; like some huge worm wriggling down into the dark, dark earth. Then, as he tried to get round the final part of the bend, he realised with horror that he was stuck. One arm was trapped awkwardly against his body and he couldn't seem to free it. He twisted his torso and strained to pull his arm out but it just wouldn't budge, and he could feel a thousand pins and needles sticking into the flesh of his forearm and hand.

The minutes passed by and still he remained where he was, his thigh muscles shaking as his legs pressed up against the sides of the chimney, holding himself in place. In his twisted position, he could no longer breathe properly, each breath too shallow, too fast. He was feeling light-headed, and he closed his eyes and pressed his forehead up against the brick that was cold as the grave against his sweat-soaked skin.

His body was growing numb and he gave in to the feeling. He was so tired. So tired. He could sleep a little. Just a little. Just for a while. He felt as though he was drifting and he thought of his old friend the cormorant, soaring through the air, wings outstretched. Then he thought of his sister, of her solemn eyes and how they had lit up when they danced together, of how he had held her hand when she was a little girl, and he told her he would find her.

He opened his eyes and, with a surge of strength he didn't know he had, he pushed himself up, twisting as he did so, so that his arm came free and he could breathe more deeply. He cried with relief, the tears washing some of the grit and dust out of his eyes, then with a last push with his legs and feet he squeezed up and round the bend into the next section of the chimney. It was slightly wider than what had come before, and as he tipped his head up to look ahead, he saw a small circle of sky and felt a draught of cold air on his face.

But he wasn't free yet. With a new surge of fear, he saw that the chimney pot was far too narrow for him to get through. Reaching up, he felt around the base of the pot with his fingertips. Where it met the top of the flue, he could feel the grainy texture of mortar which was holding the pot in place. He slid one hand down the side of his body and felt for the metal file which Joe had given him. Carefully, ever so carefully, he pulled it out. If he dropped it now, he'd be well and truly done for.

The mortar was quite soft and as he scratched it away, pieces of it started to crumble off and fall back down onto his face. He closed his eyes and dug frantically with the blade, desperate now to get out. He had to get out. Stabbing blindly above him, he felt something give and heard the pot topple over and roll away down the roof. If anyone had heard that, he was in trouble, but at this moment he didn't even care. He just had to get out of this blasted chimney. He heaved himself up and out of the opening he had made, collapsing onto the cold and welcoming leads of the roof.

He lay there for several minutes, taking huge gulping breaths of air, before he gingerly sat up and looked around. It was late by now and almost completely dark. He could see the river stretching out below and behind him: the forest of masts, the huge hulking warehouses.

Keeping low, he edged along until he could just about peep down onto the street below and made the whistling sound that was the agreed signal. But there was no reply. Had he taken too long to climb up? Had Joe left, thinking perhaps that Mat had changed his mind? He'd have to do this on his own then. Just in case, he whistled once more and this time, to his great relief, he heard Joe's answering whistle and saw Joe himself step out of the shadows across the street and give him a cheery wave.

Mat waved back and Joe pointed to indicate which way Mat needed to head to get onto the roof of the boat-mender's. He crawled along the roof, trying to ignore the pain in his knees and his hands and, well, every blessed part of his body, until he came to the place where the two roofs met. He climbed across and made his way slowly to the edge, lying on his stomach to look down to the street below. He was three storeys up and there was no way that even Mat the Cat could jump that distance.

There was a row of dormer windows along this side of the building that protruded out from the roof. That'd be a good place to start, but there were no other footholds or ledges for some way down from there, from what he could see. He didn't want to get this far and then end up splattered on the cobbles below. He'd seen men injured and even killed after falling from the top of a mast, and it was not a pretty sight. He pitied the injured more than the dead in some cases; at least the dead 'uns had been put out of their misery.

Mat uncoiled the rope that was still around his waist, a little frayed but still in one piece. He leaned out and looped one end around the ornamental finial that sat atop the pitched roof of the nearest window. After tying it in a bowline knot, Mat threw the other end out so that it snaked down the side of the building. His fingers burned from the climb up the chimney but he had to be quick. What if someone noticed he was gone?

He tugged on the rope a few times. It felt pretty secure, but just as he was preparing to climb over and begin his descent to the street, he heard Joe's warning whistle and he froze. Looking down, he saw two river pigs walking down the road towards the building, one holding a lamp up ahead, both of them with cutlasses hanging from their belts. Were they on to him already?

He held his breath and crouched, silent and still as a gargoyle, on the edge of the roof. The two men were walking towards him and he willed them not to look up. He had nowhere to hide. Then a shout from across the road took the officers' attention. It was Joe. He beckoned them over and Mat could see him gesticulating wildly in the other direction as he spoke to them. A moment later, the two officers headed back up the street – whatever Joe had told them had obviously worked. He certainly had the gift of the gab.

Joe whistled again so he knew he was safe to go on, and without further thought or hesitation, he grabbed hold of the rope and climbed out over the edge. He managed to swing himself to the edge of the window and, as quickly as he could, began to make his way down the side of the building, facing in towards the wall, his bare feet kicking against the bricks, his arms and shoulders burning with exertion. He got to the second row of windows and paused. Light was shining out from within; someone was in there. But he had to go on, and so, as soundlessly as possible, he skirted down past the window frame, praying that whoever was inside wouldn't decide to peer out at that moment.

Once safely past, he looked down and saw that he was now only about ten feet off the ground. Joe was below him, checking this way and that for any passers-by, looking up at Mat with a grin. The rope, however, was about to run out and he realised he was going to have to jump. He whistled to Joe who looked up to see Mat, clothes tattered, hands and feet bleeding, dropping towards him. He put out his arms just in time and the two men fell in a heap to the ground, Mat almost laughing, almost crying with relief.

'Come on,' said Joe, dragging Mat to his feet, 'we need to get you out of here!'

Chapter 32

Mercy got out of the carriage and ran towards the Egyptian Hall, narrowly avoiding several other vehicles as she did, their drivers shouting at her in irritation. She thought back to her first visit here. She had been so in awe of the Stephenses then, of how cultured they were, how wealthy, how happy they were together. She had felt so proud to be on the doctor's arm. Now that felt like a world away; the thin veneer of their lives had been scratched off to reveal the tarnished truth within.

She paid her penny entrance fee to the man on the door and went through the hallway, this time not stopping to look at the objects and exhibits. It was a weekday and so the museum was much quieter than before. Her footsteps echoed as she walked through the halls. As she approached the Géricault room she wondered if she'd got it wrong. Dr Stephens could be anywhere in London. But no, there he was.

He had his back to her and was sitting on a bench in front of the painting. He wasn't looking at it, though; he had his head in his hands, much like that night she had come upon him in the kitchen. That night when he had held her hand and she had felt so special.

Mercy watched him for a moment or two, unsure now how she should begin. Perhaps it was all a huge mistake, a misunderstanding. It must be. She glanced up at the painting that had so disturbed her that last time. It still turned her stomach but she forced herself not to look away.

As she looked at it, once again she felt that she could smell the sea-soaked wood of the raft, the death and decay of the bodies strewn across it, that she could feel the splash of sea spray on her face, hear the cries of despair and desperation. She let out a gasp and Dr Stephens turned to her, his face etched with misery, his skin blotchy.

'Mercy,' he said and stood to face her. 'Whatever are you doing here?' He struggled to adopt his usual wry manner, but she could see that he was surprised to see her.

'You asked me once what I dream about, do you remember?' Mercy asked him.

The doctor nodded, bewildered.

'I lied,' she went on. 'I think I told you that I dreamed about Hamblin but that wasn't true. I dream about a woman, not much older than I am now, a woman with gentle hands and slim arms wearing bracelets. But I can never see her face. She's my own mother and yet I don't remember her face, or her voice, or anything about her.'

'That's very sad,' the doctor said. 'It is very hard to lose one's parents so young.'

'I didn't lose them,' she said, feeling incredibly calm. 'They were taken from me. Or rather, I was taken from them. But then you already know that. Don't you?'

'Mercy, I don't know what you mean. Your father died—'

'Do you know what else I dream about?'

He said nothing but he looked – what? Afraid. Yes, he looked afraid.

'I dream about arms reaching out for help. I dream about water and darkness and overwhelming fear. That's what you dream about too. Don't you?'

'I don't know what…' He took a slight step backwards and she advanced towards him.

'What happened? On the ship, on the *Duke of Buckleigh*?'

Now he looked as though he had seen a ghost and his eyes flicked towards the door; but Mercy was between him and the way out.

'Tell me what happened! I know most of it. I know you took me, separated me from my brother. I know you were on that ship. The ship's doctor. Ha! Tell me, how can a doctor, one who has vowed to care for people, to make them well, how can he whip and beat and starve those in his care?'

His eyes darted from side to side like a caged animal. 'I had to do it. Had to.' He held his hands up to his face. 'Oh God, how I wish it could be otherwise.'

'What do you mean?' she demanded, going to him now, seizing his arm, forcing him to look at her.

'I've made amends, haven't I? I've made amends.' He gripped her arms now, his face desperate. 'But it's not enough, is it? I can never do enough, and now he's coming for me. Just like he came for Dudley and Booth. There's no escape. He'll find me in the end. And I deserve it, I suppose.'

What did he mean? Matthew had said that Stephens killed Booth – and probably Dudley too – so who was he talking about? Was this all part of his derangement? She glanced back towards the door. Would anyone come if she cried out for help?

'Come, let's sit down,' she said, leading him back to the bench. 'I don't understand. Who is coming for you?'

'He's one of them. It's impossible, I know, but he's come back for vengeance.'

'Who? Tell me what happened.'

He looked at her and his eyes were full of tears. He shook his head and a few drops were dislodged and rolled down his face. He did nothing to wipe them away.

'You were always so beautiful,' he said. 'The others mocked me for it. Thought there was something unnatural in my interest in you. But it wasn't like that. I could see you were special. And you were so good-natured. Such a ray of light in that most miserable of places.'

'The ship?' She spoke gently; he seemed so fragile and she knew she must tread carefully, try not to anger or provoke him.

'I never wanted to be there. My parents had died – I didn't lie to you about that – they died when I was young, and there was no money, you see? And in this world, what are you if you don't have money? I managed to train as a physician, with the help of an uncle, but once he too passed away there was no one to help me.'

Such self-pity, thought Mercy. He and Mrs Stephens were well matched after all. Each thought only of themselves. But she needed to know so she said nothing, simply nodded, encouraged him to go on.

'I only made a few voyages. I hated it from the start. Hated everything about it. The cramped conditions, the food, the stench, and most of all, the people. The vicious captains who thought they ruled the world, and the crews – God, you've never seen such a bunch of degenerates. And there was I, a doctor, a man of learning, cooped up with them, forced to take part in that foul business.'

'Slave-trading.' The phrase wasn't enough, Mercy thought as she spoke the words. Slave-trading. As though it were just the same as any other kind of buying and selling.

'That trip was to be the last,' Dr Stephens said. 'I had sworn that before we set sail. I'd met Catherine, you see.' A smile flashed briefly across his face as he remembered. 'She loved me. And she was so good, so truly good, and I thought, I must get out of this. I must get out of this and she can never know, and I'll put it all behind me and be a different man. A better man. Stupid. You can never escape your past, can you?'

They held each other's gaze in silence. He had tried to escape his past; hers had been ripped away from her.

'So, what happened, on that last trip?' she said at last.

He sighed, a long, ragged sigh, and then continued. 'Everything was normal. Well, as normal as it could be in such a godforsaken place. We'd picked up our cargo over the course of several weeks and we were making our way to the West Indies – to Jamaica – where we were due to offload before starting our journey back to England.'

'And I was part of the *cargo*, I suppose,' Mercy said. Those words again. Cargo. Trading. Language itself couldn't do justice to this… abomination.

'You were the most diverting little thing,' the doctor said, turning to her. 'You were so young that we allowed you up on deck, you see, with one or two of the other young ones. I took a shine to you, I suppose, tried to teach you a word or two of English, gave you scraps of food from our table from time to time, that sort of thing.'

Mercy felt sick and looked away, forcing herself to stay calm. She had to hear everything, however much it hurt.

'One evening, Dudley called me and Booth into his cabin. He often did that – for a glass of brandy or a game of chess – but this time it was different. He was pacing about and he locked the door behind us. Asked us to sit down. He said – I'll always remember it – he said, "How'd you like to make a bit more money, lads?" And we said yes, of course we would. I was desperate, you have to understand, desperate. If I could just make some more money, I could marry Catherine and get out of this horrible business.'

He stopped, took a deep breath.

'Go on,' said Mercy. 'Then what happened?'

'Then he told us what we had to do. It was for the insurance, you see. We would wreck the ship, lose the cargo, and then the owner could make a claim and would see that we were handsomely rewarded. There'd be another ship passing nearby so we were in no danger – we would be rescued.'

She could see them now, those bodies in the sea. The arms reaching out for help that would never come. She remembered the creaking of wood, the crashing of wave after wave. She remembered being lifted up, hoisted over someone's shoulder, cries and shouts echoing in her ears. It was the first time she had remembered this and yet it was now as vivid as though it had happened yesterday.

'You saved me,' she said.

'I did.' He turned to her and clutched both her hands in his, and it was all she could do not to be sick. 'I did. I saved you. When it came to it, I couldn't let you go. Dudley and Booth thought I was mad but I felt that if I could just save you, then something good would have come of it all. So I saved you and I brought you back to England.'

'You gave me to your cousin, to Mrs Whitworth.'

'That's right. I received quite a hefty sum from the ship's owner for keeping quiet and so I gave her some money to pay for your upbringing. And look at you now! A refined young lady. I know that what I did was wrong, but look at what it has meant for you – an education, a better life than you could ever have expected!'

Mercy tore her hands away from his and stood. She could feel every part of her shaking with a rage she had never known before.

'You should have let me die,' she spat. 'I would rather be dead. I would rather have sunk below the waves with the others than live with the knowledge that I owe my life to you. That I was saved and they were not. That I could live and breathe because they died. I despise you.'

She rushed at him then, barely aware of what she was doing, and pushed him hard in the chest. He staggered backwards and she came at him again with clenched fists and a savage anger. He let her do it, didn't try to defend himself, and after a moment her fury waned and she found herself slumping to the floor, her limbs turned to lead.

Neither of them spoke for a minute or two. Dr Stephens reached his hand out towards her but she moved away.

'What has Sir Jonathan to do with all this?' Mercy asked. 'I know he's involved. I found the note.'

Dr Stephens sighed. 'You may as well know everything,' he said. 'Sir Jonathan was the owner of the ship. Of course, most members of the House were involved in the trade in one way or another. Interesting how so many of them have now reinvented themselves as abolitionists.' He laughed, a dry, humourless laugh. 'Sir Jonathan went a step further,' he went on. 'Dreamed up the insurance scam to make himself even richer. And paid us off in the process.'

So Sir Jonathan Hazelwood, that benevolent supporter of the 'great campaign', was in actual fact a former slave trader and a callous murderer. Mercy found that she wasn't much surprised.

'It may have been his idea,' she said, 'but you didn't have to go along with it. That was your choice.'

'I know,' he said. 'And I'm sorry. It's all over, anyway, he'll be coming for me. I've seen him in the streets. He's getting closer.'

'Who? Sir Jonathan?'

'No, no. A spirit. A ghost. The figure of a young black man. One of those I killed. It sounds impossible, but I have seen him. Booth saw him too. He told me so but I wouldn't listen. Dismissed it as the ravings of a drunk. But now I believe him.'

'You saw this figure outside Booth's house?' Mercy asked, lifting up her head. Did he mean Matthew?

'I did. First Dudley, then Booth. And next, me. A spirit seeking revenge.'

'That was no spirit. That's my brother. He came to find me,' Mercy said.

'Your brother?'

'You gave him a brooch. Remember?'

'I – I...' He thought for a moment, then: 'Yes, I remember. The boy on the beach.'

'Was it supposed to be payment? "I'm taking your sister but here, you may have this bit of metal in exchange"?'

'No, no. He just looked so sad. I wanted to give him something. The brooch was all I had. How did you...?'

'He was here, in London. He came to find me. But he's gone now. And he didn't kill anyone.'

'Are you sure?'

'Yes, I'm sure. He told me it was you who killed Dudley and Booth. He was the one who warned me about you. And I didn't believe him. I drove him away because I thought he was lying.'

'But if he didn't kill them, and I didn't kill them, then who did?' the doctor asked.

Mercy looked at him, his face pale with fear, eyes red-rimmed. A little boy scared of ghosts. How pathetic. She was sure that it was Sir Jonathan who was behind the murders; he was certainly capable of it and he wouldn't want such a damaging truth to come out. How could Dr Stephens not see that? She pulled herself to her feet, dusted down her dress.

'I don't know who killed them. But whoever it was, I hope they find you. I hope they find you soon.'

And she turned and walked away, the click of her heels and the swish of her skirts echoing through the room as she went.

Chapter 33

They ran down the street full pelt until Joe pulled Mat into a narrow alleyway that led down towards the riverbank.

'Here, put these on,' he said, unwrapping a bundle of clothes onto the floor. 'Quick!'

Joe kept watch while Mat stripped off his tattered and filthy clothes and struggled into a clean shirt and trousers.

'Where are your boots?' Joe said, turning to look at him.

'I left them as a souvenir,' Mat said. 'Couldn't get up the chimney with them clodhoppers on, could I?'

'Blimey, you look bad, my friend,' Joe said, taking a proper look at him for the first time, seeing Mat's face that was caked in dust, his skin that was grazed and bruised all over.

They tore his old trousers in two and wrapped them around each foot, creating a pair of makeshift shoes. They would have to do. Then Mat wiped as much of the dirt as he could from his face and hands onto his old shirt, before chucking it into the river.

'Will I do?' he said, facing Joe arms outstretched, before turning a full circle.

'You'll have to,' Joe replied. 'Now, we don't want to draw attention to ourselves so we'll just walk normally, blend in.'

'Right you are,' Mat said. The adrenaline was beginning to wear off now and he could feel every cut and bump he had sustained in his escape. A slow walk sounded like a good plan.

Then they heard the ringing of a bell from the direction of the police office, followed by yells and running footsteps.

'Scrap that,' cried Joe. 'Run!'

They legged it through the warren of streets until they came out onto a main road where they managed to hail a carriage. The driver was none too pleased about taking Mat as a passenger, but luckily Joe had brought money with him and the driver was soon persuaded that it would be worth his while.

'Where to?' Joe said.

'Cowley Street. I need to see my sister,' Mat replied, and they set off west, each trot of the hoof putting more distance between themselves and the scene of their crime.

Bridget answered the door, and her surprise at seeing Joe was quickly overtaken by her shock at the sight of Mat.

'I thought you'd gone! Oh Lord, look at the state of you! Come in, come in.' She led them into the kitchen. 'We need to clean you up,' she said. 'Here, sit down.'

She pulled one of the benches up near the fire and Mat sat down, stretching out his legs and peeling off the now bloody rags from around his feet.

'What happened?' Bridget asked, and she put a pot of water on the stove to heat up and began searching for some cloths and a bowl.

'It's a long story,' said Joe, sitting down on the other bench.

'Is Malu – sorry, is Mercy here?' Mat asked.

'No,' said Bridget. 'She rushed off with Mrs Stephens a while ago. I don't know where they've gone but something odd's going on. Martin said Mrs Stephens had a face like thunder. Said he heard them rowing.'

Joe and Mat exchanged glances.

'I'm sure they'll be back soon,' Bridget went on. 'And she won't want to see you looking like that! Here, take this. Looks nasty.' She pointed at his toe as she passed him a bowl of warm water and a cloth.

Mat winced as he dabbed at his injured toe with the wet cloth. It had just about stopped bleeding, but the entire side of his foot was a mess and it stung as though he'd been attacked by a man-o'-war.

'You know what would help take the pain away?' he said and Bridget smiled at him, hands on hips.

'Let me see if I can guess.'

Bridget fetched them both a beer and then went to the larder to get them something to eat. He and Joe sat wordless, exhausted, listening to the crackle of the fire and enjoying the best beer they had ever drunk in their lives.

Not long after that, they heard the sound of the front door from upstairs and all three turned towards it. Was it Mercy? Mat stood up and they listened as they heard footsteps going along the hall, then a woman calling, 'Mercy? Mercy?'

'It's the mistress,' said Bridget, jumping to her feet. 'You have to get out of here. She'll go spare if she catches you two here drinking her husband's beer!'

They clumsily grabbed their things; Mat reluctant to go back outside with no shoes on his sore feet, Joe fumbling to put on his jacket, which he'd slung onto the table. They were almost out of the back door, whispering hurried goodbyes to Bridget, when the kitchen door flew open and a woman appeared.

'Bridget, have you seen—?'

She stopped and gaped at them like a netted cod.

'Ma'am,' Bridget said, 'these gentlemen were just delivering some—'

'Meat,' said Joe. 'And now we'd better be off, enjoy!'

He tipped his hat at the woman but she had her eyes fixed on Mat. He must still look a sight, he supposed, and perhaps she was wondering why a delivery man had no shoes on. Then she pointed her finger at him.

'It's you, isn't it?' she said.

Mat hesitated. Did she know he was an escaped prisoner?

'You look so alike.'

She smiled then and her pointed finger became an open hand which beckoned him towards her. Without thinking he found himself walking towards her. She sure was a fine-looking woman. She touched his face and looked him over.

'Yes,' she said. 'The same eyes, the same shaped chin, the same little dimples. So, it really is true. You really are Mercy's brother.'

'Yes, ma'am, that's right,' Mat said. 'I'm Mat. Matondo.'

'Well, Matondo, we have a lot to talk about. Bridget, please bring tea to the parlour, would you? Once you've said goodbye to your *friend* here, that is.'

She smiled again and gestured for Mat to follow her upstairs. Mat nodded at Joe and shrugged before doing as he was bid. What a day this was turning out to be, he thought, as he walked down the hallway, feeling a soft rug beneath his feet. Whoever would have thought that he'd have woken up in a cell that morning and be sipping tea with a fancy lady by evening?

*

He was awkward at first, more aware than ever of how much he must stink. He saw Mrs Stephens glance down at his bare and injured feet but she said nothing. She invited him to sit by the fire and it did feel good to sink into a soft chair. But he wasn't sure if he could trust her. How much did she know about her husband's past? He needed to stay on his guard.

Once Bridget had left them alone with a pot of tea, Mrs Stephens sat down on the other side of the fire.

'Matondo, I was very sorry to hear about – well, about my husband's activities. I had no idea about any of it. It has all come as quite a shock.'

She sipped her tea and he thought he saw tears glinting in her eyes. Hadn't Bridget said she was one of those abolitionist types? It can't have been much fun for her to find out what her old man was really like. She went on to explain that Mercy had told her everything and that they had gone to confront her husband but hadn't found him.

'And then she just disappeared!' Mrs Stephens said. 'Took the carriage and vanished!'

'Did the driver say where she'd gone?' Mat asked.

'Piccadilly, apparently, though I've no idea why. The poor girl was obviously most upset. And who can blame her? You've both been through such a lot.'

'I should go and look for her,' he said, although his aching body was reluctant to rise from this soft chair.

'Have some tea first. I'm sure she'll be back soon and if not, yes, we can arrange a carriage.'

Mrs Stephens had a kind face, Mat thought, and such a pretty smile. And she was so easy to talk to. He soon found himself telling her his whole story; about their childhood in Africa, their brutal separation from their family and from each other, and how he'd come to London to take revenge on the men who took his sister. She listened carefully, nodding sympathetically and encouraging him on.

'Tell me what happened when you got to London – how did you find the men from the ship?'

He was much warmer now and felt a heavy tiredness tugging at him, urging him to sleep, but Mrs Stephens poured him more tea, adding an extra lump of sugar, and urged him to go on with his story. She seemed quite taken with him, truth be told, but then he'd always done well with the ladies. He told her how he and Joe had tracked down Dudley and how that had led him to her husband.

'Incredible!' She was hanging on his every word. 'And did you recognise him? When you saw him again in London?'

'I've only seen a glimpse of him. Not enough to be sure. But then I found the diary, you see.'

'I see.' She nodded. 'But other than the diary, there's no proof, I suppose?'

'No, I suppose not.'

'Go on, what happened next? How did you end up in such a state?'

He told her about the stolen tobacco and his escape from the river police; she seemed quite impressed and he suspected he may have exaggerated the height of the building, the danger of the climb.

'Goodness, you've had quite a day! You must be exhausted. You stay here and finish your tea, and I'll ask Bridget to find you some clothes and we must get you a pair of shoes – I'm sure Martin will have something you can borrow.'

She left him then and he settled back into the cushions. What a nice woman. She would know what to do. She would help him and

Mercy, and somehow they could put all this behind them. Maybe he could move in here with them. Get a job. Drink tea every afternoon by the fire. He laid his head back and closed his eyes. Just a little rest. Just for a moment.

The sound of the front door banging shut woke him and it took a moment for him to recall where he was. Then the parlour door swung open and it was Malu, and she looked genuinely pleased to see him.

'Matthew!' She rushed towards him. He stood and they faced each other awkwardly.

'I don't know whether to call you Malu or Mercy,' he said, feeling shy all of a sudden.

'Mercy, I suppose. It's the only name I remember. And should I call you Matthew or Matondo?'

'Call me Mat,' he said. 'Call me whatever you want. I'll answer to anything.'

She smiled and the years fell away and she looked so young, so like the little girl he remembered, who would run to him when she fell and grazed her knee.

He opened his arms and she came to him, laid her head on his shoulder and put her arms about his waist. He wrapped his arms around her; she was so small and slight. They stayed like that for a long time, with only the sound of their breathing and the beating of their hearts to break the silence. When she lifted her face it was wet with tears and he brushed them away, just as he had done so many times before, when they were children.

'I can't believe you found me,' she said.

'I promised that I would,' Mat replied and kissed her on the forehead.

Chapter 34

Mr and Mrs Alford were happy to see them and welcomed them in without hesitation. Mercy couldn't bear to spend another moment in the doctor's house and so they had left, despite Mrs Stephens's protests. They were both worn out by the time they arrived, but Mrs Alford insisted they join them for dinner and they both realised how hungry they were once the food arrived.

Mercy tried not to notice how Mat talked with his mouth full, how he picked up a piece of meat with his hands and licked the gravy from his fingers, smacking his lips together after each mouthful. At least he looked a bit more presentable now that he had on a pair of Martin's old shoes and one of the doctor's old jackets. She was so glad to have found him, and yet she couldn't help but flinch at his slightly too loud laugh and the way he spoke.

After dinner, and once everyone had retired to bed, Mercy was alone with him. Lucy had left a lamp on for them and the fire still burned in the hearth. They sat opposite one another, watching the flames. Despite being as tired as she'd ever been, Mercy found that she didn't want to move, didn't want to be on her own.

'Tell me about them,' she said. 'Tell me about our parents.'

Mat told her about the games they used to play with their mother, about the food she used to make for them, their trips to the market.

He spoke about their father, a quiet man who was a skilled carver and who used to make them little toys out of wood when he wasn't busy with his animals.

'He was an artist then,' said Mercy, glad that perhaps she had inherited something from the man who was her father. Maybe that was why she had been so drawn to the drum in Dr Stephens's cabinet. Had she had such a drum, carved for her by her father?

'Do you really not remember them at all?' Mat asked gently.

'I get flashes of memories sometimes. But I don't know if they're real or not. I was told a story of my life for so long that it became the truth. Now I don't know which memories are real and which aren't. I thought I was some sort of princess. I pictured my father in gold robes riding around on a camel.'

'A camel?' Mat laughed. 'We definitely didn't have any of those. Goats, yes, camels, no.'

Mercy laughed too but her laughter turned quickly to tears. It was as though she had a great wound inside her, a wound that had been bandaged over for many years but that had now been ripped open, and she didn't know how to begin to heal it. She took out her handkerchief and wiped her eyes. It was the one that Mrs Stephens had given her on that first night, with the ivy leaves embroidered all around it. How grateful she had been, how easily bought. She threw the square of fabric into the fire where it caught and smouldered.

'Don't cry, Malu,' Mat said, 'it's all over now. We're together. You're free.'

'Free? How can I be free? He bought me, he named me, he paid for my upbringing, gave me a home, a job. He owns everything. He owns me.'

'No, don't say that.' Mat leaned forward in his chair and took hold of her hands. 'You don't ever have to go back there. You don't ever have to see him again.'

Mercy squeezed his hand. It wasn't as simple as that. After all, where else could she go? Mat could always get a job, but what could she do? And who would employ her? A black woman educated above her station. There was nowhere she could fit in.

'Tell me about our home,' she said. 'Describe it for me exactly.' There would be time enough tomorrow to think about the future.

'Very well,' Mat said, and he leaned back in his chair and began to talk, describing the squat, round house that she had drawn in her sketchbook so many times without even realising it. She leaned back in her chair too, closing her eyes as she listened, tears gently rolling out from under the lids, her lips in a soft smile.

They eventually went to bed at around two in the morning and the next day were both bleary-eyed at the breakfast table. As Lucy poured coffee, Mr Alford came through from the shop where he had gone to open up.

'You have a visitor, Mercy,' he said.

'But no one knows we're here,' she said, feeling suddenly fearful and finding herself looking to her brother for reassurance.

'Mrs Stephens,' he said, and she remembered that of course she had given Mrs Stephens the Alfords' address before they left, just in case she needed to contact them.

'It's not a lady,' Mr Alford said. 'It's a gentleman. Shall I get rid of him?'

Who could it be? Probably Martin with a message.

'No, I'll come through,' she said and followed him into the shop.

Standing on the other side of the counter, pale and dishevelled, was Dr Stephens.

'Mercy,' he said.

She took a moment to collect herself. Her blood still quickened when she saw him, even now, even knowing everything she knew.

'What do you want?' She felt her fingers nervously fiddling with the fabric of her dress, forced herself to be still.

'I just wanted to talk to you. I have some rather important matters to discuss.'

'Mercy, you don't have to.' Mr Alford stepped forward. 'I can ask this gentleman to leave, if you'd prefer?'

'No, thank you, Mr Alford. I shall hear what he has to say.'

'Could we step outside?' the doctor said.

'Very well. Please tell Matthew that I won't be long.'

She followed Dr Stephens out into the street and they walked towards the river in silence until they came to a bench and sat, looking out over the grey water.

'Mercy,' he said. 'I have come to tell you that I am going to hand myself over to the authorities.'

That was not at all what she was expecting. She was prepared for an apology, an entreaty to keep everything she knew to herself, a plea not to ruin his life and the life of his darling wife. But not this.

'Why?' she asked him.

'I was thinking all night. Racking my mind to work out who could have killed Dudley and Booth. How ludicrous that I could think it was a ghost. Booth's madness must have infected me for a time.'

'So you worked it out?'

'Yes, it must have been—'

'Sir Jonathan Hazelwood.'

His eyes widened a little in surprise. 'You knew?'

'Not for sure,' she said, 'but who else could it be? He's the only other person who knows what happened.'

'Exactly,' Dr Stephens said. 'It has to be him. I went to see him yesterday. To ask him if he knew what had happened to Booth. He warned me off and I realise now that it was because he was responsible for his murder. With Booth mouthing off to anyone who would listen about retribution and making amends, he must have known it was only a matter of time before the story came out. And of course Booth had my diary. Your brother presumably got it from Booth?'

He looked at her and she nodded. She had forgotten about the diary. Had she left it with Mrs Stephens? Not that it mattered now.

'I suppose Hazelwood decided he would get rid of you all to prevent the truth from coming out,' Mercy said.

Dr Stephens sighed. 'Yes, I suppose so. And next he'll be coming for me. It's inevitable. He'll make it look like an accident or a robbery gone wrong. Catherine will find me with my head caved in and that will be that.'

'Don't,' Mercy said. Whatever he had done – and despite what she had said to him the day before – she didn't want him to come to harm.

'The only way out is for me to hand myself in, tell the magistrate everything. At least then I'll die with some dignity intact. Anyway, I want you to have this. Open it later.' It was a piece of paper, sealed with wax. 'I am sorry, Mercy. I know you said yesterday that I should have let you die all those years ago but I'm glad that I didn't. I think it's the thing I'm most proud of. I think it may be the only truly good thing I have ever done. Goodbye, my dear.'

He placed his hand briefly on her cheek, then walked away. Mercy clutched the piece of paper and watched as he disappeared into the distance, tears streaming down her face. She couldn't be sure if she was crying for herself, or for him.

She walked back slowly, the paper still unopened in her pocket. As she walked, she tried to think about what she and Matthew could do next. They couldn't stay at the Alfords' forever. Perhaps she could find work in a shop and Matthew could go back to his job at the docks? They could find a little house. They wouldn't have much money but they would survive. She could teach him to read and write. They could get to know one another properly.

She knew straight away that something was wrong. The gate to the back yard was open and as she approached she could see two men, rough-looking and armed with clubs and cutlasses, standing in the yard. The back door was open too, and from inside the house Mercy could hear raised voices.

'What's happening?' she cried as she ran towards the house.

One of the men held out his arm across her path and firmly pushed her aside.

'Out of the way,' he barked, as she stumbled, shocked, across the yard.

Now, out of the house came two more men, and hoisted between them was Mat, arms pinned behind his back. He had a cut on the side of his face, just over the cheekbone, and blood was dripping down onto his collar.

'Mat!' Mercy tried to go to him but the brute who had pushed her wouldn't let her through.

They manhandled Mat out into the yard and Mercy could see the Alfords behind them, pale-faced and silent. Behind them, Lucy and Mrs Bryson held onto one another, sobbing.

'Where are you taking him? What's going on?' Mercy could feel her heart hammering in her chest.

But the men said nothing. They pulled Mat across the yard and out of the gate.

'Malu, I'm sorry,' Mat said, and she tried again to go to him.

'Stay back,' said one of the men, brandishing his cutlass at Mercy.

She longed to rush at the men, to tear at their eyes, to pull their weapons from their hands. She felt she had the strength to do it. Like a tiger fighting for its cubs, she felt she could do anything in that moment.

'Mercy!' It was Mrs Alford. She came to Mercy's side, put an arm around her. 'Come on, it's no use.'

'But—' She couldn't let him go.

'Mercy, there's nothing you can do.'

She let out a cry of impotent rage as she watched her brother being dragged down the alleyway, oblivious to the heads that had popped out of neighbouring windows to watch the commotion, oblivious to the rain that had now started to pour down around her, oblivious to the cold cobbles beneath her as she sank to her knees.

Chapter 35

They shackled him this time. Iron cuffs round his wrists and ankles. They weren't taking any chances. And it wasn't a cosy little cell with two meals a day and a blanket to keep him warm. This was Newgate and it was about as foul a place as he'd ever been. He was in a long, low-ceilinged room with scores of other prisoners. It was dark, and the floor and walls were cold and damp. The air was thick with piss and shit and sick.

Mrs Stephens. He cursed her a hundred times. Apart from Joe and Bridget, she was the only one who had known where he was. Why the hell had he told her everything? How could he have been so stupid? Bragging about how he'd escaped. Trying to impress her with tales of how brave and strong he was. *Idiot*. He thought he could trust her but as soon as she had the chance, she'd sent word to the magistrates about where he was.

There'd been no time to run, no time for proper goodbyes. The officers had dragged him out of the house before he'd even realised what was happening. He could still see Malu's face – eyes round, mouth open, as she watched him being carted off like a prize pig. There was nothing she could do, nothing anyone could do, and before he knew it he'd been trundled into a cart and seen his last glimpse of daylight for who knew how long. Possibly forever. He'd heard they blindfolded you before the gallows.

He kicked again at the shackles on his legs but they were locked tight as a miser's purse. Maybe he could slip his hands out through the bands on his wrists. He tried, twisting his hands this way and that, forcing his flesh against the metal until it bruised. He sat back, defeated. Somewhere in the gloom a man was singing; another was sobbing like a baby. He sighed and closed his eyes. This time he was out of ideas and out of luck. Nine lives don't last forever.

He was due to be sentenced the next day. The prisons of this city were so full that they didn't hang around. And it was a pretty cut-and-dried case, he couldn't deny it. Theft was one thing; escaping from prison, quite another. There was no chance they'd be lenient on him now. No, all he could hope for was a quick death. And at least he had got to see his sister, to talk to her and know that she was safe. That was all he'd ever wanted. And she'd probably be better off without him in her life. She could find a nice man, get married, have a family.

'Oy, snowball!' It was the turnkey, a miserable-looking fellow who seemed to enjoy his job far more than was necessary. 'Visitors.'

Mat hauled himself to his feet and followed the man, shuffling awkwardly because of the heavy chain on his legs. It was Malu and Joe.

'How d'you manage to get in?' he asked them, hardly able to believe they were here.

'You can achieve anything for the right price,' said Joe, but for once his smile seemed forced.

'How are you?' Malu said. She was trying to hide her shock and disgust at the state of the place – and the state of him – but she wasn't doing a very good job.

'Been better.' He tried to smile but it felt more like a grimace.

'We'll do everything we can to help you,' she said. 'Mr Alford might know someone.'

'Then they'd better be quick. They're sentencing me tomorrow.' He didn't want her to harbour false hope. Better that she understood. 'Malu, it doesn't look good.'

She stretched out her hand and he took it. Joe looked at them both and took a step back.

'I'll give you two a minute,' he said. Mat noticed he was wiping his eyes as he turned away.

'What did he want?' Mat asked. 'The doctor? What did he want to talk to you about?'

She sighed, then held up a piece of paper. 'He wanted to give me this. He's decided to hand himself over. To tell them everything. He'll go to prison. Maybe worse.'

They looked at each other. Both thinking the same, both afraid to say it. The doctor wasn't the only one who could be facing the noose.

'He's given me the house in Hamblin,' Mercy said. 'It's where I grew up. He inherited it from Mrs Whitworth and he's signed it over to me. And five hundred pounds.'

'You don't sound happy about that.' Blimey, he'd be dancing a jig to be given that much money.

'I don't want anything from him. Anything at all. I suppose that's why Mrs Stephens told the authorities where you were. She's losing everything she cares about, so she wants me to lose everything as well. I'd give up the house and the money if only it would get you out of here.'

'Then you're sillier than I thought,' Mat said, squeezing her hands. 'All I ever wanted was to keep you safe. I couldn't do it when we were children. I wasn't strong enough. But to see you now, safe and secure, that means all the world to me. And if I have to die – no, stop that'– she was crying now – 'stop that. If I have to die, then so be it. I'll die happy knowing that my little sister is safe.' He could feel his own tears coming now. 'Joe!'

Joe turned and came back to join them.

'Look after her, won't you?' Mat said, his own voice uneven now as he too fought to keep himself together. 'Look after my little sister?'

'Of course I will, Mr Matondo. My friend, my brother, of course I will.' He hugged Mat hard. 'Take care, Mr Matondo. We'll do what we can.' He nodded. He must know it was hopeless.

Mercy hugged him too and then the turnkey shouted that it was time for them to leave, and it was all he could do not to hold on to his sister, to beg her to take him with her, to holler the whole place down. But he managed it. Joe gently pulled Malu away. He watched them leave, Malu looking over her shoulder once before she turned the corner and was gone from his sight. It was only then, when they were completely out of view, that he crumbled, and he wept and he wept and he wept.

Chapter 36

As she walked away from Newgate, the stench of the place still in her nostrils, the wretched sight of Matthew still in her mind's eye, Mercy racked her brains as to how she could save him. She needed someone with influence to speak for him. But who? She considered Sir Jonathan – could she confront him? Threaten to tell the world what she knew if he didn't help her brother? But who would believe her? And in any case, if Sir Jonathan was capable of dispatching both Booth and Dudley – not to mention the many innocent souls before that – then he would have no scruples about doing away with Mercy herself. No, that would never work. There had to be another way.

'Are you all right? That's quite a pace you're setting!' Joe interrupted her thoughts as he struggled to keep up with her brisk steps.

'I have someone I need to speak to,' she said, stopping and turning to face him. 'You go on without me. I shan't be long.'

'Are you sure? You look quite shaken and I promised Mat I'd look after you.'

'I'm sure, Joe. Honestly.'

After a little hesitation he left her, and Mercy turned westwards and set off for the place she had once called home, 17 Cowley Street.

*

Her hand hovered over the knocker and she thought back to the night she had arrived here, full of hopes and dreams, desperate to impress. She took a deep breath – this was Matthew's only chance – and she knocked. Bridget had already handed in her notice, said she couldn't bear to stay after what had happened, and so Mercy wasn't surprised when Mrs Stephens herself opened the door. She wasn't her usual polished and perfect self; her hair hung in uneven curls and her dress was creased in places. Her eyes widened when she saw Mercy at the door.

'Oh,' she said. 'It's you.'

'Yes.'

'You'd better come in.'

'I'd rather not,' said Mercy. She didn't want to step foot in the place. Would burn the whole house down if she could. 'What I have to say won't take long.'

'Very well,' said Mrs Stephens. 'Go on.'

'I don't believe you're a bad person, Mrs Stephens,' Mercy began. 'Indeed, it was you who taught me about justice and equality. You taught me that we have to fight to make the world a better place. My brother doesn't deserve to die, Mrs Stephens. He committed a crime, yes, but we both know that there are those who have committed far worse who go unpunished.'

Mrs Stephens looked away, lips pursed.

'I am not too proud to beg,' Mercy went on. 'And I am begging you now. If justice means anything to you, if I meant – mean – anything to you, please, please, help me save my brother.'

'It's nothing to do with me,' Mrs Stephens said. 'I can't help you.'

'Please, Mrs Stephens!'

Mercy reached out to take Mrs Stephens's hand but she backed away.

'I'm sorry,' she said. 'I'm sorry.'

Mrs Stephens closed the door with a thud and though Mercy knocked and knocked, it remained resolutely shut. With no other choice, she walked away from Cowley Street, anger and despair tearing at her heart in equal measure. Mrs Stephens had been her last hope – Matthew's last hope. She had played her only card. And she had lost.

When the day came, just over a week later, Bridget and Joe had insisted she have some breakfast. Mercy's appetite had deserted her this past week and she knew that she was becoming thin, her ribs visible and her face gaunt. She picked half-heartedly at her bread, sipped a little of her coffee.

She wasn't sleeping much either. Last night, knowing that today was the day, she hadn't really slept at all.

Over the last few days, it was as if someone had taken the stopper out of a bottle and her memories, good and bad, were pouring out uncontrollably. She would wake in a cold sweat, convinced she was back on the ship, or in happier moments she would swear she could feel her mother's arms around her as she drifted in and out of sleep.

The Alfords had been happy to let her stay. They had enveloped her so completely with love and care, she didn't know how she would ever thank them. Joe and Bridget had been wonderful, too, encouraging her out for fresh air, insisting that she eat. Mercy had never seen a pair so well matched. Just yesterday, they had announced their intention to wed. Mr Alford had agreed to take Bridget on in the shop and they were going to save up for a place of their own. But today, they were here at her side.

'You don't have to come,' she said, as once more she returned her bread uneaten to the plate.

'Of course we're coming,' said Bridget, and she squeezed Mercy's hand and exchanged a glance with Joe.

The clock struck the quarter of the hour. It was nearly time.

The day was unseasonably warm, and as they made their way through the streets towards Newgate, it seemed impossible that what was going to happen would really happen. The sky was so blue, the air so fresh. How could death intrude on all this?

There was already a large crowd when they arrived. People chatting and laughing as if it was a summer fair. Mercy caught sight of the platform with the wooden gallows upon it and she stumbled. Bridget and Joe, one either side of her, held fast to her arms.

'I feel sick,' she said, feeling the coffee rising up in the back of her throat.

'You don't have to, you know,' Joe said. 'He would understand.'

'No, no,' Mercy insisted. 'I have to be with him.'

Joe nodded and they moved a little further into the crowd.

When the prisoners emerged from a side door there was a murmur of excitement through the crowd and cries of 'Hats off!' Those at the front removed their hats so that the people behind might have a better view. There were eight prisoners to be hanged today but Mercy only had eyes for one. He looked so small. His arms were bound in front of him and he wore a white cap on his head. She saw his gaze darting from side to side like a captured animal, watched him nervously licking his lips.

'Oh God,' she whispered, and Joe squeezed her arm tighter. Mercy could hear Bridget sniffing back tears but she herself was dry-eyed. Numb.

The prisoners were led up the steps to the platform and positioned beneath their ropes. Then his eyes found hers and she felt as though the baying crowd, the gallows, the prison walls, all melted away. It was just the two of them. Malundama and Matondo. He smiled at her and she smiled back. She was lost and now she was found.

As the hangman prepared to begin his unholy work, there was a commotion and a man, red-faced and sweating, came flying out of the side door with a shout.

'Halt! Halt!' he cried, holding onto his hat with one hand, while the other waved a piece of paper in the air.

All around, people shuffled and murmured. Who was this, disturbing their day's entertainment? Mercy looked to Joe, who shrugged. The man was now talking animatedly to the officials, gesturing towards the prisoners who stood, dumbstruck.

'What is happening?' said Mercy, to no one in particular. She searched for Matthew's gaze but he had turned his head, trying to listen to the frantic conversation going on at the foot of the gallows.

One of the officials, having looked at the paper thrust at him by the red-faced man, turned to his subordinate and whispered something to him. Mercy watched in disbelief as he approached the prisoners, took Mat by the arm and led him down from the platform. There was some booing from the crowd but within a few moments, the prisoners were lined up once again. This time there was one rope too many.

'I don't understand,' said Mercy. 'What does this mean?'

'A pardon,' said a voice at her shoulder.

She turned to see Mrs Stephens standing behind her. She looked older, smaller, than she had before.

Mercy was without words for a moment. 'A pardon?' she repeated. Elation lapped at her but she couldn't give in to it entirely. She needed to be sure she had heard correctly.

'Not a full pardon,' said Mrs Stephens quickly. 'That would have been too much to hope for. But your brother's sentence has been commuted. He will be transported to Australia instead.'

Mercy heard Bridget let out a cry and she turned to hug her and Joe, who had tears streaming down his face. The three of them held each other tightly and Mercy was glad of their arms around her, as she was sure she would fall without them to hold her up. Then she turned back to Mrs Stephens.

'Let's get away from here,' Mercy said. 'Somewhere we can talk.'

The executions were about to begin and they were all glad to turn their backs on the dismal scene, elbowing their way through the throng of onlookers. When they got to the street, Mercy indicated to Joe and Bridget that they should leave her; she wanted to talk to Mrs Stephens alone.

The two women walked in silence towards St Paul's, where couples strolled around the churchyard; a world away from the horrors of Newgate.

'Was it you?' Mercy asked at last. 'Who petitioned for a pardon?'

'Yes,' said Mrs Stephens. 'When I betrayed Matthew to the authorities, I did it out of anger, out of a desire for revenge. And you were right – I believe in justice and this would not have been just.'

'Thank you,' said Mercy. She was grateful, of course she was. And yet, she couldn't shake her own anger just yet; if it wasn't for Mrs

Stephens, Matthew would never have come that close to— She could still see that noose, swaying in the breeze.

'He will be transferred to one of the prison ships at Woolwich,' Mrs Stephens went on. 'It may be a few weeks before they sail, I understand. And I hear they're allowed visitors before they do.'

Mercy's heart leapt at that. She could see him again.

'I only ever wanted to do good, you know, Mercy,' said Mrs Stephens. 'I think when we are young, we all want to do good, don't we? As children, we see the injustice in the world and we can't understand it. We want to do something about it. But as we grow older, we close ourselves off from all the pain, the injustice. It becomes too daunting, I suppose. But I have never turned away from it. I have always fought – and will continue to fight. I have made some mistakes. Some terrible mistakes. But I will try to do good, Mercy. I really will.'

Mercy turned and offered Mrs Stephens her hand to shake. They held each other's gaze for a moment or two.

'Thank you, Mrs Stephens,' said Mercy. 'And good luck. With the campaign.'

Mercy turned and walked away, glad that she would never have to see that woman ever again.

Chapter 37

The prison hulk was called *Discovery* but all Mat had managed to discover so far was that it was a rat-infested, lice-ridden, stinking cesspit of a place that made Newgate gaol seem like Kensington Palace. At this rate, he'd be lucky to make it onto one of the convict ships, let alone all the way to Australia. But luck was the one thing he seemed to have, and after his last-minute rescue from the gallows he knew that anything was possible. Mat the Cat just had to keep his head down and try to stay alive.

He'd be here for anything from a few weeks to several months, apparently. Having lived at sea for most of his life he could cope with the cramped conditions, the hard work and the unsavoury characters he found himself surrounded by. What he couldn't abide was the food – or lack of it. They were up at dawn every day and set to work lugging crates on the docks, and all they got to fuel them was a bit of bread and a concoction known as 'smiggins', which was purportedly made from beef and oatmeal but resembled something that might have come out of a baby's rear end. Tasted like it too. Hunger was Mat's constant and unwelcome companion. He found himself dreaming about lamb chops, fatty and pink; about huge mounds of mashed potato lathered in gravy, and what he wouldn't do for a tankard of ale.

But at least they were allowed visitors. He'd been there a week when one of the guards called him away from his paltry lunch to take him up on deck. Leaning out over the side, he saw a small vessel bobbing in the murky waters below.

'Malu!' he cried.

There she was, beaming up at him. They couldn't touch but they could shout to one another.

'It's so good to see your face,' she called.

'What? This ugly mug?'

They both laughed but then the guard indicated that they only had a few minutes, and it suddenly seemed as if there was both too much to say and not enough.

'I'm sorry,' Mat shouted down to her, but Malu shook her head.

'No, I'm sorry. If you hadn't come looking for me, none of this would have happened.'

'It was worth it,' he said, and he meant it too. 'It was all worth it to see you again. To know that you're well. I just wish we'd had more time.'

'Me too.'

'But it's not forever,' Mat said. 'Fourteen years, that's all.'

'It's no time at all,' she said, still smiling but with eyes bright with tears.

The guard was pulling at his arm now.

'I love you, Malu!' She looked so far away, so small down there. The guard hauled him off and he heard his sister's voice on the wind.

'I love you too! I'll visit again! As soon as I can.'

But a second visit was never to be, for the very next week Mat was marched off the *Discovery* and transferred to the *Adamant*, the ship that would be his home for the next few months. The *Adamant* was around four hundred tons, Mat calculated, and not too shabby. There was something comforting about stepping aboard. He was back in his element. He'd be stowed below decks of course, for most of the time, but with good behaviour the crew might let him up on deck – especially once they knew he was one of them. And he'd heard that some folks did well over in Australia. He'd serve his time, make some money, then he and Malu could be reunited. He'd found her once; he could do it again.

As he shuffled along in his shackles and chains, he looked up for his last sight of the grey English sky. He saw a bird flying overhead, long neck and wings outstretched in the shape of a cross. His cormorant.

So, you're here, old friend. Come to guide me.

He arrived at the hatch that led below deck and rough hands undid the shackles at his ankles. With one last glance to the heavens, Mat stepped down, sure-footed as a cat, into the darkness below.

Epilogue

May 1821

Mercy knocked at the door, butterflies skipping in her stomach. She adjusted her hat and smoothed down her skirts. This was one of several new outfits she'd bought: a sea-green dress with matching bonnet and gloves. Her boots were of the latest fashion; a blend of wool and silk with Morocco leather at the heel and toe. An outfit worthy of a princess, in fact. Mercy had to admit she still felt slightly self-conscious – as though she were wearing a costume.

After a moment, the door opened and she was shown up to the drawing room. Mr Northbury greeted her with affection.

'Mercy! How wonderful to see you!' he said.

'Thank you,' she said. 'And thank you for answering my letter. I wasn't sure you would remember me.'

'Of course I remember you,' he said. 'Agatha, this is Mercy.'

Mercy now saw a woman step forward, her dress simple but elegant, her hair greying at the temples.

'Mercy, this is my wife, Agatha Northbury.'

'A pleasure to meet you, Mercy,' Mrs Northbury said with a warm smile. 'Don't worry, I shan't intrude. I know you two have matters of business to discuss.'

She retreated to a high-backed chair in the corner of the room and took up some embroidery, her head bent so that she might catch the light coming in from the window.

'Now,' said Mr Northbury, 'let's sit down and we'll have some tea.'

Mercy was still clutching her portfolio, wrapped up in paper and secured with string. Mr Northbury gestured for her to put it on the table. 'We'll have a look at that in a minute,' he said. 'First things first.'

The maid poured them some tea and left.

'So, Mercy,' Mr Northbury said. 'How are you keeping?'

'I'm very well,' she said. She had better broach the subject. It was sure to be on his mind. 'After all the... unpleasantness with the Stephenses.'

'Indeed,' he said. 'It was a great shame. And there were no signs leading up to it? He always seemed, well, quite sane to me.'

'And to me,' Mercy replied. 'It seems he had some kind of – episode. He became convinced that he'd taken part in some awful business on a slave ship. The doctors think that he was suffering from a form of mania.' She sipped her tea. The lie was well-rehearsed.

'I see,' said Mr Northbury, his face grave. 'And I understand he is now in Bethlem Hospital?'

'That's right.' Sir Jonathan had made sure of that. There was no way he would let the truth come out after all these years.

'Poor old Stephens.'

'Indeed.' She sipped her tea again, hiding the involuntary smile that sprang to her lips. She'd heard that some of the treatments at Bedlam were less than gentle.

'Exhaustion, probably. And spending all that time on Catherine's campaign – must have put ideas into his head, I suppose.'

'Yes, I imagine so.'

'Well, well, poor old Stephens. Now,' he said, and slurped the last of his tea. 'In your letter you mentioned your desire to be an artist.'

She felt embarrassed, hearing it said out loud. Who was she to think she could call herself that? But she drew herself up, gathered her courage and said, 'Yes, that's right. I believe I have a talent. And I believe that with a little instruction, I might grow to be quite good.'

He stood and took hold of her drawings, began leafing through them with a finger and thumb. Here and there he nodded or grunted. Mercy held her breath, waiting for his verdict.

'Your hand is a little heavy here,' he murmured, looking at a sketch of St Paul's.

She should never have come. What was she thinking?

'Your portraits are better,' he went on. 'Yes, you have a good eye for people, for expressions. This one, I like. Who is it?'

He held up the paper. It was Mat. His cheeky grin, complete with dimples, his large eyes that could say so much with just a look.

'Just someone I saw in the street,' Mercy said, the lie slipping easily from her lips. It was better for Mat to remain her secret for now. 'I thought he had an interesting face.'

'Very good, very good.' He put the drawings down. 'Mercy. Let me be honest. You do have a talent. But it is very unusual for a lady – and particularly for a lady of your...' He waved his hand vaguely at her, unsure how to phrase it. 'A lady like yourself, to take up such a profession.'

'I know,' she said. 'But I know there have been lady artists. Artemisia Gentileschi. Maria Cosway. And plenty more, I'm sure. And if I learned anything from Mrs Stephens it was not to let my sex prevent me from fulfilling my ambitions. She certainly never has.'

He laughed. 'Well, there you are quite right. Remarkable woman. Well, how can I help you? Would you like a recommendation for a tutor or...?'

'I would like to be your student,' Mercy said.

'Ah.'

'I have money,' she blurted out and immediately felt foolish. 'I mean, I can pay – to be your student, if you'll have me. My father was a prince, you see, back in Africa. When he died he left me some money. I can pay my way.'

This at least didn't feel like a lie. It was what she had believed for so long, after all. And she had come to realise it was the version of her life that she preferred to the truth. She looked at him expectantly. If he said no, she wasn't sure what she would do.

'Mercy, my dear, I would happily take you on as a student.' Her heart leapt a little but then he went on. 'But unfortunately you have caught me at a time of flux. I have decided to move abroad – to Italy, as it happens, where I shall be setting up a small studio. I expect to be there for a year at least. In fact, my family and I are leaving tomorrow. If that wasn't the case then...'

'I see.' She began to wrap her drawings back up, keeping her face down to hide her disappointment, her desolation. She should have known it would come to nothing.

Mr Northbury, no doubt sensing her hurt feelings, moved away, loudly poured himself another cup of tea. As Mercy slid the pictures back into place, her eyes lighted on Mat's portrait once more. He gazed out at her with a determined look. He had let nothing get in his way of finding her. He had refused to give up. She needed some of his daring now.

'Mr Northbury,' she said. 'If you would allow it – if you would allow it, I should like to accompany you to Italy. I can be your student there.'

He blustered for a moment, opening and closing his mouth like a goldfish. He cast a look at his wife who had paused in her stitching and sat, needle in hand, watching them.

'Please don't say no,' Mercy went on. 'Months ago, when we first met, you told me that art is what sustains us, and I took those words to heart. And you were right. Art is what sustains us. It's what sustains me. Please.'

There was a moment of silence in which it felt to Mercy that her very life hung in the balance.

'James, dear.' It was Mrs Northbury, rising from her chair and coming towards them. 'Forgive me for interrupting, but I believe Mercy's idea is a good one.'

Mercy felt her breath catch in her throat as she looked from husband to wife.

'She clearly has talent,' Mrs Northbury went on. 'And having an assistant on board for our travels would certainly make my life easier! No more cleaning brushes and mixing colours for you when I have plenty to do as it is.'

Just then the door opened and a girl came in, probably around the same age as Mercy. She was the very model of her mother, the same open face, the same warm smile.

'Ah, Mercy, this is my daughter, Mabel,' said Mr Northbury. 'Mabel, this is Mercy.' He paused for just a moment, threw another look at his wife who gave a small nod. 'She is my student. And I'm delighted to say that she will be accompanying us to Italy.'

*

That night, Mercy carefully packed her belongings, ready for the journey. Mr Northbury had said he would send a carriage for her in the morning. When he'd asked her for her full name for the tickets, and so on, she had hesitated. Whitworth no longer felt right. Not any more.

'Matthews,' she had replied. 'My name is Mercy Matthews.' It had a good ring to it.

She folded up her stockings, her gloves, her scarves, placed each one into her case. This handkerchief had been a present from Bridget, embroidered by her own hand with forget-me-nots. As if she could ever forget Bridget, she thought with a smile.

They had held an impromptu farewell dinner for her; Bridget and Joe. They'd been married four months now, and Bridget was wearing the secret smile and rounded belly of a new wife. The Alfords came too. It was so good to see them all again. The Alfords had begged her to stay with them while she was in London, but she'd chosen these private lodgings instead. She found that she wanted to be alone.

She had spent the last few months in Hamblin, organising the sale of the house and all its furnishings. For a time, she had thought she could perhaps live there. Settle in the country, live a quiet life. But there were too many memories. The place was tainted now with the knowledge of how she had come to be there. The very walls were steeped in lies.

But then wasn't her whole life just a collage of half-truths and untruths? The difference now, she supposed, was that she could choose her own lies. Be whoever she wanted to be.

Her bag was almost packed. This would be her first time at sea – well, the first time she would remember anyway. She hoped she would manage. At least she wouldn't be alone; Mr Northbury, his wife and their three boisterous daughters would be with her. And Mr Alford had given her some lozenges made of ginger, which he said would hold any seasickness at bay.

Her hand lighted upon the ribbon that Dr Stephens's gift had been wrapped in all those months ago. The ribbon she had once held to her lips just because she knew his hand had touched it. She still felt a hot rush of shame whenever she thought of it. She would give it as a gift to Mrs Northbury; she couldn't bear to wear it any more.

Had she forgiven him? She knew the Bible taught her that she should. But surely there were some sins that cut too deep ever to be forgiven? She had reconciled herself to accepting his money, accepting the house in Hamblin – that was small recompense for what he'd done. But forgiveness, well, that still seemed a long way away.

Bag packed, Mercy began to get ready for bed. She let out her hair from its pins, then wrapped it up in a muslin cloth. She unpinned the brooch from her dress and placed it on the bedside table next to her.

Once she was under the covers, she reached for the brooch again, rubbed its smooth front and bevelled edges between her fingers, as she did every night. She had removed the piece of Mrs Stephens's hair – had burned that on the fire – and had replaced it with a lock of Matthew's. He had sent it to her before he set sail.

Mercy opened up the brooch now and touched the soft hair within, then closed it back up. She wondered where he was now. He might be almost there. She tried to picture Australia but her imagination failed her. It was simply so far away.

Fourteen years. It was a long time but it wasn't forever.

'Matondo,' she whispered into the dark, holding tight to the brooch. 'I will find you. I promise.'

A Letter from Lora

Dear Reader,

I want to say a huge thank you for choosing to read my debut novel, *Daughter of the Shipwreck*. If you enjoyed it, and would like to keep up to date with all my latest releases, just sign up at the following link. Your email address will never be shared and you can unsubscribe at any time.

www.bookouture.com/lora-davies

Daughter of the Shipwreck was inspired in part by a painting by J. M. W. Turner called *The Slave Ship*, which was based on a real-life event in which more than 130 enslaved people were thrown off the British slave ship *Zong* as part of an insurance scam in 1781. I have always been fascinated by history and particularly by the people and events that have typically been marginalised or suppressed. Through my fiction I want to bring these hidden stories to the fore. With *Daughter of the Shipwreck*, I also wanted to write a gripping and moving story, and once I had created the siblings, Malundama and Matondo (or Mercy and Mat), they took me on a whirlwind ride which I do hope you enjoyed reading as much as I enjoyed writing.

While Malundama and Matondo are fictional, there were millions of people taken from their homes in Africa, including from the area now known as the Democratic Republic of the Congo, where the siblings are from. Their names are from the Kikongo language spoken in this area. Matondo means 'thanksgiving' and Malundama means 'that which is hidden'; an appropriate name for this character whose true identity is hidden from her. I like to think she will go on to have a happy life as an artist and will be reunited with Mat one day.

Thanks again for reading *Daughter of the Shipwreck*. If you enjoyed it I would be very grateful if you could write a review. I'd love to hear what you think, and it makes such a difference helping new readers to discover one of my books for the first time.

I love hearing from my readers – you can get in touch through Twitter, Goodreads or my website.

Thanks,
Lora

 @DaviesLora

www.loradavies.com

Acknowledgements

While *Daughter of the Shipwreck* is a work of fiction, it is rooted in reality and it was of great importance to me to thoroughly research all aspects of the novel. To this end, I consulted a number of books and articles, too many to mention them all but chiefly those listed below.

For information about the slave trade: Marcus Rediker's *The Slave Ship: A Human History*, James Walvin's *The Slave Trade*, *Equiano's Travels* by Olaudah Equiano (ed. Paul Edwards), and *An Account of the Slave Trade on the Coast of Africa* by Alexander Falconbridge. For general information on London in the period: *Georgian London: Into the Streets* by Lucy Inglis, and Peter Ackroyd's *London: The Biography*. On Géricault's *The Raft of the Medusa* and the true story behind it, Alexander McKee's *Death Raft* was invaluable. Frederick Charmier's *Life of a Sailor* and Brian Lavery's *Jack Aubrey Commands: An Historical Companion to the Naval World of Patrick O'Brian* helped me to enter the world of a nineteenth-century sailor. David Olusoga's book *Black and British* was also a great inspiration and resource throughout the writing of this book.

Several museums were of great help, including the Museum of London and the Museum of London Docklands, the National Maritime Museum and the International Slavery Museum in Liverpool. A special thanks also to the Thames River Police Museum and the wonderful Rob Jeffries who showed me around this gem of a place – all inaccuracies surrounding Mat's arrest and subsequent escape are purely my own. I would also like to thank Anne Marie Wamba, Muadi Mukenge and Professor Nancy C Kula for their help with queries about the Kikongo language.

So many people have supported and encouraged me over the three years it took to write this novel. First, my agent Hannah Weatherill and editor Therese Keating, whose dedication, eye for detail and belief in the book have been invaluable. I am incredibly grateful to you both and to all the teams at Northbank and Bookouture.

This novel sprang from a small seed planted while on a creative writing course at the wonderful Bookseller Crow bookshop in Crystal Palace, London, and so I would like to thank Karen MacLeod for her support and encouragement in those early days. Thanks must also go to my tutors at Royal Holloway, Eley Williams and Anna Whitwham, who helped me to hone and develop the idea for the book over the course of my Master's. My fellow students were also a great help with their feedback on early chapters of the novel, and I certainly couldn't have written it without the ongoing support, constructive criticism and friendship of Bethany Wren and Judith Wilson. Thank you both so much.

A huge thanks to my parents, my step-parents and my brother, who have always believed in me and who have provided so much support over the years. An extra-big thank you to Carmel – my stalwart and unwavering supporter. Thanks also to Neal who has put up with me spending half my time in the nineteenth century over the past few years, who has cheered me through the hard times and celebrated with me through the good. This novel is dedicated to my creative and inspirational aunt, Rosalind, who is very sadly missed.

Printed in Great Britain
by Amazon